ELEVATOR TO OBLIVION

"Maybe it's stuck," Renie said impatiently. "It does that sometimes."

She gave the button an extra hard push. The elevator doors seemed to resist, then creaked open with a shudder. Judith and Renie started into the car and stopped. Judith gasped and Renie squealed. The elevator wasn't empty. Sprawled on the tweed carpet was a black form that looked like a giant spider.

It was Bob-o, the popcorn man, with a neat, ugly bullet hole in his tasseled cape.

Judith shivered. "I don't understand. Why would anyone want to shoot a popcorn vendor?"

"I told you his popcorn was lousy," Renie replied. She glanced into the elevator, flinched, and turned away. "Well . . . maybe not *that* lousy."

MARY DAHEIM

Fowl Prey

A BED-AND-BREAKFAST MYSTERY

AVON BOOKS
An Imprint of HarperCollins*Publishers*

AVON BOOKS
An Imprint of HarperCollins*Publishers*
10 East 53rd Street
New York, New York 10022-5299

Copyright © 1991 by Mary Daheim
Excerpt from *Just Desserts* copyright © 1991 by Mary Daheim; *Fowl Prey* copyright © 1991 by Mary Daheim; *Holy Terrors* copyright © 1992 by Mary Daheim; *Dune to Death* copyright © 1993 by Mary Daheim; *Bantam of the Opera* copyright © 1993 by Mary Daheim; *A Fit of Tempera* copyright © 1994 by Mary Daheim; *Major Vices* copyright © 1995 by Mary Daheim; *Murder, My Suite* copyright © 1995 by Mary Daheim; *Auntie Mayhem* copyright © 1996 by Mary Daheim; *Nutty as a Fruitcake* copyright © 1996 by Mary Daheim; *September Mourn* copyright © 1997 by Mary Daheim; *Wed and Buried* copyright © 1998 by Mary Daheim; *Snow Place to Die* copyright © 1998 by Mary Daheim
Inside cover author photo by Tim Schlecht
Library of Congress Catalog Card Number: 91-92052
ISBN: 0-380-76296-X
www.avonbooks.com

First Avon Twilight printing: July 1999
First Avon Books printing: November 1991

Avon Trademark Reg. U.S. Pat. Off. and in Other Countries, Marca Registrada, Hecho en U.S.A.
HarperCollins® is a trademark of HarperCollins Publishers Inc.

Printed in the U.S.A.

20 19 18 17 16 15

To all those empty places at the Thanksgiving dinner table—we miss you. Lots.

ONE

JUDITH GROVER MCMONIGLE brought her full weight down on her suitcase and jumped. Angling one foot carefully, she clicked the lock shut and let out a sigh of triumph. She was ready.

Hopping off the handsome brown leather case, she smiled in anticipation. It wasn't a honeymoon in the Bahamas as she might have hoped, but even a three-day trip to Canada with Cousin Renie would be a treat after the past two years of struggling to get the bed-and-breakfast under way. Hearing the squeal of tires in the driveway below, Judith knew that Renie had arrived on the dot of nine.

Judith paused, gazing around the third-floor bedroom under the eaves of the old Edwardian house on Heraldsgate Hill. Her last-minute inspection took in her handbag which contained her birth certificate, the dark green leather coat over her arm, and the brown suitcase which was finally shut.

And moving.

Judith couldn't believe her eyes. The finely tooled

1

case she'd received the previous month as a birthday present from Renie and her husband Bill was sliding across the braided rug. Not an earthquake, surely: November in the Pacific Northwest usually held no seismic terrors. Judith's big black eyes stared at the mobile luggage. Then she pounced.

Flipping open the latch, she swore aloud as the contents heaved, a growl erupted from the vicinity of her neatly stacked underwear, and Judith's cat, Sweetums, emerged with teeth bared and scraggly fur on end.

"Insufferable mange-ball!" cried Judith, diving in vain after the cat.

"What are you doing?" demanded Judith's mother, Gertrude, who was standing in the bedroom door. "Customs won't let pets in, you dope! You want to start a war with Canada?"

Judith made another swipe at Sweetums who was now tearing around the room, leaving a trail of tangled clothing. In an orange and white blur, the cat raced for the door, sailing between the legs of Gertrude's walker—and Gertrude.

"I'll kill him!" Judith vowed, flinging scattered apparel back into the suitcase. "How'd he sneak in there? No wonder I couldn't shut the blasted thing! I wish I'd squashed the little fleabag!"

Gertrude staggered slightly in the wake of Sweetums's flight. "Probably sniffed that new perfume you got in there. Smells like rat bait to me," she declared in her raspy voice. "But then," she added, her beady eyes narrowing at her daughter, "that's who you got it for, I'll bet. The Rat."

Judith gave her mother a baleful glance, but avoided the verbal trap. "You know I got it from Mike for my birthday."

"Hunh!" snorted Gertrude. "My grandson has screwy taste in perfume. What's it called, Obnoxious?"

"Obsession, and I love it," replied Judith, closing the suitcase a second time and brushing the salt-and-pepper curls from her high forehead. "There's Renie at the doorbell. Move it, Mother."

But Gertrude was deliberately barring the way with her walker. "A fine thing," she muttered, "you and Serena running off to a foreign country like a couple of gallivanting hussies! Just before Thanksgiving, too. I suppose I'll end up doing all the work. As usual. You've probably even got paying guests coming here while you're gone."

"Of course I don't. Nobody's booked until the day after Thanksgiving." Judith tried to wedge her way out into the little foyer that had once been part of the servants' quarters in a bygone era of Grover affluence. "Mother—you know I've got everything ready for Thursday. We'll be back early Wednesday evening. All you have to do is make the creamed onions."

Gertrude's small eyes darted up at her daughter. "And the cranberry sauce. I suppose Deb will be too puny to fix the green beans and Renie will ruin the gravy again."

"Renie will break down the door if you don't move it," said Judith, using her statuesque size to nudge her mother's walker a couple of inches to the right. "Do you realize that except for visiting my mother-in-law in Arizona this is the first vacation I've had in over twenty years?"

"Big deal. It's not my fault you married a lazy slob." But Gertrude gave way as Renie's buzzing turned to banging.

Judith raced past her mother and down the short flight of stairs to the second floor with its four guest rooms and two baths. Taking the front staircase, she called out to Renie to hold on. The pounding stopped. Sweetums poked his head around the corner of the living room and hissed. Judith ignored him.

"Hi, coz," greeted Renie, looking amazingly alert for a woman who didn't usually function in a human capacity until after ten a.m. "Where were you?"

"Upstairs, packing my cat. Here," said Judith, swinging the suitcase across the threshold, "let me put this in my car. Then I'll go out to the toolshed."

Suddenly solemn, Renie shook her head. "I'll do that. I already put my stuff in your trunk. It was open."

"I know, I was just coming down." Judith peered out the front door, briefly savoring the crisp scent of autumn. "Give me your keys so Mother can turn them over to Bill when he collects your car tonight."

"Right. I'll load your suitcase, then I'll go get . . . *the box.*" Renie and Judith exchanged meaningful gazes along with luggage and keys. The Jones family sedan would be picked up that evening by Renie's husband after his daily stint as a professor of psychology at the university. The two-and-a-half-hour drive to Port Royal would be made in Judith's blue Japanese compact.

Renie disappeared around the corner of the old house while Judith watched with an anxious eye. It was just as well that Gertrude hadn't gotten downstairs yet. Judith preferred that her mother didn't know what Renie was doing in the toolshed.

After a final check of the kitchen, Judith was back in the entry hall when Gertrude clumped down the stairs. "Where's that moron of a niece of mine?" she growled around the cigarette she was attempting to set off with an ancient red lighter bearing the inscription Harold's Club or Bust. "That little screwball never did learn any manners from Deb. Can't she say hello to her old aunt?"

"She's loading the car." Judith avoided her mother's gaze, glancing out the window in an attempt at distraction. "See, the Rankers are up and about. Carl's just leaving for work." She waved; their favorite neighbors waved back. "Don't worry, they'll keep an eye on you."

Gertrude puffed away, looking vaguely appeased. "Arlene's making lasagne tonight. It's better than yours."

"Arlene's a super cook," Judith agreed, willing to concede any point to keep the peace before departure. "She and Carl are super people. I'll call tomorrow after five when the rates go down. You *will* answer, won't you?"

Gertrude turned cagey. "If I hear it ring." She hated the telephone, and resented the fact that Judith not only had six of them installed in the house, but two separate lines, one for business and one for the family.

In deference to her mother's professed hearing loss, Judith gave a thin smile. "I'll hang on until you get there, okay?"

Renie sailed through the back door, making straight for her aunt. "Hi, you ornery old coot," she said, giving Gertrude a big smack of a kiss. "You look good enough to eat—if I were a grizzly bear."

"You look like Mrs. Astor's horse, rear view," retorted Gertrude, taking in Renie's red wool blazer, navy slacks and white silk blouse. "It's Thanksgiving, not the Fourth of July. You're getting as daffy as your mother."

"Hey," replied Renie, tugging on the baggy green and orange cardigan that Gertrude wore over her garish Hawaiian print housecoat, "at least I don't glow in the dark. You take care of yourself while we're gone. Mom will call you."

"At least fifty times," muttered Gertrude. Her sister-in-law's obsession with the telephone was as great as her own antipathy. "All right, all right," Gertrude moaned, clumping after them to the back door, "go off and leave a pair of old widows, live high on the hog, get drunk as skunks, pick up sailors—but don't worry about your mothers! Our day is done, our sun is set, we're over the hill . . ."

"You're over the limit," broke in Judith, giving her mother a hug and a kiss. "See you day after tomorrow. Try to keep from getting arrested for impersonating a helpless old person, okay?"

Looking miffed, Gertrude stood on the back porch, watching her daughter and niece get into the car. As the blue compact reversed and started to back out the driveway, she lifted a limp hand in farewell. "I could go at any minute," she called after them. But the car was already heading down the street that led to Heraldsgate Avenue.

"Nitwits," breathed Gertrude. "It'll serve 'em right. I forgot to tell them not to drink the water." At her feet,

Sweetums weaved in and out, making importunate noises. "I *am* a helpless old person, dammit." For an instant, her small, wrinkled face crumpled. Gertrude enjoyed her solitude, but she didn't much like being left alone. Not that she'd ever admit as much to Judith. Along with "I appreciate you," "I need you," and "I love you," such phrases had long ago been excised from her vocabulary, if not from her heart. Gertrude looked down at the cat which came to rest next to the walker, whiskers drooping, green eyes narrowed. "Okay, hairball, it's just you and me," she growled with an effort to straighten her stooped shoulders. "Why the hell can't you learn to play cribbage?"

The long stretch of interstate highway was crowded for the first twenty miles out of the city as Judith and Renie headed north. Having expended all her early morning energies, Renie now lapsed into silence. Judith checked the digital clock on the dashboard, noted that it was 9:33, and decided to let her cousin's brain fog over until her mental alarm clock went off at its regular time.

The distance between Heraldsgate Hill and the Canadian border already seemed great. Judith hadn't been to Port Royal since before her marriage. The city, Renie assured her, had changed a lot, evolving from a frumpy colonial outpost into a cosmopolitan gateway to the Pacific. Having seen little outside her own hometown except for her mother-in-law's retirement village in the Arizona desert, Judith was excited at the prospect of three days of relaxation at the Hotel Clovia on Prince Albert Bay. It was not the autumn outing she had planned, of course. In winter, with snow on the ground and hope in her heart, she had nurtured vague plans for a honeymoon with Joe Flynn. But the six months that Joe had asked her to wait had turned into ten. The Catholic Church's wheels ground slowly when it came to granting annulments.

She had seen Joe only once since he'd investigated the fortune-teller's murder at Hillside Manor Bed-and-Breakfast in his official capacity as a homicide detective.

Indeed, their only encounter since had been by accident, when Judith had been buying Mike's birthday present in August at Nordquist's men's department. The six months had already slipped by. When she came eyeball-to-eyeball with Joe over a rack of leather jackets, Judith had been angry. He had been embarrassed. It probably would be the first of the year before he heard anything definite, he'd told her. For one thing, his wife, Herself, wasn't cooperating. For another, the shortage of priests in the archdiocese made the entire process more difficult. And, Joe had asserted, his round face looking unusually earnest, he had not wanted to come to her until he was actually free. Did she believe him?

She didn't. She wasn't even sure she believed he was getting an annulment. Almost a quarter of a century earlier, they'd gone together for over three years, had been passionately in love, and experienced more fun than two squirrels on a peanut farm. Then, inexplicably, Joe had dumped her. On the verge of their planned trip to Mexico, he had married another woman. Judith had neither forgiven nor forgotten. Worse yet, she had never stopped loving him. If she had, she'd always reasoned, she could have done both. Yet the shock of his elopement to Las Vegas with Herself, a thrice-married divorcee and the mother of two children, had never worn off. Judith had never understood what had happened to change her life and send her into a disastrously hasty marriage with Dan McMonigle. Joe had promised to explain it all someday. But if his past promises were anything to go by, Judith wasn't going to hold her breath.

Nor could she see why Joe would leave his wife at this late date. Her logical mind made hash of his pie-in-the-sky pledges. Besides, she was too old for illusions. So when she'd accidentally run into him last August, Judith had rebelled against Joe Flynn and the world at large by purchasing Mike two cashmere sweaters, four pairs of slacks, and a half-dozen designer shirts. Her son had never had such a lavish birthday.

Judith slowed down behind a logging truck as Renie stirred in the seat next to her. The stands of fir and hemlock now grew close to the highway, orderly rows of dark green ranged against the clear blue sky. They were almost to the turnoff for the cabin.

"You're sure you want to do this?" Renie asked somewhat dubiously.

Judith kept her strong profile looking straight ahead at the red flag on the end of the cedar logs. "I promised Dan I would. He really liked the cabin."

Renie shrugged and stretched, her toes peeking out through red leather pumps. "Okay. I'd better put on my boots. It's going to be wet by the river."

Judith pulled off the interstate at the turn for Glacier Falls. The car wound through farmlands where cows grazed and dogs slept, among the foothills to the rugged mountains that divided the state in half, past sawmills and RV campgrounds and little stores with signs that read Food–Beer–Bait.

They slowed down to pass through the tiny town of Glacier Falls, stopped at the only light, and turned left. The car seemed to drive itself down the long hill leading to the bridge by the falls that gave the town its name, then curved upward and eastward, climbing higher into the foothills where Judith and Renie caught their first glimpse of Mount Woodchuck. Dusted only slightly by snow, its craggy pillars stood sentinel over the river valley. The familiar sight was reassuring, and both cousins smiled. They had been coming to the family cabin since they were babies, gathering every summer weekend with the rest of the Grover clan. Then, as the older generation passed into history, the get-togethers became less frequent. Bill Jones preferred the ocean; Cousin Sue's husband frequented the racetrack; only Dan McMonigle had enjoyed rusticating at the river.

But, Judith thought to herself, Dan had enjoyed rusticating just about everywhere. And working not at all. Dan preferred eating himself into a mound and drinking himself into a fit, tasks which he had accomplished most successfully by the time he died at the age of forty-nine. If ever a man had committed suicide with an overdose of sour cream, it was Dan McMonigle. He had known exactly what he was doing—Judith was convinced of that. And in the process, he had made the request to have his remains scattered in the Glacier River. Now, over three years after his death, Judith finally had the time and the opportunity to honor his wishes. Meanwhile, he had reposed in the toolshed, awaiting Judith's first free moment from refurbishing the old family home and setting it up as a profitable bed-and-breakfast.

The gate to the Grover property sagged on hinges older than either cousin. Renie got out of the car, retrieved her boots from the trunk, and put them on. With a mighty heave and an impatient curse, she managed to shove the gate open, fighting against the long, damp grasses that had overgrown the driveway.

Five minutes later, Judith and Renie were at the riverbank, in the shadow of Mount Woodchuck. Behind them, the sprawling shake and shingle cabin that had hosted four generations of Grovers stood with its homemade curtains closed and a big padlock on the only door. The cousins would not go inside: For the time being, they had all the memories they could handle in the big plastic garbage sack.

With an air of solemnity, Renie handed the bag over to Judith. "I put the box in this, just in case your mother looked out," she said.

"Good." Judith gave Renie a wan smile. "We have to be careful. The undertaker warned me that ashes aren't exactly what you think . . . Hey!" She hoisted the bag effortlessly. "What . . . ?" Frowning, she set the bag down and opened it. "Hell!" exclaimed Judith, glaring at Renie. "This isn't Dan, it's my begonia tubers, you dope!"

Renie clamped a hand to her chestnut curls and uttered several one-syllable obscenities. In the background, the river rumbled on, crystal-clear waters over moss-covered rocks. "Oh, coz, I'm sorry! You said it was a shoe box!"

Judith gritted her teeth. *"Boot,* not *shoe!* You think I could get Dan into a shoe box? Jeez, the man weighed four hundred pounds! It wasn't like ashes, it was more like rubble!''

Renie let out one final, fading expletive. "I didn't know . . . I should have . . . Oh, damn, I feel awful!'' She turned a miserable face up to her cousin.

But Judith had recovered, taking this mishap, like all others, in stride. "Forget it.'' She swung the plastic sack over her shoulder and started back for the car. "Let's face it, coz,'' she noted with a wry grin, "at least the begonia tubers will come back to life. We'll let Dan go on doing what he always did best—nothing.''

TWO

RENIE MAY HAVE been wrong about the shoe box, but she was right about Port Royal. Skyscrapers gleamed at the edge of the bay, sprawling condos dotted the islands that nestled among the coves and inlets, bold new homes marched up the hill overlooking the city, and even the older residences displayed a rediscovered dignity. Judith was impressed.

The Hotel Clovia, however, was another matter. A mile from the city center, it stood dowagerlike on Prince Albert Bay, with a magnificent view of the water and Empress Park. The setting was perfect, with a broad street sweeping past, and handsome apartment buildings at each side. But the Clovia itself remained an ivy-wrapped citadel of stodginess in a high-tech sea of luxury.

"It's a historical landmark," Renie explained cheerfully, as Judith tried to negotiate the impossible confines of the Clovia's underground parking garage. "They couldn't change it if they wanted to."

"What did they build this place for, horse carts?"

asked Judith, finally guiding the compact into a stall between a mini-van from Alberta and a sports car from California. "How the hell do you and Bill get your big Chev in here?"

"We don't," replied Renie. "We park out back and walk. Sometimes Bill even carries the luggage."

Judith emitted a growling noise that sounded not unlike Sweetums. "I can't wait to see our room. Do we sleep standing up?"

"Oh, no," Renie answered blithely, squeezing her diminutive form between Judith's car and the van. "The rooms are quite big. They're not standard, though. I mean, as often as Bill and I've stayed here, we've never been in a room that was quite like any of the others."

"I'll bet," muttered Judith, trying to figure out if she should risk tearing her gray slacks on the car's grillwork or simply vault over the California sports coupe. "How's the food?"

"Great," said Renie, grabbing Judith's hand and bodily pulling her between the cars. "At least breakfast is. We usually eat somewhere else for lunch and dinner. Port Royal has so many terrific restaurants. We should try the Prince Albert Cafe down the street tonight. Just avoid Bob-o on the way. His popcorn will kill you."

"Who," Judith asked as they unloaded their suitcases, "is Bob-o?"

"The popcorn vendor. He's a real character, been out there on Empress Drive forever. But his popcorn could create its own oil slick. It's just horrid. Look." She paused, halfway to the elevator. Through the breezeway, they could catch a glimpse of the street and the bay. "There he is now, talking forty-to-the-dozen to some unsuspecting tourist. That's the other thing, he's like a wind-up toy. Once he starts blabbing at you, he won't shut up."

Judith peered at the rotund figure shrouded in a billowing tasseled cape with the popcorn wagon at his side. In the noonday sun, Bob-o was a dark silhouette, reminding Judith of a giant spider rendered by Arthur Rackham.

His customer looked like a dancing bear. A sharp crack echoed off the concrete walls of the parking garage. Judith jumped.

"What was that? The popcorn exploding? Or did somebody blow up Bob-o?"

But Renie was unperturbed even as a series of loud reports sounded from outside the building. "Crackers, for Guy Fawkes Day. You know," she explained, pushing the elevator button, "like our Fourth of July firecrackers. The Canadians celebrate Thanksgiving the second Monday in October, then Guy Fawkes Day on November 5. That just warms them up for the rest of the holiday season. They keep right on shooting those suckers off through New Year's."

"Swell," Judith remarked as the elevator door opened, revealing a bearded man of middle age with an unlighted pipe. He nodded vaguely as he got out and the cousins got in. The cables creaked and the small car groaned. Judith was alarmed until she noted Renie's composed features.

"It always does that," said Renie with a little shrug. "Wait until you hear the Heat Pixies in the radiators. Oh, and the Clovia boiler has a mind of its own. When they're working on it—which seems to be often—room temperatures can vary by 40 degrees in a single day."

"No wonder this place is so cheap," murmured Judith as the door jerked open onto the lobby.

"They can't raise the prices," said Renie. "I told you, it's a historical landmark. And it's always jammed."

Judith was about to ask why but one look at the lobby partly answered her question. The furnishings were old, but solid and handsome. Stately vases with fresh flowers, red-striped velvet sofas, high-backed oak armchairs with needlepoint seats, paintings which were either originals or excellent reproductions, filled the small lobby. So did at least a dozen guests, hovering around the desk. Even the life-sized lamp in the shape of a turbaned Nubian serving boy had a certain charm, his hand outstretched as if in welcome. The fact that some puckish soul had put an old

toothbrush in his palm did nothing to diminish Judith's
enchantment. She smiled in spite of herself.

"Wait here," said Renie, putting down her suitcase.
"I'll check us in. There's Doris." She gave an airy wave
in the direction of a stoic redhead who was stamping the
bill of a departing guest.

Judith stepped aside to let a giggling young couple pass.
Honeymooners, she thought with a pang, then steeled her
spine and set her jaw. To hell with romance. From the
wrong side of forty, True Love had to be an illusion. Or
so Judith kept telling herself. She was trying to absorb the
idea when a tall, dark-haired woman in a sable coat came
into the lobby from an entrance which Judith assumed led
out onto the street. Judith stared. The woman turned and
stared back.

"Judith!" she exclaimed, her handsome face breaking
into a big smile. "Judith Grover!"

"Maria!" The two women rushed to embrace, both of
a height, one reed-thin, the other full-figured. Judith swore
she could feel the bones under the sable and was reminded
of Dan in the boot box. She actually shuddered.

But her long-lost friend didn't seem to notice. "Judith,
I can't believe it! After almost thirty years!" Maria held
Judith at arm's length. "You look wonderful! What are
you doing here?"

Judith glanced over at the desk to get Renie's attention.
But Renie was engaged in deep conversation with Doris.
"My cousin—I'm not sure you ever met Serena, she was
a couple of years ahead of us in school—and I came up
for a few days before the holiday season sets in. I run a
bed-and-breakfast on Heraldsgate Hill and I—" She
stopped, taking in the sleek black hair pulled back into a
chignon, the shimmering pearls, the smart taupe dress under the expensive fur coat. "But you've retired from dancing, right? And married to . . ." The name eluded Judith.
Maria Filonov's husband was a big luminary in the theater, a producer, or something.

"Max Rothside," said Maria graciously. She gestured

with a gloved hand toward the desk where Renie was still consulting with Doris. "In the fedora."

"Ah." Judith took note of the tall, distinguished man with the silver moustache and cashmere overcoat who was collecting messages from a dumpy blond. He had a cane over his arm and an attache case in one hand. "I remember now. I read about it in the paper. Ten, eleven years ago?"

Maria adjusted a pearl earring. "Almost thirteen, actually. Lucky thirteen," she added, perhaps a bit too hastily. "They've been exciting years, even though I retired about the time we got married. We've gone all over the world and been involved in some really extraordinary ventures. But there!" She put a hand to her flat bosom and looked abject. "What about you? I'm sure you've had some thrills along the way as well."

Judith reflected that if working two jobs, getting evicted, and having your husband blow up at the age of forty-nine constituted thrills, then she'd had them, all right. But the lobby of the hotel Clovia wasn't the place to say so. "I'm a widow," she blurted, saw Maria's face fall, and gave her friend an encouraging smile. "I have a wonderful son who's in college, I moved back with Mother, and the B&B is doing very well. That's my life." She paused, then shrugged. "That's what I want. For now."

If Maria heard the doubt in Judith's voice, there was no opportunity for her to remark upon it. Renie was storming across the lobby, all but knocking over a stout white-haired woman with a Dandie Dinmont on a leash.

"They screwed up our reservation! It's never happened in the fifteen years Bill and I've been coming here! I told Doris I want to see the manager!" Renie was worked up into one of her rare but explosive rages, heedless of the other guests, oblivious to Maria Filonov Rothside. Her short chestnut hair all but stood on end and her brown eyes flashed. "I refuse to stay in one of those ghastly antiseptic glitzy horrors downtown!"

Judith wasn't quite sure how a hotel could be both glitzy

and antiseptic, but this wasn't the moment to query her cousin. "Calm down, it's just a little past noon. They may have a cancellation."

But Renie shook her head with vigor. "Never. Nobody ever cancels at the Clovia. It's a historical landmark!"

"Oh, shut up!" snapped Judith, grabbing her cousin by the lapels of her blazer. "Settle down, meet Maria Filonov, the dancer. Remember her from grade school?"

Renie's rages tended to die down as quickly as they built up. "Maria!" she beamed and put out her hand. "Yes, I do. You were the awkward kid who fell off the stage doing the minuet for the George Washington's birthday assembly! I never could figure out how you went on to dance with Balanchine and win international acclaim!"

Maria had the grace to laugh. "I think that incident taught me a lesson. I've never fallen off a stage since." She sobered a bit and relinquished Renie's hand. "Actually, the Clovia does have the occasional cancellation." Her wide-set gray eyes rested on each of the cousins in turn. "Max and I have taken the entire eighth floor—they're suites, you know—for a reunion of theater people he calls his Sacred Eight. But one couple can't make it, so if the two of you would like their room, I'm sure we could arrange it."

Judith and Renie exchanged questioning looks. "I don't know," Judith began. "It sounds as if we'd be imposing . . ."

"Nonsense." Maria tossed her sleek head, very much the prima ballerina. "In fact, I think it would be wonderful fun. These are really Max's friends, and I'd enjoy having someone of my own on hand. We'll talk to the desk and arrange it. You'll join us for cocktails at six, of course."

Judith felt as if she were being given a royal command. She shot a look out of the corner of her eye at Renie, who seemed equally cowed. "Well . . . okay, sure, if you don't think Max will mind," said Judith.

Max, in fact, was approaching, swinging his cane and

doffing his fedora. Introductions were made all around, and Judith was much taken with his expansive manner.

"Heraldsgate High School," he said with a nostalgic catch in his deep voice. "How often I've heard Maria mention that name! And the grade school, what was it, something about drunkards?"

"SOTS," replied Judith, "for Our Lady, Star of the Sea. It was—is—a parochial school, attached to the parish."

Max Rothside beamed. "Delightful. We must make a pilgrimage some day. Heraldsgate Hill is about the only place we've missed over the years. But of course Maria's parents have been dead for some time now."

Maria looked appropriately solemn, then took Judith and Renie by the arm. "Let's get you checked in. You'll be in 804—no, wait, I put Birdwell in there when Jonny and Clea couldn't come" She rocked gracefully on her suede high heels, tapping a manicured red nail against her chin. "That's all right, Birdwell isn't here yet. We'll give him 802. It's smaller, and he'll complain, but he always does. He's a critic, you know."

"Birdwell de Smoot?" inquired Renie. She saw Maria nod. "He's a crank! My husband Bill says that if you look up the word 'negative' in the dictionary, you'll find that the definition is—"

"We expected a smaller room anyway," Judith interrupted, riding right over Renie's latest recital of The Word According to Husband Bill.

But Maria forced the large suite upon them. Since Renie had originally requested a much cheaper room, Doris and the Clovia's management insisted that the rate remain the same, despite the upgrade in amenities. To the elation of both cousins, Suite 804 was furnished not in forty-year-old bits and pieces, but elegant First Empire. There were two bedrooms, a sitting room, a kitchenette, and a huge marble bath set in mahogany. The view of Prince Albert Bay was unrestricted. They could even see Bob-o, plying his trade and chattering like a magpie to a trio of punk rockers. The Heat Pixies, however, did not defer to price. Even as Judith and Renie unpacked, the clatter and clang of the radiators threatened to deafen them.

"So tell me about Maria," inquired Renie half an hour later as they sat down to lunch in a small French restaurant three blocks from the hotel. "She's too skinny, I can see that. Makes her look older."

"Dyes her hair, too," said Judith, sampling a warm wedge of *tarte a l'oignon.* "But she certainly had a wonderful career. I used to try to follow her rise to fame before I got married. Then I had enough problems following my own."

"Which involved two jobs at once," murmured Renie over her lamb's lettuce salad. "but let's not be bitter. You never could dance worth a lick."

"I still wanted to," said Judith as the waiter poured more Vouvray. The restaurant had been built to resemble a cave, with bottles of wine shoved into every conceivable crevice. "I envied Maria a lot, especially when she went to Europe to study. We wrote for a while, but then one of us stopped. I forget which."

"And Max produced plays from Athens to Zimbabwe. He's a Canadian, as I recall, though his earliest successes were in New York." Renie shot Judith a smug look over her mache-betterave.

"How do you know that?" queried Judith.

Renie grinned, heedless of the wine she was spilling on the tablecloth. "I just finished designing a commemorative brochure for the university's acting program. Max Rothside was listed among the three greatest theatrical impresarios of the twentieth century. You know me, I may be just the designer, but I don't trust anyone else to proofread. There isn't a soul on that campus who can spell. Including Bill."

Judith tipped her head to one side. "Maria did all right for herself for a pudgy kid from Heraldsgate Hill. I wonder whatever happened to Spud."

Renie's eyebrows lifted. "Spud? Who's that?"

"Spud Frobisher. He played football for Heraldsgate High and Maria was madly in love with him. Beefy kid, no speed, but lots of desire. Some of it, I heard, was for Maria." Judith leered slightly above the rim of her wineglass. "He got a football scholarship somewhere after he graduated. As I recall, both he and Maria were broken-hearted over the separation."

Renie made a face. "They probably forgot all about each other as soon as they left town." She put aside her salad plate, leaving most of the cubed beets in a little pile. "Then this was Maria's first marriage, I take it? No kids?"

Judith shook her head. "I doubt it. Where would she put one with that scrawny frame of hers?"

A suave waiter, who looked more Pakistani than Gallic, removed their starter plates and refilled the bread basket. The cousins had already demolished the crusty rolls along with most of the butter. Judith mentally kissed her pre-holiday calorie counting goodbye and verbally abused Renie for eating like a pig and looking like a pole.

"Metabolism," explained Renie for what she calculated as the thousandth time in over four decades. "Nervous energy. I pour it all into my fabulous graphic designs."

"I pour it all into my gut," lamented Judith. She patted her midsection, which actually was nowhere near as ample as she made out. "It's aggravating. Look at Maria—she's as tall as I am and weighs about half as much."

"I'll bet she's got thighs like a linebacker." Renie paused as the waiter returned with her quenelles of pike in chive sauce and deposited Judith's mackerel poached in cider. "You'll note her oh-so-simple-but-chic dress came damned near down to her ankles."

"True." Judith looked for her fork and realized it had gone off with the first course. Leaning back in her chair, she tried to signal to the waiter, but he had been diverted by the burly customer at the next table. To Judith's surprise, the customer, rather than the waiter, sprang to attention.

"Excuse me," he said, clumsily edging in between the

wine racks which separated the tables, "I eavesdropped. Did you mention Spud Frobisher?"

Judith and Renie exchanged curious glances. "We did," replied Judith, warily surveying the intruder. He was middle-aged, with thinning blond hair, a fresh pink face, and pale blue eyes. "We were also about to mention a missing fork."

Deftly, the waiter supplied the proper utensil. The burly man leaned on the table, causing it to sway slightly. "*I'm* Spud Frobisher," he said, with a diffident smile. "You could be . . . oh, heck, I'm not sure . . . Joanne? Jennifer? Julia?"

"Judith. My God!" she exclaimed, her memory clicking into place, "you *are* Spud Frobisher! What is this, old home week?"

Spud guffawed as if Judith had made a hilarious joke. "Yep, in a way." He gestured to his table where a gray-haired man with a goatee was paying the bill. "Let me see my friend off and then I'll tell you the story of my life. The short version," he added, noting the look of alarm on both cousins' faces. "I'll be right back."

"Well, well," remarked Judith, starting in on the mackerel. "What is this, the land of coincidence? I feel like singing the old high school fight song. If I could remember it."

" 'Fight on ye Harbingers,' " sang Renie in a mercifully soft off-key voice, " 'bring the news of victory . . .' "

Judith grimaced. "No wonder I forgot it." She thought it best to change the subject. "Do you suppose Spud heard what we said about him and Maria?"

Apparently unfazed by her cousin's implied criticism, Renie responded with a quizzical lift of her eyebrows. "If he did, it didn't seem to bother him."

"True," agreed Judith. "He hasn't changed all that much, really. Bigger. Balder. Bolder. Spud always spoke in monosyllables."

"I don't think I ever talked to him," said Renie. "He

was, after all, only a sophomore. The only reason I talked to you was because we were related."

"And then you acted like a snot if there was anybody else around," Judith reminded her cousin with a hint of reprimand.

"It's not my fault you were a nerd. All sophomores were nerds. It was a new word then." Renie lapped up her pike, while somehow managing to devour yet another roll almost simultaneously.

Having parted with his companion, Spud was wheeling back to the table. He hauled his chair over with a loud clatter and sat down, much like a water buffalo submerging into a lake. "Judith. Let me think . . ."

"Don't," urged Judith, who didn't remember brains as being Spud's strong suit. "McMonigle now, Grover then. This is my cousin, Serena Grover Jones. She was two years ahead of us and a snot."

Spud eyed Renie with apparent awe, as if the magic spell of high school hierarchy still lingered. "Sure! You were a cheerleader!"

Renie all but bolted from her chair. "I was not!" she protested, as if accused of some heinous crime. Judith smirked, figuring it served her cousin right for remembering the loathsome Heraldsgate fight song. "I was president of the Honor Society!" shrieked Renie.

"Oh, gee!" Spud was mightily embarrassed, his pink face turning crimson. "Gosh, I'm sorry, it's been awhile. I must have gotten you mixed up with someone else." He gave Judith and Renie a sheepish, engaging grin. "I haven't been back to Heraldsgate Hill since I graduated. Dad got transferred and my folks moved to Denver that summer."

"And you got a football scholarship," said Judith, attempting to put Spud at ease. "So what have you been up to? Coaching?"

Spud emitted his boisterous laugh. "Well, yeah, sort of. But not football." He leaned forward, his face earnest, his knees pushing the table a good two inches across the stone floor. Judith and Renie clung to their plates. "I got that scholarship all right, to Nebraska, but I separated my shoulder in the first game against Oklahoma. That ended my playing days." He paused, eliciting sympathetic looks from Judith and Renie. "But that was okay. I wasn't all that crazy about football. I'd gotten in with some of the drama students and they had a good theater program at UN. I tried acting, but I was too clumsy on stage. Still, I really loved the theater. All those words—I didn't know there were so many, or that you could put them together like that!" His face glowed like a baby's; he was suddenly the eager undergraduate once again. "My folks weren't much for culture," Spud confessed. "My dad worked for the phone company."

"That explains it," said Renie, who'd had her share of run-ins over various presentations to the telecommunications industry's top brass. "Most of the officers think *Hamlet* is an egg dish."

Spud howled. "Right," he agreed, all but wiping his eyes, and beaming at Renie as if they had suddenly become soul mates. "So it was all new to me. And since I couldn't act and the technical stuff was too hard and I was no writer, I had to take what was left." He lifted his wide shoulders. "I became a director. It *is* like being a coach, you know."

A dim light shone somewhere in Judith's mind. In almost 19 years of marriage to Dan McMonigle she hadn't had the time or opportunity to keep up with the American theater scene. And widowhood's responsibilities with raising a son and running a bed-and-breakfast had prevented her from catching more than the occasional movie. But somewhere along the line, the name of Frobisher was known to her other than in the guise of Spud, Heraldsgate High School lead-footed fullback. "Not *Kent* Frobisher?" she asked in astonishment.

Spud pounded the table, rocking china and cutlery. "That's right, that's me! Isn't it a hoot?"

Renie was aghast. As season ticket holders to the repertory theater, she and Bill knew Kent Frobisher was one of the most outstanding directors in the country. "Why, you've won a Tony! Or two! Good grief, how come the local media wags have never claimed you as their own?"

"Well," Spud replied, turning ruminative, "I'm not sure they know I'm theirs. You see, we moved around a lot because of my dad's job, and I was only in town for the four years I was in high school. Then, when I went away to college in Lincoln, it turned out that a lot of Nebraskans work in the New York theater. I made all my contacts through them when I went back East. Everybody in the business thinks of me as a Cornhusker. Somehow, that Midwestern farm boy background was good for my image. Heck, even 'Spud' fitted somehow, with all due respect to Idaho." He leaned back in the chair, looking ingenuous, and threatening to tip over onto the wine rack.

Judith studied him with new appreciation. The bumptious exterior obviously masked a great deal of intelligence and cunning. Not to mention genuine talent. Spooning up the last bit of cider, Judith shook her head. "Amazing. Really, it is. The reason we were talking about you was because we'd just run into—" She caught Renie's warning glare and stopped. "Actually, we just met someone else who went to Heraldsgate High and it made me remember . . ."

Spud broke in on Judith's fumbling explanation. "Maria, right?" He jabbed Judith in the upper arm, knocking the spoon out of her hand. "Oops, sorry. I know, that's what I mean about old home week. My wife and I are here for Max Rothside's Sacred Eight reunion. We're staying with them at the Hotel Clovia."

Suddenly, the resurfacing of Spud and Maria didn't seem like such a coincidence after all.

THREE

FOLLOWING SPUD FROBISHER'S announcement, Judith and Renie had eyed each other surreptitiously. Old home week indeed, Judith was still thinking, and knew Renie would agree. The waiter had returned, whisking away the empty plates and pouring more wine. Spud groped at his wristwatch. "Hey, it's going on two o'clock! Gotta run, I'm supposed to meet the wife at some boutique on Queen Charlotte Street. Maybe we'll see you around."

"You can't avoid it." In brief, Judith summed up the cousin's plight over lost reservations and Maria's gracious invitation. Spud seemed delighted. They'd have a real hoedown come the cocktail hour, he asserted, and almost knocked over the Pakistani waiter on the way out.

"This is the genius who directed that highly acclaimed revival of *Long Day's Journey into Night?*" gasped Renie over coffee. "I don't believe it!"

But Renie had no choice. Spud might be a Midwestern rube, but it appeared that professionally he was a city slicker. Or so Judith contended as the cousins prowled the small, smart shops of Prince Albert Bay. Two hours later, with feet dragging and arms full, they headed back to the hotel, taking Renie's shortcut through an alley that led from the neighborhood's commercial strip.

"Are you sure Bill's Cuban cigars won't get confiscated?" Judith asked dubiously as a sleek Siamese cat that bore no resemblance whatsoever to Sweetums arched its back next to a dumpster.

"They never do," Renie answered blithely. "Bill's been buying them up here for years."

Judith said nothing, her mind veering off onto Joe. He, too, was a cigar smoker, and policeman or not, no doubt would have been elated with a gift of contraband Havanas. But Judith and Joe weren't exactly at the present-giving stage. Maybe they never would be, she told herself, and felt Renie stiffen at her side.

"What's wrong?" asked Judith, but a glance at the other end of the alley answered the question. A rotund figure in a tasseled cape pushing a popcorn wagon was heading straight for them.

"Pretend you don't speak English," hissed Renie. "Act like you're deaf and dumb. Hold up a plague sign. Just don't let Bob-o get started or we'll be here all night."

But the warning was in vain. Within ten feet of the cousins, Bob-o began his spiel, the sound of Bow Bells in his singsong voice. "Pretty ladies, spent every 'aypenny, now it's time for tea. What 'ave you got there, something nice for me?"

Judith opened her mouth to reply, but Bob-o had barely paused for breath: "Got me a parakeet, pretty as you please. Speaks like a proper lad, sits in the trees. Born on Armistice Day, when we beat the Kaiser. Been all over 'ell and gone, growing old and wiser. 'Ad me a collie dog, when I was . . ."

The voice rattled on as Judith and Renie stood imprisoned next to a pile of packing crates. Tuning out the words, Judith studied Bob-o and recognized that at least he was probably right about his Armistice Day birthdate:

His blotchy face showed all of seventy years and the watery gray eyes looked unfocused. Sprigs of white hair stood up around the bald spot at the back of his head. He was of medium height, and perhaps not really as fat as he looked in the billowing cape. His boots were old and worn, yet his brown wool trousers looked new, if cheap. As the words kept tumbling out, Judith had the feeling that Bob-o wasn't talking to her and Renie so much as he was babbling on cue. Judith snapped her fingers. Bob-o shut up.

"Nice to meet you," said Judith, with a nod. "If you'll excuse us, we have to go do brain surgery."

The watery eyes suddenly focused. "No! Not on me, you don't!" He held both hands up in front of his face, as if warding off attack.

Renie took advantage of the gesture to attempt escape, but couldn't surmount the popcorn wagon. Judith, however, was stricken with remorse. "I didn't mean that," she insisted. "I meant we had to be someplace. For tea," she added rather wildly.

Bob-o slowly lowered his hands, peeking out between his fingers like a child playing a game. "Tea? Well, there now!" He crooked a gnarled finger at them. "Come on, don't be shy, I've plenty of tea and biscuits, too. Tootle loves company, 'e does, and so do I, especially when they're pretty lasses."

"Hold it," cried Renie, digging in her heels.

But Bob-o had turned into a doorway next to the packing crates. "Shortbread, straight from Scotland, and some loverly creams. 'Ere we go." The door swung open and he made a lavish bow, ushering his guests into the ground-floor entrance.

Judith gave Renie a helpless look. Renie's face hardened, but she knew her cousin too well. Judith was a real sap when it came to people. She actually liked most of them. To Renie, it was often a flaw, yet it was also the reason Judith was such a success in the bed-and-breakfast business. Renie surrendered, and tramped along behind Judith into Bob-o's tiny apartment.

It was everything they might have imagined, with newspapers stacked all over the floor, dirty dishes on the table and in the sink, grease running down the grimy stove, dust webs in the corners, and furniture that looked as if the Kaiser's men had plundered it before running up the white flag in 1918. There were dozens of objects strewn about, all of them old and battered—an accordion, a broken drum, leather ice skates with missing laces, even a conical cap with stars. Photographs, many of them framed, were plastered on the walls and sitting on whatever flat space was available. To Judith's surprise, they were recognizable: Olivier, Gielgud, the Lunts, the Barrymores, Noel Coward, and Beatrice Lilly.

"Hi, sluts!" The voice came from on high. Startled, Judith and Renie looked up in unison. A turquoise parakeet with a sour expression perched on top of a faded floral lampshade. "Tarts, trollops, hussies!" the bird chirped, then flapped its wings and flew off to the refrigerator.

"That's Tootle," said Bob-o, blowing the bird a kiss.

"Gee, I thought it was Gertrude," murmured Judith, wondering if they should attempt sitting down.

"I'll kill you for this," Renie whispered back. "He's nuts, and so are you."

But Bob-o was filling a kettle and turning on the stove. Judith removed a foot-high stack of newspapers bearing dates from five years earlier, and cautiously sat down on a rickety chair. Renie remained standing.

"Nice and easy does it, 'ere we go, ducks," said Bob-o, shoving a tartan biscuit tin in front of Judith. "Shortbread, just like I promised. Tootle ate the creams."

"Tootle's a scamp." Judith remarked, exchanging hostile looks with the parakeet, who was doing something disgusting on top of the refrigerator. Fleetingly, Judith wondered what would happen if Sweetums and Tootle were left locked up together in the same room. The prospect was ghoulish, but not entirely displeasing.

"You must be a great fan," Judith remarked to Bob-o's back as he fiddled with the knobs on the stove.

"Fan!" Bob-o turned halfway around. *"Friend."* He undid the cape and tossed it onto a pile of old phonograph records. "Knew them all, I did. Larry. Jack. Bea." His thumb jabbed at each famous face in turn. "A wonderful woman Bea was, nobody like our Bea. Used to leave my dog with 'er." He picked up a smaller photo which had been lying facedown on an old magazine. "There's Viv. Beautiful. But troubles, lots of troubles." He flashed the picture of Vivien Leigh in the cousins' direction. "Poor Larry, she gave 'im a rare bad time. " 'E was a saint, really 'e was."

The kettle hadn't whistled, but Bob-o poured the water anyway. Renie shifted uneasily, keeping a wary eye on Tootle. The bird flapped his wings, then burst out with a parody of his master: "Daddy put the kettle on, wearin' o' the green; Mummy come for biscuits, says we don't keep clean!"

Tuning Tootle out, Judith nibbled at the shortbread and was relieved to discover it was relatively fresh. "You knew them all in London?" Judith hazarded a guess, relieved that at least Bob-o, if not Tootle, had stopped rattling away like a nursery rhyme.

"Mostly." Bob-o was nonchalant, dipping a single tea-bag in and out of the ceramic pot shaped like a sheep's head. "Cream? Lemon? Sugar?"

The cousins declined any risky additions. Bob-o poured the pallid tea into three unmatched cups. "Cozy, eh, ducks?" He winked at Judith and smiled, revealing two broken teeth. "Nice to have ladies to tea. People 'ere in Canada aren't as friendly as they're said to be. 'Ard to make new friends when you're old."

Nuts or not, Judith was touched by Bob-o's candor. "People get too busy. They're afraid to be friends sometimes. But you must meet lots of folks in your . . . uh, job. I think that would be quite pleasant."

Bob-o cocked his head to one side, looking not unlike

Tootle. "They come. They go. It's not like the old days."
He sighed, then took a deep drink of tea. "Nothing's like
it used to be." He waved a hand, taking in the entire
squalid room. "They're all gone." His voice dropped and
his watery eyes came to rest on a picture Judith didn't
recognize, a lovely young woman with golden curls and
seductive eyes. "All gone," he repeated under his breath.

"We should be, too," interjected Renie, putting her
cup down on an ancient television set. "It's been very kind
of you," she added, guilt finally catching up with her more
fastidious nature. "We'll come by tomorrow and get some
popcorn."

Judith regarded Renie with approval. "We certainly
will. I'll see if I can find some of those creams when we
go shopping, okay?"

Bob-o's face lighted up. "Now what a fine idea!" He
put out a hand and clutched at Judith's fingers. "I knew
you were a kind lady, I could see it in your eyes. 'Appy
eyes, I call 'em." He shot a glance at Renie. "Some as
'as 'em, some as don't."

To Renie's credit, she kept her smile in place. Judith
thanked Bob-o again, let him see them out the door, and
remembered to call a farewell to Tootle. The parakeet
hopped off the refrigerator and landed on Bob-o's head.
"Four ducks on a pond, the drake's on the make! So
long, strumpets! Don't forget your key!"

"With any luck, I'll forget I've been here," Renie muttered as the cousins trudged through the alley. "Damn,
how could you do that to us, we've probably been poi-
soned! That place smelled like the old outhouse up at the
cabin! Our English ancestors used to take tea with Queen
Victoria and the Prince of Wales! You get us stuck with a
loony popcorn vendor and his dirty bird!"

Judith was unperturbed. "I did it because we didn't
have any choice," she asserted, stopping at the Empress
Drive entrance to the Clovia. Admittedly, the red ivy on
stout, twisting vines clawing its way up the walls was an
impressive sight in the fading autumn sun. Judith paused

to admire the Clovia's stolid exterior with its mellow old brick and evergreen shrubbery. Brushing a tiny crescent-shaped bit of glitter from her slacks and giving thanks that her person hadn't collected something more disagreeable during their visit to Bob-o, she continued her self-defense: "And I'm glad. I don't know why, but there's something about him that upsets me. I guess I just feel sorry for the poor old guy."

"You feel sorry for everybody. Except me." Renie grumbled all the way up to the eighth floor. Only a session with toothbrush and mouthwash, a hot soak in the tub, and a stiff rye and water improved her disposition. It also revived her brain. "By the way," she said, rubbing her hair dry with a thick towel, "did you notice the picture of Maria?"

"Maria?" Judith looked up from the Port Royal visitors' guide she'd been perusing. "Hunh. Well, she was a big star in England, as well as over here."

"Was Bob-o talking nonsense all the time?" Renie inquired, plopping down on the plush sofa and retrieving her drink.

Judith was trying to track down a bicycle specialty shop for Mike. "What? Oh—probably." She scribbled out an address, then glanced at her watch. "Hey, it's almost six. Let's get going. Didn't you make the dinner reservations at the Prince Albert Cafe for seven-thirty?"

"Right." Renie was scrutinizing her travel wardrobe. "Shoot, what do we wear to something called the Sacred Eight?"

"Not much choice, with one suitcase apiece," said Judith, then jumped as a series of explosions rattled the windowpanes. "Damn! More crackers?"

Renie nodded, less concerned with the revelers out along Empress Drive than her social dilemma. She finally wrapped herself in a reversible blue-green blouse and skirt that hadn't traveled as well as the Donner & Blitzen sales clerk had promised. Judith settled on a tailored ivory silk shirt and black velvet trousers. Shortly after six p.m. the cousins approached the door of Suite 800 at the far end of the hall. Judith's knock was answered by Maria, looking divine in a black suede jacket trimmed with gold over red jersey harem pants. Her gold and ruby earrings looked like spaceships. Judith and Renie were properly impressed.

"My dears!" Maria welcomed them, against a backdrop of art deco furnishings and Cole Porter on tape, "come in, meet three-fourths of the Sacred Eight. The Castles got held up in Hong Kong. Jonny's new picture ran over schedule."

"Jonathan Castle and Clea Rome?" echoed Judith, recalling Maria's earlier reference to the missing couple. "The movies' gorgeous hunk and the hot mama of hard rock?" She boggled at the thought of replacing two such mega-stars.

"Yes," sighed Maria, steering Judith and Renie toward Max Rothside and the bearded man the cousins had seen coming out of the elevator upon their arrival, "it's a shame. Max was so hoping the reunion would be complete. Weren't you, darling?"

Max Rothside bowed over his cocktail glass and flicked ash from his cigarette into a crystal bowl atop the white baby grand piano. Everyone was smoking; in fact, the room seemed to be divided into Smoking and Heavy Smoking sections. Judith felt herself weakening despite her long months of total abstinence, but caught Renie's dark glare and repented.

"I lament the Castles' absence, but there's no perfection in an imperfect world," Max was saying, looking even more distinguished in his dinner jacket and black tie than he had in the lobby. At sixty, Max was still a handsome, well-preserved man whose silver hair and moustache only enhanced his masculine charm. By comparison, the shorter, somewhat younger man at his elbow seemed insignificant. The assessment, however, was utterly wrong. Maria introduced the cousins to Alabama Smith, the Pulitzer Prize–winning playwright whose works had electrified audiences for over two decades.

"A pleasure, I'm sure," declared Alabama in a carefully articulated voice that indicated he'd worked hard to rid himself of Dixie speech patterns. "You must meet my wife, Desiree Sinclair."

A mane of copper hair swung around from the Cubist sofa on which Desiree reclined, champagne glass tilted toward her red lips, green eyes shrewdly surveying the newcomers. No threat, her glance seemed to convey, and she flashed the famous smile that had dazzled her stage and screen admirers for more years than she probably cared to admit.

"Hot damn!" she exclaimed in the well-known throaty voice that had uttered lines for such diverse characters as Auntie Mame and Lady Macbeth. "Fresh blood. You're friends of Spud's as well as Maria's, I gather."

"Well," said Judith, trying to remember the name of Desiree's last hit, "we knew them both in high school."

"Cute." Desiree swung her copper mane at the mousy woman who sat next to her on the sofa. "Did you go to high school, Mildred, or did the superintendent just order you a diploma because you were such a kiss-ass?"

The painfully plain woman named Mildred seemed to scrunch even further into the plush cushions. "I worked very hard in school. I always work hard," she said in a whiny voice. "I don't know why you pick on me, Desiree. You never talk like that to Maria or Evelyn. Next time, let one of them lend you her Epilady shaver!" Her pale blue eyes squinted at the lavishly framed portrait on the end-table next to the sofa. Judith took a closer look: It was Max and Maria with the Sacred Eight, including the missing Castles, photographed in the Place Vendôme. They appeared delighted to be together, and Judith decided that the camera could lie.

She was being officially introduced to the mousy Mildred, whose last name was Grimm and whose job was described as Max's assistant, when a gnomelike man burst into the room pumping away at an atomizer. "Good grief," whispered Renie, "I thought it was bug spray, and he was trying to zap the other guests."

He was, in fact, Birdwell de Smoot, the respected theater critic and enemy of tobacco smoke. "You're all killing yourselves," he announced, his pointed ears twitching and his tuxedoed chest puffed out like a penguin's. "And me." He stopped squirting the air spray long enough to stand on tiptoe for his welcoming kiss from Maria and to give Max a jerky handshake. He then plopped down on the sofa, landing between Desiree and Mildred. "Mildred, your dress is out of date. Pastels don't become you. Why don't you get a new hairstyle? Desiree, your perfume doesn't go with your personality. You need to lose five pounds. You should never have taken that role in *It's His Toupee.*"

"Go screw yourself," said Desiree with a yawn.

Birdwell de Smoot ran a small hand over his bald head. "Who's spitting on my scalp? I hate it when people speak and spit on me!" Behind his thick glasses, he turned sharp dark eyes up to Judith and Renie. "Who are you? What do you do? Act? Write? Sing?" Before either cousin could answer, he was on his feet. "Never mind. I need a drink."

Maria extended a graceful arm, as if to haul him back. "Birdwell, dearest . . ." Ignoring his hostess, the little man zeroed in on the makeshift bar, which stood in front of a mirror decorated with a frosted leopard motif. Maria turned to Judith. "Birdwell's rather difficult, but most critics are. There, my dears, Max has your drinks."

Max did, with scotch for Judith and rye for Renie. He also had Mildred trailing after him. "Max," she inquired in her whiny voice, "are the hors d'oeuvres satisfactory? Should I get more liquor? Is there something I can fetch you?"

Ever courtly, Max took her hand. "Everything's wonderful, Mildred, as always. You've met Maria's friends?" His expansive smile took in not only Mildred, but his wife and the cousins as well. "Without Mildred," he asserted, patting her limp hand, "my life would be chaos." He

beamed down on his assistant, whose answering smile was
halfhearted. Maria maintained her gracious exterior,
though Judith could have sworn that the briefest of daggers
had passed between the two women.

"Max is so modest," said Mildred in that whining
voice. "He brought me out of nowhere."

"Actually," put in Desiree, who had risen from the sofa
and come to join them, "it was Cleveland. Same thing,
though, isn't it, Mildred?" She gave a toss of the copper
mane and a shrug of emerald-green satin.

"At least it wasn't Brilliant, Alabama." Mildred's small
blue eyes finally came to life and darted a venomous look
at the bearded playwright, who was studiously avoiding
the little group and chewing thoughtfully on an anchovy.
"Is it true, Desiree, that your husband got his start by
writing an ode to Bear Bryant's hat?"

"There was more drama in the Bear's hat than in Alabama's last play," asserted Birdwell, who had somehow
materialized between Renie and Mildred. Even with lifts
on his shoes, Birdwell barely came to Judith's chin. Fascinated, she stared down at the top of his bald head and
had an intense desire to spit.

"Rot," replied Desiree, fitting a green cigarette into a
long holder and deliberately waving it in Birdwell's indignant face, "*G-52* is a marvelous work. It's the first time
anyone has explored the social and theological implica-
tions of bingo in the Catholic Church."

"Birdie's a Presbyterian, remember?" Max's smooth
voice should have had the effect of balm, but instead, Desiree laughed derisively and Birdwell snorted loudly.

The exchange was cut short, however, by the arrival of
Spud Frobisher and a svelte woman with brown hair fitted
close to her head like a cap. "Well, look at all these swell
people! Are we having fun or *what?*" demanded Spud,
long arms spread out to embrace the entire room. "Evelyn, we gotta get to drinking and catch up with the rest of
them. How about a cream soda?"

"How about piping down," murmured his wife. With

a resigned sigh, she gave Spud a little push toward the
bar, then allowed Max to kiss her cheek and Maria to offer
a stilted hug. "You must be Judith and her cousin, Serena," said Evelyn Frobisher, not wasting time with proper
introductions. "You made Spud five minutes late meeting
me this afternoon."

Judith was about to apologize when she noticed the glint
of amusement in Evelyn's hazel eyes. "We had thirty years
to cover," Judith said with a smile. "I guess it took more
than five minutes."

The others were drifting away, Birdwell still arguing
with Desiree, Mildred plying Max with canapes, and Maria joining Alabama by the window. Out on Prince Albert
Bay, the lights from a dozen freighters shone in the clear
autumn night air as their captains awaited pilots to guide
them into the inner harbor. Spud was carrying two glasses
of mineral water and spilling one of them on the deep pile
of the carpet as he bumped into a chrome and leather
footstool.

"Here, sweetie, no cream soda. Will this do?" He
handed the full glass to Evelyn and gave her a puppylike
look.

Evelyn wore a faintly weary air. "Of course, if it's all
there is in the nonalcoholic line." She raised the tall glass
at Judith and Renie. "Spud and I don't drink. My father
died of cirrhosis of the liver when he was thirty-nine. My
mother died of a broken heart six months later."

"That's why Evelyn became an agent," interjected
Spud, draping an arm around his wife's neck. He saw Evelyn's lifted eyebrow and revamped the statement: "I
mean, she had to quit college and go to work. She was
with William Morris when we got married, then she started
up her own agency, didn't you, sweetie?"

"So it seems," responded Evelyn with a resigned expression. "The truth is," she said to Judith and Renie, "I
quit to have our first child. Then a couple of clients—no
names, please—who were unhappy with the Morris agency
asked me to represent them. Of course I always was Spud's

agent. Now Desiree is with me and Jonathan and Clea and several other big names. Mostly New York, though I have a few clients in London and L.A.'' She summed up her career with the same brisk efficiency that she used to brush a piece of lint from her deep blue crepe dress.

"Impressive," remarked Judith, thinking that Evelyn Frobisher's polished, no-nonsense manner was totally different from her husband's ah-shucks, down-home persona. "What about Alabama Smith?"

Evelyn's gaze traveled across the room to where the playwright was now engaged in a heated discussion with Birdwell de Smoot. "Alabama is a writer. Ergo, he has a literary agent." She smirked. "If I were Birdwell, I wouldn't stand too close to that window. It's a long drop to Empress Drive."

"Birdie would bounce," said Desiree, sidling up to Evelyn and Spud. "Listen, Ev, one more role like the Queen of Thrace, and I'll put you out there with him. That's the last time I play a part wearing a costume made out of furnace filters. Let's get a little more selective, hmmm?" The green eyes glinted at Evelyn, then shifted to Max, who appeared to be refereeing between Alabama and Birdwell. "Maybe I should start sleeping with Max again. The best parts I ever had were under him. So to speak." The heavy eyelids and thick lashes dipped in a sly, langorous motion. Spud actually blushed.

"Golly, Desiree, you wouldn't want to upset Maria! She and Max have been married a long time now." He sounded quite stern, like a Sunday school teacher lecturing preschoolers in a little church on the prairie.

"Oh, cut the corn, Spud!" snapped Desiree, coming out of her indolent state. "I was married to Max almost as long as Maria has been. We still work well together." Her crimson mouth twitched slightly. "In many ways."

"At least you're all friendly," Evelyn put in, watching her husband turn an even deeper red. "Usually."

"Sure," said Desiree is that husky voice. "I suppose what I ought to do is inspire my brilliant pork rind from

Brilliant to write something to showcase my talents. That's assuming he can still write at all. I'm getting sick of defending that stupid bingo turkey.'' Her green gaze cut across the room like a laser just as Alabama grabbed Birdwell by the lapels and shook him violently. ''Oh, damn!'' exclaimed Desiree, grasping her emerald satin skirt and hurrying to her irate husband. ''Put the little twerp down, 'Bama. Nobody reads his wretched stuff anyway!''

''You're a bitch! He's a liar!'' Birdwell was turning blue. ''I'm number one! There's not a critic in North America who can touch me! Help!''

''Well, Ah'm touchin' you now, Birdie ol' boy,'' said Alabama, his carefully cultivated accent gone as he lifted the little man off the floor. ''How would you like to go for a nice ol' swim in Prince Albert Bay?''

''Max! Maria! Help! I'm blind!'' Birdwell's glasses had fallen off into the clam dip. Max was grappling with Alabama while Maria tried to calm Birdwell. Mildred stood by the telephone, ready to summon reinforcements. Evelyn was concerned; Desiree, bemused. Judith and Renie edged toward the door, prepared to beat a hasty retreat to the Prince Albert Cafe.

Spud lurched across the room, knocked a bottle of gin off the bar and smashed his shin on the coffee table, but still managed to reach Birdwell and Alabama before further harm could be done. Somehow circumventing Max Rothside, Spud picked the critic up in one hand and the playwright in the other.

''Hey, you guys, this is a *party!* We're having *fun!* Look, you've ruined the ice sculpture!''

Sure enough, the graceful swan, apparently carved in honor of Maria's famous role, lay on its side with its head broken off. Birdwell was unmoved. Alabama, however, looked vaguely ashamed.

''My apologies, Maria. It was a pretty piece of ice.'' He gave Birdwell a hard stare, then put out a hand. ''Sorry, Birdie, but you get under a man's skin. Back home, you'd have been lynched forty years ago.''

Birdwell accepted the apology with bad grace. Spud released both men and slipped on the swan's head, falling to the floor with a terrific thud. Evelyn rushed to his side, but her sympathy was perfunctory. "He falls down a lot," she said to Judith over her shoulder. "If you knew him way back when, you probably remember."

Judith didn't, exactly, but took the comment as her cue to depart with Renie. "This has been . . . interesting," she said to a shaken Maria. "But Renie and I have a dinner reservation."

"In Guam," muttered Renie, surveying the damage wrought by falling bodies, melting ice, overturned furniture and spilled drinks. "Thanks a lot, have a nice day.'Bye."

"But wait!" Maria's voice bordered on panic. She grabbed Judith's hand and came so close their toes touched. "Judith," she whispered, "I must talk to you. Alone. When will you be back from dinner?"

Startled, Judith glanced at Renie, who was looking increasingly thunderous. "Well, um, I suppose around nine-thirty or so. Shall I ring your suite?"

Maria's padded shoulders slumped in relief. "Yes. No, I'll ring yours. We have to feed these people." She sounded as if she planned on tossing out raw meat at the zoo. Leaning forward, she brushed her cheek against Judith's. "Thank you, my dear. Thank you. I'm so glad you're here!"

Puzzled, Judith looked past Maria's sleek black head to Renie, who was on the verge of an explosion. "We won't be late," Judith promised, and gave Maria an impulsive hug. "Don't worry."

With a wave that no one else seemed to notice, the cousins were gone. Renie was already swearing a blue streak, employing words learned at her father's knee. Since Cliff Grover had been a seafaring man for much of his life, the language his daughter used all but seared the paint off the Clovia's walls.

"That's it!" Renie announced when she'd finally polished off her stream of obscenities. "No more invitations! No old chums, no popcorn vendors, nobody but us, you lamebrained knothead! We came up here so you could relax. It's been one goofy disaster after another." She paused, running out of steam. "Now we have a nice, quiet dinner. Tomorrow we shop. Then we have another nice, quiet dinner. Then we go to bed. And we'll have more fun, quiet times before we head home Wednesday. Okay?"

"You've got clam dip on your blouse."

"Oh, crap!" Renie started to work herself up into another rage, then collapsed against the glass box that housed the fire extinguisher. "I'll have to change. What time is it?"

"Actually, it's not quite seven. We've got half an hour. Why don't we go down to the bar and have a drink and watch the ships in the bay?"

"We can do that at the restaurant," replied Renie, using her key to unlock their door. "If we deviate from our schedule—*my* schedule—we will end up meeting someone you knew out on Thurlow Street who runs a crack house or is a pimp or used to hustle you when you worked at the Meat & Mingle. Worse yet, we might meet one of our relatives. That's the only drawback to visiting Port Royal, I'll have to admit, you always bump into people you know."

"It seems like we have already," Judith remarked perching on the bed while Renie tried to sponge off the clam dip. She failed, swore some more, and finally slipped out of her reversible wrap. "You said you saw the Rankers up here once," Judith remarked, suddenly realizing that though the night was young, she wasn't, and if she remained on the bed too long, she might topple over and go to sleep. It was clear that her idea of a vacation didn't quite jibe with her cousin's. Renie's boundless nervous energy couldn't be contained in a single hotel suite. Judith, however, would have been content to loll about in bed and let room service cater to her every whim. She'd been giving to other people for too long not to enjoy being on the receiving end for a change. But this probably wasn't the moment to say so to Renie. "Do Carl and Arlene often stay here?" Judith asked instead.

"I doubt it," replied Renie, wriggling into a mauve wool jersey with a drape across the bodice. "I think they move around a lot. They were staying at Victoria Place then. Arlene cold-cocked the doorman."

"Good old Arlene," murmured Judith. "She should have been here tonight."

"I wish she had, instead of me. What a bunch of—" Renie gripped the suede belt to her dress with both hands and Judith had to brace herself with her high heels as a tremendous *whump!* seemed to shake the hotel's historical foundation. The cousins stared at each other, then waited for ensuing tremors.

But only the sound of traffic down on Empress Drive reached their ears. "If that's a Heat Pixie, I'm checking out, " said Judith.

Collecting herself, Renie fastened the belt in place, annoying Judith by using the last hole. "No, more likely a giant cracker. I guess." Shrugging off the loud report, she glanced in the mirror and picked up her purse. "I don't know why you'd complain about Heat Pixies when you keep dragging us into situations that make the Middle East look like Disneyland." She took out her lip-liner and made a less than perfect pass around her mouth. "Sometimes, coz, I can't understand you. Don't you like peace and quiet? You've spent a lifetime in chaos. Give yourself a break."

Judith knew that Renie's little lecture was the product of genuine concern. "That's exactly what I'm trying to do. All I did was accept a cup of tea and a scotch on the rocks. I don't call that searching out trouble."

"No," Renie conceded. "Maybe trouble seeks you. It always has."

The cousins grew quiet, Renie reapplying blush and powder, Judith brushing her hair. "All right," Renie said at last, "what have you heard from Joe?"

Judith had been waiting for Renie to ask, but even when the question was finally posed, she wasn't prepared. "Joe? Joe who?"

Renie tossed her mascara back into her handbag. "Oh." The ensuing silence would have been awkward between most people. But Judith and Renie were too much in tune to be uncomfortable with each other's emotions. "Bill says the chancery is overwhelmed with annulment requests these days," Renie remarked after at least a full minute had passed. "He thinks it's a good sign, really. People may want out of their marriages, but they also want to stay in the Church."

"I don't know why Bill has to ask his students or his clients any questions," Judith said with a touch of asperity. "He's so damned smart, he can read their minds."

Renie absorbed the criticism of her mate without comment. "It took Cousin Marty almost two years, remember?"

"Marty's a moron. He thought all he had to do these days was call 555-SPLIT at the chancery and the archbishop would send the annulment back on a picture post-card of the Pope." Judith stood up and went to the closet to get out her leather jacket. "The real question is, what happens when—and if—Joe is free?" Her anxious expression begged Renie for the right answer.

But Renie was fresh out of pat solutions. "Wait and see. It'll all come out in the wash," she said, ducking behind one of Grandma Grover's favorite all-purpose platitudes.

"I've been waiting. For ten months." Judith's black eyes snapped.

"Then you won't have to wait much longer," Renie said blithely. She put on her black raincoat, searched for the belt in the pockets, and came up empty-handed. "Let's go. We've both waited long enough for dinner. I'm starved."

At the elevator, the old-fashioned dial pointed to 7. "Let's hope it's not going down," said Renie. "Everybody in Port Royal goes to dinner about this time."

But the metal hand stayed put. Judith became restless; Renie grew impatient. "Come on, let's walk down one flight," said Renie, heading for the stairs. "Some idiot may be holding it. Or maybe it's stuck. It does that sometimes."

They tramped down the old worn stairs, their high heels echoing loudly in the stairwell. But on the seventh floor, there was no one at the elevator. Renie gave the button an extra hard push. The doors seemed to resist, then creaked open with a shudder. Judith and Renie started into the car and stopped. Judith gasped and Renie squealed. The elevator wasn't empty. Sprawled on the tweed carpet was a black form that looked like a giant spider.

It was Bob-o, and somehow both cousins knew he was dead.

FOUR

A BRIEF, IF terrifying, examination proved that their instincts were correct—Judith could find no pulse, and the discovery of a neat, ugly hole in Bob-o's tasseled cape suggested that the shattering noise they had heard in their hotel room was not fireworks, but a gun.

Unlike more modern versions, the Clovia's elevator had no telephone. Fighting down panic, Judith searched for the button which had been set to hold the car on the seventh floor. It was large and dull red. She pressed it, the doors inched shut, and the cables went into their groaning act. The cousins stood transfixed, staring helplessly at each other over Bob-o's corpse.

"I'll call the front desk from our room," Judith said in a low voice, as if she might awaken the late popcorn vendor. "You stay here and hold the car." Renie's nod was barely perceptible.

The hotel seemed ominously quiet. Judith entered Suite 804 cautiously. A murderer was loose, after all, and a vacant room was an ideal hiding place. But only the sounds of traffic from Empress Drive met her ears.

With unsteady fingers, she dialed the desk and informed Doris that there had been an accident.

"The police are on their way," Judith reassured Renie in a breathless voice. A glance down the hall told the cousins that no one else on the eighth floor had—as yet—been alarmed by the unusual noise.

"They were probably too busy trying to kill each other," remarked Renie, who was now propping herself up against the corridor wall. "Jeez, coz, now I feel crummy." She gave Judith a long look that was full of affection as well as admiration. "Just think, you made that poor old nut's last afternoon happy."

Judith shrugged off the compliment. "I just wonder who made it his last afternoon, period. Why would anyone want to shoot a popcorn vendor?"

"I told you his popcorn was lousy," replied Renie, then looked vaguely ashamed. "Well, maybe not *that* lousy . . ." She glanced back into the elevator, flinched, and turned away.

"How will the police get up here?" asked Judith "There's only one car."

But Renie was pointing across the hall, into a little alcove. "There's a freight elevator. They use it for housekeeping and room service. Gee, I wonder, do they send the Mounties?"

Judith shook her head. "How would I know? You're the Sage of Canadiana. I'd guess they have some kind of metropolitan police force. Or would it be a constabulary?"

"Beats me. Bill and I've never gotten arrested in Canada." She grimaced suddenly at Judith. "My gosh, coz, we're foreigners! Should we call the American consul?"

"We should call the Prince Albert Cafe and tell them we'll be late," said Judith. She caught the billowing folds of Bob-o's cape out of the corner of her eye and bit her lip. "I'm being callous. Damn. But this is my second body in less than a year!"

"Don't forget Dan. Just think, we almost brought him along."

"Yeah, and he was always such fun." Judith paused, hearing the groan of cables in the recesses of the Clovia's walls. "That must be the freight elevator. *En garde,* coz."

Four uniformed policemen, looking not unlike their American counterparts except for extra buckles and a bit more brass, erupted into the hallway. A fifth man remained by the freight elevator, sending it back to the lobby.

"Medics," he said, "not that they're needed, we're told." His voice had a soft Scots burr.

"Stand aside, please." An older officer, presumably in charge, made straight for the passenger elevator and went down on his knees. His examination was only slightly more thorough than Judith's. "Shot through the chest. Death was instantaneous, I'd guess." His dark eyes took in Judith's anxious face, then Renie's nervous fidgeting. "Did you know him?"

"Didn't you?" Judith blurted. Seeing the policeman's startled, faintly annoyed reaction, she waved a hand in the direction of the body. "It's Bob-o, the popcorn vendor. I'm told he's been around the neighborhood for years."

"We ask the questions here." The policeman's eyes narrowed and his long nose seemed to grow sharper. "You say you knew the victim?"

Renie stepped forward, her short chin jutting. Finding a corpse in the elevator had not helped her disposition. "Everybody around here knew Bob-o and his popcorn wagon," she said. "What's your beat—Mars?"

The policeman did not take kindly to Renie's flippant tongue. "Be careful, madame, or I'll charge you with insolence."

"Insolence!" shrieked Renie. "How about inconvenience? We were on our way to dinner!"

"Coz . . ." Judith began, but was interrupted by the arrival of the white-coated medics who were crowded into the elevator.

"Are you two guests of the hotel?" the senior policeman inquired stiffly.

"Yes," answered Judith, elbowing Renie out of the way. "We're in Suite 804. Right there." She pointed to their door.

The officer nodded curtly. "Let's step inside where we can conduct this investigation in a more peaceful atmosphere."

The decision was made just in time. Not only were the medics busily at work on poor Bob-o, but the door to the stairway had opened, revealing several curious Clovia employees and at least a couple of guests. At the end of the hall, Max, Alabama, and Desiree gaped at the congregation of emergency personnel. Judith and Renie whisked inside their room with the policemen at their heels.

"The homicide detectives are on their way," the officer announced, making a quick survey of the suite, "I'm Constable Guildford, and this is Patrolman Forbes."

The young Scot acknowledged the introduction by striking his fist against his leather belt. Judith offered seats which the policemen refused, while Renie commandeered the damask-covered armchair and looked sullen.

"Names?" asked Constable Guildford as Forbes whipped out a notebook and Judith remained standing by the gas-lit fireplace. Spellings ascertained, the cousins were required to give their addresses.

"Americans," Guildford said, as if that explained a great deal, at least about Renie. He glanced at Forbes. "We may have to check in with the RCMP."

"Really?" Renie's demeanor changed dramatically. She shot forward in the chair and all but beamed. "You mean, just like in the movies?"

Guildford's long nose twitched as he regarded Renie coldly. "Not precisely. At least, not the way you imagine it, madame." He took a deep breath and made an effort at civility. "Here in Port Royal, we call in the RCMP only under certain circumstances. One of these is when foreigners are involved. Since you are from the States and acquainted with the deceased, consultation may be necessary.''

Renie's smile faded. "Oh, we didn't know Bob-o. I mean, not as a person. We just knew *of* him, if you get what I mean.''

Constable Guildford exchanged a bleak glance with Patrolman Forbes. "I see. I think. You knew Bob-o as a vendor, correct?''

Renie nodded. "Correct.''

Forbes made a notation. Guildford resumed his routine questions: "You arrived in Canada when?''

Renie was still giving the answers. "This morning. Just before noon, actually.''

"How long do you intend to stay?'' inquired Guildford, his tone growing more pleasant with each satisfactory response.

"Until Wednesday.'' Renie leaned back in the chair, crossing her legs at the knee. "We have to be back home by eight p.m.''

"Wednesday?'' The constable lifted his dark eyebrows. "Day after tomorrow?'' He saw Renie nod again. "Hmmm. That may not be possible. It will depend on the course of the investigation.''

"What?'' Both of Renie's feet slammed onto the floor. Even Judith let out an astonished exclamation. "We have to leave!'' protested Renie, yanking at the folds of her mauve skirt. "Thursday is Thanksgiving!''

"*Your* Thanksgiving,'' said Guildford, as if Judith and Renie should take the blame for their country's celebrating a month late.

A knock at the door prevented further debate over national holidays. A bulky man in a classic trenchcoat entered the room, taking off a battered hat to reveal dark hair combed over his forehead. Despite his easygoing manner, he exuded a mournful air, as if his calling required him to remain in a perpetual state of grief. "Murder at the Clovia!'' he remarked in feigned shock. "What next, porno stars in Parliament?''

"I thought we had one, sir," murmured Forbes, "from West Fortescu."

"Eh?" The bulky man turned around to stare at the young patrolman. "So we do, I forgot about Ms. Labelle." He cleared his throat and put out a hand. "I'm Detective Angus MacKenzie, Port Royal Homicide Division. You poor young ladies discovered the body, I take it?"

"We did," replied Judith, warming to Angus MacKenzie at once. "We were going out to dinner and the elevator came and there was Bob-o. Dead." She held up her hands in a helpless gesture.

"Dead indeed, poor old soul." MacKenzie shoved his hands into the pockets of his trenchcoat and whistled a few dirgelike notes. "You recognized him, eh?"

"Oh, yes," Renie put in. "My husband and I—he's not here this trip—have been coming to the Clovia for years."

"Indeed." Angus MacKenzie nodded approval. "The Clovia has staunch fans, especially among you Yanks." He glanced at Forbes, who produced the notebook. "Yes, I see . . . names, addresses, very good." The detective lumbered over to the window and looked out in the direction of Prince Albert Bay. "Lovely night. Frost by morning, I should imagine." He whistled again, soft and unrecognizable. "Well." He swiveled about, the dark hair falling almost into his eyes. Judith judged him to be about fifty, and clearly an old hand at homicide. "Did you hear the shot?" he asked in a voice that sounded as if he'd surprised himself with such a sordid question.

The cousins exchanged glances. "I think so," said Judith. "It was more like a thud. Or a whump. We thought it was firecrackers."

MacKenzie nodded and chewed on his long upper lip. "That makes sense. I don't suppose you noticed the time?" He sounded apologetic.

Again, the cousins made a visual consultation. Judith hazarded a guess: "About seven? I know we got back to our room just before the hour. Renie couldn't get rid of the clam dip so she changed, and that was when we heard the noise, right?''

"Right," agreed Renie, her spirits on the rise with the advent of Angus MacKenzie. "Clam dip has an oil base. The elevator was on the seventh floor. We walked down."

"Nasty stuff, clam dip," mused MacKenzie. "On seven, you say? Locked to stay put, eh?"

"That's right," replied Judith. "Whoever shot Bob-o must have gotten out there. I suppose the question is, was he coming up or going down?"

"Indeed." MacKenzie prowled the sitting room, studying the breakfront with its collection of English bone china, the silver wall sconces shaped like fleur de lis, a Turner print of Venice. "Very observant." He gave Judith and Renie the benefit of a toothy smile. "You heard nothing else? Saw nothing unusual?"

Judith shook her head. "No. We'd come down the hall just before seven, from Suite 800. Maybe five or ten minutes before we heard the noise. Nobody was around when we went out to the elevator."

MacKenzie frowned, then turned to Guildford and Forbes. "Would that mean that no one in this entire hotel used the elevator for—what?—ten, fifteen minutes?"

The other two policemen looked blank. "It's possible, sir," Guildford finally replied. "It's really quite a small place. Under a hundred rooms, I believe. But of course they may have tried to call for the car, given up waiting, and used the stairs. As Mrs. McMonigle and Mrs. Jones did."

"Indeed." MacKenzie let out a heavy sigh. "Thank you, ladies," he said with an apologetic smile. "I'm sorry you had such an unfortunate incident spoil your visit. Please don't let it warp your opinion of Port Royal. Basically we're as law-abiding a community as the next."

"Of course," agreed Judith, her sympathy with the detective almost goading her into a confession that she had unwittingly given shelter to a murderer in her very own home less than a year ago. But it was probably best not to say so. Unlike Constable Guildford, Angus MacKenzie didn't seem inclined to detain the cousins in Port Royal. "Will there be an inquest?" Judith asked, just to make sure.

MacKenzie picked up a glass paperweight from the end table next to the sofa and whistled some more. "Don't worry about it," he said at last. "We'll have someone bring a form for you to sign tomorrow. Except for the approximate time of death, we won't need anything else from you ladies. If we do," he added with his apologetic smile, "you're only a hundred and twenty miles away."

"True." Judith put out her hand as Guildford and Forbes started for the door. "I wish we could have been more help."

Angus MacKenzie's jowls jiggled in denial "Nonsense. You've done everything you could for us. Now we'll do what we can for poor old . . . what was it?" He saw Guildford mouth Bob-o. "Oh, yes, yes, Bob-o. Bob-o, indeed. With hard work and a bit of luck, we'll find the murderer. For now, we must find his next-of-kin. Mrs. Bob-o, poor lady, is in for a shock."

"Oh, no," blurted Judith. "There isn't one. There's just Tootle."

All three policemen, who had been standing in the doorway, gaped at Judith. "Tootle?" echoed Angus MacKenzie. "Who is Tootle?"

Renie was glaring furiously at Judith. "Ah . . ." Judith found it easier to deal with the Port Royal authorities than with her cousin. "Well, as it turns out, Tootle is Bob-o's parakeet, and what we forgot to tell you was that quite by accident this afternoon, Renie and I were invited to . . ."

In a belabored account, Judith rendered her explanation. MacKenzie listened with apparent disillusionment over Yankee candor, while Renie tried to recover from her near-apoplexy. The cousins were then given a stern warning to remain not only on Canada's side of the border, but within the immediate call of the Port Royal Homicide Division and, since they were not citizens, the Royal Canadian Mounted Police. At that point, Renie didn't think it was anything like the movies.

Angry with herself for letting the truth slip out, Judith felt it was more like a nightmare. It was bad enough to incur the wrath of Renie and the displeasure of Angus MacKenzie, but how was she going to explain to Gertrude that they might not get home for Thanksgiving? Come Thursday, her mother would roast the turkey, but Judith knew her own goose was already cooked.

Judith was in no mood for dinner out. She was torn between calling Gertrude to forewarn her of their potential delay, and simply confessing to the murder. A hanging judge on foreign soil was preferable to her mother any day.

"Don't be an ass," urged Renie after the policemen had left. "The bottom line is we happened to find a dead popcorn vendor in the elevator. We're innocent. We're on vacation. We need to eat out. Now."

Judith, who was sitting on the bed with her shoes off, set her jaw and stared with unseeing eyes at a portrait of the Empress Josephine. Josephine stared back. "The bottom line is that the sooner we figure out who killed Bob-o, the sooner we can go home."

"But we just got here!" wailed Renie.

"I mean, you dope, we can go home as scheduled. *Your* schedule, remember?" Judith fixed Renie with severe black eyes.

Renie's shoulders slumped. "Oh, shoot, coz, just because you figured out who did in that screwball fortune-teller doesn't make you Miss Marple! Once MacKenzie's feathers get unruffled, he won't care if we take off for the North Pole." Trying a more reasonable tactic, she tugged at Judith's ivory sleeve. "Don't let this screw up our vacation. You need it even more than I do. Come on, we're only half an hour late for dinner. Let's eat."

Judith, who hadn't quite given up her stare-down with Josephine, spoke out of the corner of her mouth. "What about Maria?"

"What about her?"

Finally conceding victory to the Empress, Judith looked up at Renie. "She acted scared, or at least upset, remember? Ten minutes later, somebody is dead in the same hotel. Somebody, I might add, who you said had a photograph of Maria in his apartment."

"Oh." Renie was chastened. "Well, what's that got to do with us going out to dinner?"

Slipping into her shoes, Judith slid off the bed. "I should go see her first. Then we can eat dinner."

Renie started to protest, noted the set of Judith's wide shoulders, and gave up. "I'll wait here," she said, "and call the cafe to see if we can get in by eight-thirty. We've probably lost out by being late."

"It's Monday, a slow night in the food business. The Meat & Mingle used to close from Sunday until Wednesday," said Judith, halfway out the door.

"That was because of the Health Department." But Renie's comment went unheard by her cousin, who was already going through the sitting room. At the door to the corridor, Judith paused: The police and whoever else had joined them were still there, making quite a commotion. Judith changed her mind about going to Suite 800 in person and dialed Maria on the phone.

There was no answer. Either the Rothside party had left for dinner or they were congregated out in the hall, making nuisances of themselves with the authorities. Judith returned to the bedroom. "How do you feel about room service?"

Renie was still trying to find her glasses so that she could look up the Prince Albert Cafe in the phone book. "Why? Are we under house arrest?"

Judith glared in the direction of the hall. "It's a jungle out there. Do you want to face that mob?"

"I just want to face a menu," said Renie glumly. "Hey," she brightened, dropping the phone book and going to the door which adjoined the next suite, "if we could get into 803, I think the fire escape goes out that way into Hepburn Street.''

Judith stared at the door which boasted a sturdy but old-fashioned Yale lock. She cocked her head at Renie. "Hairpin, bobby pin, paper clip? How did we do it when Cousin Sue used to lock us out of her bedroom to keep us from reading her diary?''

Renie was rummaging in the deep recesses of her handbag. "Here,'' she said, producing a turkey skewer. "You asked me to lend you some for Thursday, remember? I brought them along this morning so I wouldn't forget.''

"Clever girl.'' Judith knelt down and began probing the lock. "What was it Sue wrote about her first kiss?''

"It felt like a sink plunger,'' replied Renie promptly, summoning up the description from forty years ago. "Who was the guy, Pudge Rollins?''

"No, he was the one who got ringworm for her junior prom.'' Judith kept twisting the skewer in different directions. "I think it was Tommy Lee Bascomb, that walleyed kid who . . . Hey, I got it!'' She raised her fist in triumph.

The lock gave; the door swung open. A moment later, Judith and Renie had collected their coats and were standing in a darkened bedroom. They waited for any sign of life from other parts of the suite, but all was quiet. Judith turned on a light, revealing complete disorder. The canopied bed was unmade, clothes were strewn across the floor, cosmetics littered the Louis XV dressing table, a white fox jacket hung at half-mast from one of the bedposts, and a half-dozen magazines were scattered around the room. The air smelled of tobacco, perfume, and sensuality.

"Gee,'' said Renie, "an upscale Bob-o.'' She picked up an emerald-green Yves St. Laurent tunic from the floor. "Desiree?''

"Most likely. It's sure not Mildred.'' Judith was at the window, tugging hard. "This place needs an airing anyway. Ooops!'' She had just edged the sash up an inch when she lost her grip and the window came crashing down.

Renie, who had been perusing a closetful of glittering gowns that looked like stage costumes, let out a little squeak. "Are you okay?"

Judith surveyed a broken fingernail. There were mirrors everywhere, giving the illusion of several sets of cousins and even more disarray than actually existed. Desiree's closet, however, was more opulent than overflowing. The dazzling array of satins and silks, sequins and beads, along with all manner of shimmering decorations indicated that the actress's wardrobe traveled with her. "Quit ogling those fairy-tale outfits and give me a hand," coaxed Judith. "This window's heavy." Working in tandem, the cousins finally raised the sash. They crawled out onto the fire escape and were suddenly overcome by the rickety feeling of the metal platform under their feet.

"It's a long way down, actually," breathed Renie. Nervously, she tugged at the window to push it back in place. "I think I'll take off my heels."

"Me, too." Moving cautiously in the confined space, the cousins prepared for the descent. The ivy brushed at them, the wind picked up from the bay, the steel railing felt like ice to their touch. From somewhere close by, probably a police car parked on Empress Drive, they could hear the toneless voice of a radio dispatcher, giving notice of a vehicular accident on the St. George Bridge. By the time Judith and Renie reached the third floor, they dared to look down into Hepburn Street. A dozen or more people were milling about at the corner. Curious bystanders, Judith thought, and hoped they wouldn't look up.

They didn't. The cousins made the final leap to the ground on stockinged feet, then turned away from the little crowd. It appeared they had escaped the Clovia without mishap.

"Wow," gasped Renie, stopping at the crosswalk to put her shoes back on, "where do I get these weird ideas? Remind me never to try that one again! It's a good thing the Prince Albert Cafe's menu is worth it."

But after they crossed the street, Judith headed not for

the cafe, but the alley down the block. Renie grabbed her leather sleeve. "Hold it, you're going the wrong way!"

"Just a detour. Let's see if the police have gone to Bob-o's apartment yet."

"Coz! It's after eight-thirty! I'm going to pass out from hunger! You aren't serious about this detection crap, are you?" Renie was clinging to Judith with all her might, heels dug into the parking strip grass.

But Judith was undeterred. "Let's just look. It's right here, past the dumpster."

Renie gave in. The alley was dark. There was no sign of police activity. Judith took a small flashlight from her purse and passed it over the uneven cobbles. In the shadows, by the packing crates, something moved. Judith and Renie froze in place. A shrill cry met their ears.

"Let's get out of here!" urged Renie in a frightened whisper.

Judith held up a hand. "Wait." The packing crates moved again. Just as Judith was about to take Renie's advice, the Siamese cat stalked into the alley, blue eyes gleaming in the glow of Judith's flashlight.

"Okay, okay," breathed Renie, "so it wasn't Jack the Ripper. I still say, let's go. There's a murderer loose, remember?"

But Judith was at the door, turkey skewer in one hand, handkerchief in the other. Somewhat to her surprise, the knob turned easily. "I didn't remember it being locked this afternoon. Still, I wonder . . ."

"What?" demanded Renie, nervously following Judith into Bob-o's apartment. The little flashlight flitted from broken drum to dirty fridge to a picture of Richard Burton. The clutter seemed much the same as it had a few hours earlier. Yet Judith felt something was amiss.

"Where's that light?" she asked, more of herself than of Renie. She waved a hand in the air, finally making contact with a knotted string. The single naked bulb flooded the room with a yellow, sickly sheen. Judith switched off the pocket flash and looked around. "That kettle wasn't there,'' she said, indicating the stove. "What is it?''

Renie moved gingerly through the stacks of newspapers and around a deflated inner tube. "Mush. Or very gray meat. But don't think it's affecting my appetite. I could eat Tootle about now. Let's get out of here.''

"Tootle!'' Judith swung around, peering up at the refrigerator, the curtain rods, the cupboard over the sink. Her gaze traveled downward, scanning every inch of Bob-o's earthly possessions.

Next to a small plaster bust of Shakespeare, Judith espied Tootle. She edged closer to inspect the motionless bird. "I guess he's asleep,'' she said but the words were doubtful. Judith touched the parakeet; her hand fell away as if burned.

Tootle's neck was broken.

FIVE

"I'LL HAVE THE lox with capers and the mussels in broth and the angels on horseback," a rejuvenated Renie told their waiter. "Then I'll get the Caesar salad, and after that we'll figure out what we're going to have for our entrees. Oh—and bring plenty of your wonderful sourdough bread." She closed the menu with a big smile.

The waiter had turned to Judith, who was reading the wine list upside-down. "Madame?" he ventured.

"Huh?" Judith gave a start. "Oh! I'll have a cup of clam chowder and a petite filet, medium rare. Maybe Petunia Pig over there will throw me some scraps from her first few courses."

"Jeez, coz," said Renie after the waiter had headed back toward the cafe's kitchen, "forget the damned diet! We're on the town!"

"We're on the lam. And, unlike certain callous people I know, I can't put Bob-o and that poor bird out of my mind. I swear, if you'd gone to watch the aristocrats get guillotined, you'd have brought a picnic hamper."

Renie's eyes glazed over. "Filled with French food.

Pâté and cheeses and long loaves of bread and tiny button mushrooms with—''

"Can it. Here come our drinks. Why don't you at least have the decency to say you'd rather get sloshed about now than eat like a hog?''

Renie's ebullience faded as she zeroed in on the tragedy at hand. "Shoot, I feel terrible about Bob-o. And even that awful little bird. But starving myself isn't going to bring them back. Remember, coz, we are on *vacation.*''

"The Killer isn't,'' Judith retorted. "Why would anybody strangle a parakeet?'' She shivered, recalling the stiff little body with its broken neck. Just seconds after the discovery, the sound of squealing tires at the far end of the alley had flushed the cousins from the apartment. Fleeing in the opposite direction, they had sought refuge in the oak and brass ambience of the Prince Albert Cafe.

"Maybe Tootle fell,'' Renie suggested after the waiter had left their drinks and brought the bread basket.

Judith shrugged and sipped at her scotch. "It's weird, I'll admit. Risky, too. That's assuming whoever did in Bob-o, did ditto for Tootle. I just wish we'd had time to find some personal papers. We don't even know what Bob-o's real name was.''

"True.'' Renie smeared butter on her bread and took a big bite. "The police will find out. It'll be in the morning papers.''

"Or even the late TV news tonight.'' Judith checked her watch. "It's after nine. Maybe I should try to call Maria around nine-thirty.''

Renie looked askance at Judith, but didn't try to dissuade her. Thirty minutes later, after Renie had wolfed down her hors d'oeuvres and salad, Judith was at a phone in the ladies' room. But there was still no answer in Suite 800 at the Clovia. A shaken Doris informed Judith that the Rothside party had gone out for dinner shortly after eight-thirty.

"Have the police left yet?'' Judith asked, shielding her

words from the two older women who primped in front of a mirror.

"I beg your pardon?" said Doris with a shocked air that carried over the phone lines.

"Excuse me, I'm Mrs. McMonigle. I'm in Suite 804 with Mrs. Jones, and we were the ones who found the body in the—" She felt, rather than saw, the two women turn and stare. "Never mind, Doris. We'll try tunneling back in." Judith put the phone down, gave the curious women a cloying smile, and patted her purse. "I don't know about you, but I'm glad I'm armed."

She was still laughing to herself at the snoops' stunned expressions when something occurred to her. "Hey, coz," she said sitting back down across from Renie, who was eating more bread, "what kind of gun laws do they have up here?"

Renie reflected. "Tough. Bill says they're much stricter than we are at home. Why do you ask?"

"How many average citizens in Port Royal would own a handgun? At least compared to people in our state. That fact alone narrows the field of suspects, especially if you first limit the list to people in the hotel."

"Somebody could have followed Bob-o into the Clovia," Renie pointed out.

Judith withheld her reply until the waiter had brought her steak and Renie's whole Dungeness cracked crab. "Have you ever seen Bob-o in the hotel before?" queried Judith, giving in to temptation in the form of butter, sour cream, chives, and bacon bits on her baked potato.

"No." Renie was cracking crab with gusto.

"So someone invited him. Or else he came to find somebody. Probably that somebody was staying on the seventh or eighth floors." She bit into her steak, discovering the marvels of Alberta beef. "Mmm, you're right, starving won't bring Bob-o back."

"Why seven and eight? Why a guest and not an employee?" Now that Renie's appetite was appeased, she was throwing herself wholeheartedly into the puzzle.

"I'm not entirely ruling out employees. But if you planned to kill Bob-o—and I think it was planned because of the way it happened—why attract attention to yourself at your place of work? An employee could knock him off any time, and someplace other than the Clovia. But a visitor's opportunities are more limited." Judith paused to savor a buttered baby carrot. "As for figuring it was someone on the the top two floors, you have to assume Bob-o was meeting the murderer, okay?" She saw Renie nod over a crab claw. "You don't ride up and down with your victim, gun in hand. You either get in with him and shoot him and then get out, or you shoot him as soon as the door opens, and then you reach into the car to set the button on Stop."

Renie swirled a big chunk of crabmeat in a cup of melted butter. In blissful ignorance, she managed to spatter the mauve drape on her dress. "That makes sense. I think. But it's sure risky."

Judith nodded. "The killer is a real risk-taker. He—or she—also had to go to Bob-o's apartment and do in Tootle."

Renie tore into more crab, sending bits of shell into her hair and onto her sleeve. "So we've got two victims, one killer, and absolutely no motive. Unless," Renie mused, unaware of the butter that had landed on her arm, "Bob-o saw something he shouldn't have in his course of work."

Judith, who had become momentarily fascinated by the wreckage of Renie's toilette, looked perplexed. "Like what?"

"Well," explained Renie, "his route covers the street across from the Clovia. He could have seen something through the window. Because of the view, everybody leaves their drapes and curtains open on that side."

"Good point," agreed Judith as the waiter came to see how the cousins were faring. Cringing at the carnage that surrounded Renie, he asked if there was anything else he could bring for their dining pleasure.

"How about a hose?" asked Judith.

They settled on two cups of decaf and a fingerbowl.

"Gee," exclaimed Renie, surveying some of the damage, "I seem to have soiled myself. Again. I'm going to run out of clothes. I'll have to go to La Strada Boutique tomorrow and pick something up.

"The last time you did that, you had Bill teaching night school for three quarters," said Judith.

"I pay for my own clothes," Renie countered. She was about to launch into a dissertation on the Jones family financial responsibilities when she suddenly made a motion with her thumb. "Hey—by the door. The Rothside party is just exiting the private dining room."

Sure enough, Max and Maria were exchanging pleasantries with the hostess, while Alabama helped Desiree into floor-length mink, Mildred allowed Birdwell to assist her with a drab brown raincoat, and Spud knocked over the brass hat rack as he tried to hand Evelyn her snakeskin jacket. The crash caused everyone in the group to turn around. As Evelyn extricated Spud from the hat rack, Maria caught Judith's eye across the room. She turned to Max and spoke rapidly. Nervously, too, thought Judith, though at such a distance, she couldn't be sure. But Maria detached herself from the others, and with less than her usual grace, moved toward the cousins' table.

"Do you mind?" Maria smiled tremulously and reached for the extra chair. "I told Max I wanted to apologize to you for the scene between Alabama and Birdwell. It was a lie, of course." She sat down gingerly, mindful of the sash on her harem pants.

The waiter returned to inquire after her needs, but she waved him away. "I feel so stupid," Maria said, a hand to her sleek head. "I was so full of my own concerns, and then that poor man got killed in the elevator. How petty we humans are!"

"As compared to what, goats?" retorted Judith, but saw Maria's dashed expression and felt silly. "Never mind, it's been a rough evening. I tried to call you at nine-thirty, but you weren't there. That's because you were here," she added, somewhat inanely.

But Maria didn't notice Judith's small gaffe. "It's probably a prank," she said, not looking at either of the cousins, but across the brass rail which divided the upper part of the restaurant from the lower level so that both halves could take in the view. "I ought to tell Max and be done with it. He'll laugh and make all my worries go away. He always does." She smiled widely, but there was something of the frightened child in her wide-set gray eyes.

Bewildered by Maria's rambling words, Judith went straight to the point. "Look, Maria, you can speak in front of Renie. We've been keeping each other's secrets since World War II. If you'd like to unload, go ahead."

Maria put a thin hand on Judith's arm. "You're a darling. You always were. I remember how nice you were to me when I threw up in geometry class and everybody else was so nasty. But dear Judith, I assure you, I've nothing to say. It was all a tempest in a teapot. I'm like that, nervy. Forgive me for worrying you." She let her hand fall away, and fixed Judith with that fragile smile.

"Well, okay, but if you ever feel like—" Judith began, but Maria was on her feet.

"I must run. Max said he'd wait outside. He didn't want me walking back to the Clovia alone. There's a homicidal maniac out there, after all." Still smiling, she blew a kiss at the cousins and then was gone, her tall, slim, red-and-black-clad figure turning several heads in the cafe.

"What was that all about?" inquired Renie, finally daring to look at the dinner bill which had been resting inside its leather-bound folder.

"Damned if I know," said Judith, getting out her wallet. "Maybe Maria is subject to nerves. Or maybe something happened in the last couple of hours. Like Bob-o getting killed."

Renie's eyebrows arched. "That's right. He had that picture of her. Gee, do you think Maria . . . oh, no." Renie checked herself. "Somehow I can't see Maria shooting that poor old popcorn vendor."

Judith was looking grim. "Somebody did. And it was

probably somebody on the seventh or eighth floor. So far, the only link we have with Bob-o is Maria.''

Renie considered her cousin's words. "If you've got Maria, you've also got Max," she noted, putting on her glasses to sort out the bill. "For the moment, let's move on to the next mystery."

"What's that?"

Renie's lips moved as she toted up figures. "The exchange rate. What's eighty-five percent of ninety dollars, then twenty percent for the tip?"

Judith gave her cousin a dour look. "Beats me. Whatever it is, it's too much, Petunia."

Ten minutes of calculations, including how much was owed by Renie as opposed to Judith, brought the cousins to the front door as well as to the conclusion that foreign currency was not their metier. Out on Empress Drive, they observed that all but one of the police cars was gone.

"Dare we try the front way?" Renie asked.

"Why not? They can't arrest us just because we sneaked out for dinner. Besides," Judith added as they crossed the street to the hotel and felt the sharp breeze cut through their coats, "I'd like a word with Angus MacKenzie."

"The last words he used on you were 'liar, cheat and fraud'," Renie pointed out. "Your usually glib tongue failed you, I noticed."

"I couldn't lie to a Canadian policeman," replied Judith, who sometimes had an uncanny knack for twisting the facts so that even she couldn't tell what was true and what was false. "Besides," she went on as they mounted the five steps that led up to the stained-glass hotel doors with their scenes from Arthurian lore, "I couldn't figure out any way to extricate myself. The question now is did the police find Tootle's body? Hey," exclaimed Judith, yanking on the door and discovering it was locked, "what's going on? Have they sealed the place?"

"No, no," replied Renie, pointing to small sign next to the double doors. "The Clovia doesn't encourage carousing among its guests. If you come back after ten, you have to let yourself in. If you return after midnight," she continued, running a finger under the engraved instructions, "you have to buzz and be admitted."

"With an excuse from your mommy?" inquired Judith. "Weird. How did you and Bill find this place, in a guidebook for wimps on Tour?"

Pushing the heavy door open, Renie glowered at her cousin. At the desk, Angus MacKenzie's shambling form was hunched over a pile of registration slips. A frazzled Doris was going though a cardboard box that appeared to be the Clovia's files. It occurred to Judith that although the Age of the Microchip had dawned everywhere else, it had not yet hit the Clovia.

Hearing the cousins, MacKenzie slowly turned around. "Well," he said in a somewhat frosty greeting, "the Houdini Sisters are back. I don't suppose there would be any point in asking how you left the hotel, eh?"

"Sure would," replied Judith smugly. "We flew off the roof in our moon launch. Caught any good murderers lately?"

"There's no such thing as a good murderer," MacKenzie asserted, regarding Judith with undisguised disapproval. "This investigation has barely begun. You realize we have an entire hotel to consider, almost four hundred people, including staff?"

Judith looked at him unblinkingly. "I'd narrow that down to about forty. I think you can eliminate the first six floors of guests, and the staff."

"I don't need any advice from American tourists who try to deceive the Canadian police."

MacKenzie's ferocious glare would have intimidated anyone who hadn't been married to Dan McMonigle for over 18 years. But Judith stood her ground. "You'd save yourself a lot of trouble if you did." She wavered, wondering if she should ask about Tootle. Or mention the photograph of Maria in Bob-o's apartment. But MacKenzie's men should have found both, unless they were bat-blind. And Judith felt she owed a certain amount of loyalty to

Maria. They had, after all, both danced the minuet at Our Lady, Star of the Sea Parochial School. "No early leads, I gather," she finally ventured, aware that the more suspects MacKenzie considered, the longer it would take to find the killer. Gertrude's scrawny image materialized in a haze of black cigarette smoke and blue curses.

"We don't discuss our progress with the public," MacKenzie replied, turning back to the desk. "Indeed, we don't have a coroner's report as yet." His tone shifted slightly, as if his natural affability was resurfacing.

"Have you got a name?" Judith inquired, ignoring Renie's tug on her sleeve.

"A name?" MacKenzie's heavy dark brows came together under the brim of his hat. He hesitated. "Oh. Robin O'Rourke. Born in London, November 11, 1918." His face broke into a sheepish grin. "You were right. According to his landlady, he's a widower. Wife died during the Blitz. One daughter, also deceased."

Taking advantage of MacKenzie's softer side, Judith uttered a little sigh. "Poor man, all alone in the world. Except for Tootle, of course." She lowered her lashes as if in sympathy, but kept one eye peeled on the detective.

"Well, yes. Rather." MacKenzie shuffled some of the registration forms at Doris, whose fatigue was obvious. "Plane, as opposed to car or rail. Or bus, for that matter," he said. "Get some help, ma'am. You looked tired."

Judith took MacKenzie's ambiguous reaction to the parakeet as an acknowledgment of the bird's demise. He was now rifling the cardboard box, but stopped abruptly with an exclamation of satisfaction. "You're right, they were here in February 1989."

Despite her weariness, Doris looked pleased. She was probably in her fifties, Judith surmised, a tall, angular woman who may have been accustomed to crises, but not to dead bodies in the hotel elevator. "We had that terrible winter, with all the snow. The Rothsides had to stay an extra two days because the airport was closed."

Judith glanced at Renie. So they had found the photograph of Maria, too. Otherwise, Judith reasoned, why single out the Rothsides? The detective was going through the box again. Renie gave another yank on Judith's arm. "Let's head up," she urged in a whisper. "He's not going to tell you anything."

"That's true," said MacKenzie in a genial voice, his keen ears picking up Renie's words. "What I will say is that I see you and Mr. Jones have visited the Clovia every October for the past ten years—until this one. Why is that?"

Renie gave Judith a helpless look. "Bill had a conference in mid-October in Salt Lake, and Judith's birthday fell on the first weekend, and the third one was our daughter's, and then Uncle Al gave a Halloween costume party. After that, my husband I had our birthdays—they all come at the end of the year, you see, it's such a hectic time—and I had a deadline on a presentation to the gas company, and my husband got bronchitis, and we'd given Judith a suitcase for her birthday, and she needed a rest, but we had to schedule our trip when she didn't have any guests, and now we have to go home Wednesday or Aunt Gertrude will kill us." Renie ran out of breath and explanations at the same time.

"Indeed." MacKenzie actually looked as if he'd taken everything in. "So you knew Bob-o from your previous visits, eh?"

"Of course," Renie gulped.

"Ever talk to him before today?"

"No. You didn't talk *to* Bob-o, he talked *at* you. Like a broken record." Renie's vocal pace slowed as she mounted onto firmer ground.

MacKenzie appeared satisfied, but he perused the Jones file once more. "Mr. Jones always asks for extra bath towels. You've complained six times about room service being slow with breakfast. Interesting."

"I was hungry," Renie said sulkily.

MacKenzie wore an expression of faint amusement.

"Which explains why you two exited the hotel via the fire escape." The heavy eyebrows arched a bit.

"So much for our life of crime," murmured Judith. She saw the detective's eyebrows still raised, and let out a little sigh. "Or maybe not."

But MacKenzie was finishing up with the hotel records. "My men will check these out in the morning, after you've sorted through them," he said to Doris. Bidding all three women good night, he doffed his battered hat and went out through the Hepburn Street exit.

Doris drooped on the desk. "I can't get anyone reliable to help me this late," she complained, her pinched face about the same color as her olive-green blouse. "That's the trouble these days, we have so many foreigners who can't speak—let alone read—English."

"We'll help," volunteered Judith over a groan of protest from Renie. "What does he want, how people arrived at the hotel?"

Doris looked skeptical. "For starters. But I can't ask guests to—"

"Of course you can," cut in Judith, nimbly stepping behind the desk. "I'm in the same business myself. Let's sort these into three stacks. It won't take that long."

It didn't, since each registration card was clearly marked as to what mode of transportation that particular party had used. In the case of automobiles, even the make, year, and license plate were given. With fewer than one hundred rooms, it took Doris and the cousins less than fifteen minutes to sort through the cards. In the wake of Doris's speech of gratitude, Judith and Renie headed up to the eighth floor, not in the passenger elevator, but in the car usually reserved for freight. The scene of Bob-o's murder was still off limits, according to Doris.

"So," said Judith, as the cousins undressed and prepared for bed, "Max and Maria flew in from London, arriving Saturday. Spud and Evelyn flew in from New York, arriving yesterday. Desiree and Alabama have been here for over a week, taking the plane from Los Angles."

She paused, tying her blue terrycloth robe in place and consulting the hastily scribbled notes she'd made on the back of a Hotel Clovia postcard. "Doris said Desiree was here to do a play at the King Charles II Theatre. An all-star *Christmas Carol* gala, she thought. As for Birdwell, he came yesterday on the train, hates to fly. And Mildred," she continued, trying to decipher her own handwriting, "drove in, apparently with a rental car, Oregon plates. Her home address is given as New York City."

"All of which tells us nothing," noted Renie. She was zipped into a voluminous deep purple velour bathrobe, her face smeared with something that looked to Judith like bear grease.

"Not so," countered Judith. She smirked at her cousin. "It tells us that only Mildred and Birdwell could have brought a gun along."

Enlightenment dawned on Renie. "Of course! The airlines people would have found any guns with those metal detector things."

"Right." Judith put a check next to Mildred and Birdwell's names. "But in a car or on a train, you could take a chance and sneak a gun in. Just like Cuban cigars." She gave Renie a cunning look. "And if, as you say, the gun laws up here are so tough, I doubt that any of the others could have brought one. At least not the Frobishers or even the Rothsides, since they just got here over the weekend."

Renie sat down on the sofa, going over the notes she'd made on the back of a hotel message slip. "I'm not sure I got everybody on the seventh floor. Frankly, they're an innocuous bunch. An entire family of ten who drove in from Calgary, occupying three rooms, a pair of honeymooners from San Mateo, a doctor and his wife from Saskatchewan, two priests from Quebec, a couple of young women from home who live on the other side of the lake, and three couples on a senior citizens' bus tour out of Edmonton."

"Innocuous is right," agreed Judith, still studying her

own scribbles. "Birdwell. Mildred. I can see somebody shooting either of them, but not the other way 'round."

"I can't see either of them packing a gun. Of course they both live in New York, don't they?"

Judith rechecked her notation for Birdwell's address. "True. I suppose that's reason enough." She glanced at her watch. "Damn, we missed the eleven o'clock news. It's going on midnight."

"I'm going on to bed," announced Renie, getting up and heading for her separate bedroom. "Do you think they've left police on duty?"

Judith went to the window. The ships still rested at anchor, their light showing amber in the night. The sweep of the bay curved almost as far as the eye could see, with the dark stands of timber in Empress Park faintly outlined against the sky. Down in the street, traffic had let up, with only the occasional car passing by. But just across from the hotel, in a No Parking zone where Bob-o's popcorn wagon used to stand, Judith saw the sedan with its telltale rack.

"I think we're safe," she said. "At least from the Clovia's libertine revelers trying to break down the front door."

Only partially reassured, Renie bade her cousin good night. Silence settled in over the hotel, but for Judith it brought no peace. She lay on her back in the comfortable bed with its fluted headboard and polished mahogany, staring at the ceiling. Renie, that Queen of the Creature Comforts, was probably already asleep. Judith mentally cursed her cousin and rolled over onto her side. Of course anyone could have killed Bob-o. The man was simply an admirer of theater people, filling his lonely life with famous faces. By some strange coincidence, one of them had shown up in Port Royal. For all Judith knew, any of them—Gielgud, Olivier, Burton—could have visited the city over the years. It was, after all, the hub of Canada's West Coast. And Bob-o, widowed and childless, had formed a fixation for these splendid performers. It often happened; it was a cliché.

It was ridiculous of Judith to think that she could solve the riddle of Bob-o. If she and Renie wanted to leave Port Royal by Wednesday, it was more important to prove that they had nothing to do with his death. Surely Angus MacKenzie didn't really believe that she and Renie could be implicated. The only thing they were guilty of was taking tea with Bob-o in his squalid apartment. Unfortunately, they were probably the only two people who had visited the dead man in a long time.

Except, perhaps, for the murderer.

The problem was trying to prove that neither Judith nor Renie was the killer. For on the face of it, the cousins had as little—and therefore as much—of a motive as anyone else. Judith turned over onto her other side.

She was trying to reassure herself that without any evidence the police couldn't possibly keep her and Renie in Canada, when she heard a strange noise. Judith tensed, then pulled herself up into a sitting position. Someone was knocking at the outer door. It was a timorous knock to begin with, but now it grew bolder, more insistent. Judith slipped out of bed and threw her robe over her flannel nightgown. She glanced in at Renie, but her cousin was sleeping like a log.

The Clovia had been built in an era when peepholes were superfluous. Judith slipped the deadbolt, but kept the chain on, opening the door enough to see who was calling after midnight.

"Mildred?" Judith gaped, then removed the chain. It was hard to tell which woman was more surprised.

"Oh!" Mildred squeaked and squinted. "Mrs. Mc-Doodle! Excuse me, I . . . oh, dear . . ." She was all at sea, twittering away in a pale pink wrapper with fuzzy white slippers on her feet.

"Can I help you?" Judith asked for want of anything better to say.

"No, no," insisted Mildred. "I was . . . I made a mistake. I was looking for my Epilady."

"I may have a Bic," Judith offered.

Distractedly, Mildred scanned the deserted hallway.
"Never mind. But thank you." She peered at the number
on the door. "Oh! Of course! This is 804! I meant to go
to 803, Desiree and Alabama's room! I'm a bit upset, I'm
afraid. That poor old man in the elevator, coming right on
top of the troubles with my mother. She's eighty-five and
lives alone in Sweet Home, Oregon, and can you believe
someone broke into her house last month? In Sweet Home?
Bikers, I think. She's very frail and so delicate. It's a wonder she didn't have a stroke."

"Poor thing," commiserated Judith, trying to imagine
Gertrude confronting a gang of bikers. Visions of long-
haired, drug-crazed hoodlums shaking in their biking boots
danced before her eyes. "Was anything taken?"

Mildred was still darting nervous glances in every direction. "No. Yes, the heirloom silver. We think. Mother
can't remember where she put it." With an uncertain
smile, Mildred waved both hands. "I must get to bed. I'm
so sorry I disturbed you. I'm such a silly fool!" On fuzzy
feet, she hurried off down the hall.

A disheveled, sleepy-eyed Renie was hanging on the
door to her bedroom. "Whazzit?" she muttered.

Judith replaced the chain and turned to Renie.
"Mildred, with fuzzy feet and furry legs. Or so she'd have
you believe."

"Huh?" Renie staggered slightly as she came into the
sitting room.

Judith switched on a light, dazzling Renie. "She claimed
to be looking for her Epilady. She claimed to be looking
for Desiree, who, if memory serves, borrowed it. She also
claimed to have a mother in Sweet Home, Oregon."

"Mmm?"

"Go back to bed. You're already back to sleep." Judith
sat down on the sofa, picking up the glitz-'n'-glamour
novel she'd brought along. "I'm going to read myself into
unconsciousness."

"Epilady hurts," muttered Renie. "I like it."

"Good, I'll borrow it some day and use it on Sweet-

ums. I've always wanted a bald cat.'' She flipped open
the book to chapter three. "Funny," she mused, more to
herself than the sleepwalking Renie, "I thought Mildred
was smart.''

"Unh?"

"She acted addled, as if she were some sort of brainless
ninny. That's not the feeling I got about her at the cocktail
party.'' Judith closed the book with a snap. "Of course!
That's why she was naked!''

"Huh?"

Swiveling on the sofa, Judith turned to Renie. Judging
from her cousin's blank expression, it was a lost cause,
but Judith spoke her mind anyway: "Under the pile of
pastel, our Mildred wasn't wearing a stitch. This was supposed to be Birdwell's room. I suspect she wasn't looking
for her shaver, but for a shiver. Furthermore, if her mother's house got broken into, what more natural thing to do
than buy a gun?'' Judith saw no reaction from Renie, but
had one of her own. "Except why didn't she leave it in
Sweet Home? Did she buy two, with one for herself? Or
did her mother refuse to have firearms in the house? I
wonder.''

"I like it,'' repeated Renie, and stumbled back to bed.

SIX

"YOU," SAID JUDITH to Renie over breakfast in the Clovia's small tartan-covered dining room, "must buy a frock."

"You," said Renie to Judith, looking up from the breakfast menu, "must be a freaking wacko."

"I'm serious. You are about to become Bob-o's English cousin. As you know, all English women wear frocks."

It was almost nine o'clock, an overcast November morning in Port Royal with the threat of rain heavy in the air. The frost which Angus MacKenzie predicted had never materialized. Instead, low-lying dark clouds had rolled in over Prince Albert Bay. The Clovia fortified itself against the weather with mingled smells of grilled meat and fresh-baked scones along with a roaring blaze in the stone fireplace on the far wall. The hotel's dining room was busy, with as many business types as guests crowded around the linen-covered tables. Clan crests and racks of antlers ornamented the oak partitions. A wrought-iron chandelier with light-bulbs shaped like candle flames hung from the middle

of the room. The plaid carpet was worn down by the tread
of capable waitresses and hungry diners. Renie had given
the food high marks, which appeared to be justified, judging from the number of satisfied customers stowing away
everything from kippers to kumquats.

Now that Renie had had her first cup of coffee and was
looking forward to pancakes, ham, and eggs, she was almost ready to deal with matters of the moment. But not
with buying a frock.

"Why am I Bob-o's cousin?" she inquired at the very
moment Spud and Evelyn Frobisher entered the dining
room.

"You have to be some kind of kin to ask his landlady
personal questions, that's why. Floral, with a little white
collar, maybe." Judith smiled demurely, feeling quite
smug in her matching charcoal-gray sweater and slacks.

"Yuk!" cried Renie, startling the dignified man in pin-
stripes at the next table. "I hate frocks! Can't I at least
get a cashmere sweater and a Black Watch kilt?"

"You wore that in high school when you were a snot.
I'll go along as your neighbor." Judith didn't pause for
breath as she followed the Frobishers' progress across the
dining room. "You've only lived in Port Royal a short
time, and hadn't yet managed to call on Bob-o"

"Wait a minute, why me, and not you? You're a lot
better at feeding people a line of bull than I am," protested Renie.

"Because you can do an English accent and I can't. You
used to practice when you were a snot, remember?"

Renie's shoulders slumped under her beige and navy
houndstooth checked jacket. "Here," said Judith, pushing
a scrap of paper across the table, "this is the address of the
apartment house manager. I already called while you were
in the tub. Gerda Wittelstein, on the Prince Albert Street side
of the building, first floor. She sounds very nice, if loud."

Renie contemplated the name and address without enthusiasm. "No frocks. I go as I am or not at all."

Ultimately, Judith relented. An hour later, the cousins were ringing the buzzer to Apartment 101. The front of the building bore the inscription Tudor Arms, and was a far cry from the alley side. It was a model of new Olde English, its pseudo half-timbered exterior boasting a fresh paint job and carefully clipped greenery.

Gerda Wittelstein, however, was neither new nor fresh. She was a large woman with an unfettered figure let loose in a floral frock not unlike what Judith had had in mind for Renie. Guardedly opening the door, Mrs. Wittelstein surveyed her visitors with shrewd black eyes and pursed ruby lips. Judith introduced the cousins as Margaret O'Rourke Grover and her neighbor, Gertrude Walker.

"Margaret is Mr. O'Rourke's cousin from Cornwall," Judith explained with a jab in Renie's ribs. "I called you about a half hour ago?" The statement hung as slack as Mrs. Wittelstein's shape.

"So you did." Mrs. Wittelstein manned the door, ushering her guests in like a hen shooing chickens. "Poor Robin, such a tragedy, I'm thinking. I've only a few minutes, seeing as how my son is taking me to the dentist." Her fluting voice made the appointment sound as if she were meeting with the Prime Minister.

"We won't take long," Judith promised as Mrs. Wittelstein led them into a parlor that was almost as much of a jumble as Bob-o's, except that the clutter had cost more. Ruffled pillows, knickknacks, teacups, vases filled with artificial flowers, afghans, and piles of popular magazines filled the room. Judith wondered if residents of the Tudor Arms had to qualify as pack rats.

"Margaret moved to Canada just this summer," Judith explained, accepting a seat on an overstuffed armchair complete with crocheted antimacassars. "She hadn't had time yet to call on Mr. O'Rourke."

Mrs. Wittelstein, who had planted her massive frame on a faded floral print sofa that clashed with her dress as well as the cabbage roses in the carpet, surveyed Renie with skepticism. "Has she learned how to talk yet?"

"She's shy," Judith said, giving Renie a tight-lipped smile. "Aren't you, Mugs?"

Renie was trying her best to get comfortable in a rocking chair shaped like a saxophone. "Rath-er," she said, at her most English.

"Mugs was so hoping Bob-o had made friends here," explained Judith. "Did he have much company?"

"Him?" Mrs. Wittelstein looked flabbergasted. "Hardly ever. He kept himself to himself, as they say. He had that route of his with the wagon, and talked like a parrot to anyone who'd listen. But as for friends, I'm not recalling. Then again," she added with pursed lips gone prim, "I'm not one to pry into my tenant's affairs."

"How long had he been here?" asked Judith, shooting a venomous glance at the taciturn Renie.

Mrs. Wittelstein reflected. "Before I moved in. At least ten years. More, maybe, I'm thinking. He paid his rent on time, didn't have a lot of complaints like some I could name, and was quiet. Who could ask for anything more?"

She seemed to be asking Renie. "Rath-er!" responded the ersatz Mrs. Grover. "Robin was always *terribly* self-sufficient."

Mrs. Wittelstein did not look encouraged by Renie's remark. "I don't remember you writing to him, Mrs. Grover. Are you shy about letters, too?" The black eyes bored into Renie, who squirmed faintly in the uncomfortable rocking chair.

"Rath-er." She caught her cousin's homicidal gaze and cleared her throat. "That is, I mislaid his address. Early on. Careless." Renie clucked her tongue.

Mrs. Wittelstein shifted her bulk in a shuddering motion that sent the floral patterns of frock and sofa into combat. "You found it, I see, in time to collect." She leaned forward, wagging a thick finger at Renie. "Such a thing, to neglect an old man and then hover like a buzzard! Well, I'll tell you right now, there's probably not enough to bury the poor soul. And it serves you right, Mrs. Fancy-Pants Cornwall!"

On reflex, Renie glanced down at her tailored navy slacks. "Really now!" She eyed Mrs. Wittelstein with a touch of well-bred annoyance. "Let's be sporting about this, m'dear. It's taken me weeks just to unpack my shooting trophies. For grouse," she added hastily, lest there be any misunderstanding given the nature of Bob-o's demise.

Judith, well aware that the interview was going downhill fast, intervened. "It's not like you think. I mean, the money, you see. Mrs. Grover is very well-off. It's the memorabilia she was thinking of. Bob-o—Robin—had all those wonderful pictures. And Mugs is such a fan of the theater. She knew Robin wouldn't want his treasures thrown out."

Mrs. Wittelstein's black eyes were cynical. "Worth a piece, I'm guessing. Signed by most of the great ones. What does an Oliver fetch on the autograph market?"

"Olivier?" Renie raised her eyebrows, elated at finally being able to score off Mrs. Wittelstein. "I haven't got the foggiest. I'd hang them in my conservatory. Next to the billiard room, of course."

Her hostess snorted. "I'll bet," she breathed, then sat up straight and made strange faces with her ruby lips. "I wouldn't mind having that one of Richard Burton. There was a fine piece of man. No wonder Liz was so crazy about him, poor girl. And that photo of Robin, dressed as an owl." She heaved herself to her feet and ran a hand through her hennaed hair. "The rest you can have, when the police say so. Oh, maybe I should be keeping one of his daughter. She was a lovely creature, poor thing." The black eyes scoured Renie. "About your age, I'd imagine."

Renie and Judith exchanged mystified glances. "Rath-er," muttered Renie, then gathered her nerve and hazarded a guess. "She died young. So tragic."

Mrs. Wittelstein softened. "Indeed it was. Poor husband. At least there were no youngsters."

It occurred to Judith that the beautiful young woman in the photograph must be Helen O'Rourke. "A blessing,"

she agreed, darting a wild look at Renie. "What was it?
A car crash? A plane?"

Renie burst into sobs. "Please! I can't talk about it!"
she wailed through her fingers.

Giving Mrs. Wittelstein her most appealing gaze, Judith
put her hands together in a prayerful attitude. "She won't
discuss it. Ever. It must have been terrible."

"It was." Mrs. Wittelstein had turned downright sen-
timental. "A fall on the stairs. Poor Robin wouldn't mention it, either. At least not without going to pieces. Just
like her." She jabbed a fat finger at the apparently con-
vulsed Renie. "How he went on! About ghosts and being
haunted and villains and cowards and all kinds of strange
things! I always thought," she continued, dropping her
voice, "that Helen's death unhinged him. At least a little.
I think that's why he left the stage."

Judith had just opened her mouth to pursue this line of
inquiry when the buzzer rang. Mrs. Wittelstein moved with
surprising speed toward the hallway. "It must be Herbie,"
she said.

In her absence, the cousins huddled quickly. "Helen
wasn't killed in the Blitz," whispered Judith.

"And Bob-o actually *was* in the theater," murmured
Renie.

"We've got to see those pictures again," said Judith,
and then shut up as Mrs. Wittelstein returned to the parlor
not with her son, Herbie, but with Evelyn Frobisher in
tow. All three visitors stared at each other.

"Mrs. McMonigle," said Evelyn in amazement, "and
Mrs. Jones."

"I'm Mrs. Walker," said Judith "I think you've made
some mistake, Mrs. uh, er . . . ."

As bewildered as the cousins, Evelyn tried to recover
her aplomb. *'I'm* Mrs. Brown," she asserted, "of Canadian Life Assurance, Limited."

"I see." Judith smiled blandly. "This is Mrs. Grover."
She drew the newly composed Renie forward.

"Yes," agreed Evelyn. "Of course it is."

"Rath-er," said Renie, extending a hand.

If bewildered by the confused identities of her callers, Mrs. Wittelstein didn't show it. "I can't let you go snooping around by yourself, Mrs. Brown," said Mrs. Wittelstein. "In fact, the police have padlocked the place. They let me in to look for the policy, but I couldn't find it."

Evelyn looked faintly crestfallen. "I'm sure it's there," she insisted, taking on her professional hard-bitten air. "If you can't find it, you'll have to let me look. It's company policy."

"Some company," said Mrs. Wittelstein as a horn sounded impatiently in the street. "Herbie," she breathed, going to the window. "Finally. We'll be late, mark my words. Of course he'll drive like a fiend." She turned to her visitors, a majestic sweep of her hand indicating the door. "You'll have to come back later, Mrs. Brown. Out, out, everybody, I'm on my way."

"I can't leave without the policy." declared Evelyn, avoiding the cousins' probing eyes and planting herself in the path to the hallway. "Canadian Assurance demands your cooperation."

Mrs. Wittelstein was struggling into a bright blue wool coat that looked as if it could have given shelter to a homeless family. The horn blasted again. "I'm coming already," muttered Mrs. Wittelstein. The coat tumbled into place; she bulldozed her way past Evelyn like a freight train. "My teeth demand a root canal," she said over her shoulder. "As for you, Mrs. Grover, leave your address. I'll send those pictures later." Mrs. Wittelstein rattled the door. "Let's move, let's go. Herbie hates to wait."

Reluctantly, the women trudged out of the room. Mrs. Wittelstein closed the door firmly behind them and lurched down to the sidewalk where a gaunt young man drummed his fingers on the steering wheel of a compact car. Judith wondered how Mrs. Wittelstein would fit inside. She was tempted to stay and watch, but Evelyn was already march-

ing off down the street. At the corner, she gave Judith and
Renie a challenging look. "You think I'm crazy, I suppose."

Judith shook her head. "No crazier than we are. I assume you want to get out of Port Royal, too."

"Our kids expect us for Thanksgiving in New York,"
said Evelyn, now gazing not at Judith but at a fishing
trawler out in the bay. "They're home from college on
break. We can't let them go to friends for the holiday."

She sounded reasonable, but Judith retained mental reservations. "It turns out that Bob-o actually was a performer. At least he did something in a bird suit." Judith
threw the information out like a fisherman making an ex-
perimental cast in uncertain waters.

Evelyn was expressionless. "Yes. That was a long time
ago, I believe." She swerved on her black snakeskin heels.
"I forgot, I must get downtown to meet Spud. Do me a
favor, will you?" she entreated, her usual poise failing
her on this damp and chilly autumn morning.

Judith and Renie stared at her. "What?" asked Judith.

Evelyn's fine mouth had turned into a grim line. She
actually shivered under her deep purple coat. "Don't tell
Spud I was here."

"Oh." Judith lifted one shoulder. "Okay. But tell me
one thing." She saw Evelyn give a slight nod. "Since
Mrs. Jones is with me, how come you used Brown instead
of Smith?"

Judith had expected Evelyn to laugh and break the ten-
sion. But instead, her features became more grim than
ever. "I thought of it. But before I could say who I was
on the phone, Mrs. Wittelstein told me Mrs. Smith was
just leaving."

The rain was blowing harder, shaking out the last leaves
on the horse chestnut trees along the esplanade. The cousins waited to cross Prince Albert Street, feeling the first
drizzle of the day on their cheeks.

"Evelyn isn't playing detective," said Judith. "At least not like we are. She's after something."

"She'll get it," replied Renie. "She's one very determined lady. But what was Mrs. Smith doing there?"

"Desiree, we presume?" Judith saw Renie nod. "She's after something, too. At least she used her real name. Her married name, that is, which is a ready-made alias."

"I'll bet her picture was there someplace in all that junk," Renie remarked. "Hey, what's all that?" She had paused as they reached the curb, pointing to a group of people outside the Clovia carrying placards.

"Gee," said Judith, gaping at the orderly protestors who numbered about a dozen. "They must take murder seriously in Port Royal. I thought they had a pretty high crime rate."

"They do," agreed Renie. "Breaking the law is one of the things both countries inherited from their Common Mother. It looks to me as if the criminals are about to take over. Those marchers are in uniform."

They were. Police uniforms, Judith realized and groaned. "You're kidding! The police can't go on strike!"

"They can up here," Renie said grimly. "Everybody else does. The last time Bill and I came to Port Royal, it was the post office. Before that, the truck drivers and the nurses."

The cousins resumed walking toward the hotel. The police protesters smiled and nodded, gently waving their signs. More Sterling for Coppers, Crime Doesn't Pay— For Us, and Take a Policeman to Lunch—We Can't Afford to Buy Our Own, were among the hand-lettered messages on the placards. Across Empress Drive, Judith recognized Angus MacKenzie leaning into a police car again parked at about the same spot where Bob-o had held court with his popcorn wagon. The detective straightened up, said something in dismissal to the

driver, and stepped away. Judith and Renie waited for
him to cross the street.

"Welcome to the land of the labor dispute," he said in
greeting, his long face even longer than usual under the
brim of his hat.

The trio mounted the short flight of steps into the Clovia
as the marchers made a respectful path for them. "I hope
this is a one-day walkout," said Judith as they entered the
lobby.

"Not bloody likely," grumbled MacKenzie, his hands
shoved deep into the pockets of his rumpled Mackintosh.
"It's been brewing for a long time."

Departing and arriving guests buzzed around the
desk where Doris held sway, her professional poise re-
stored. Judging from the number of newcomers, a dead
body in the elevator had done nothing to dampen the
travelers' enthusiasm. Judith recalled her own fears that
the murder of the fortune-teller would ruin her fledg-
ling bed-and-breakfast enterprise, but had discovered
that Renie had been right—notoriety was good for
business.

"In other words," ventured Judith as a Japanese family
carrying their own expensive set of matched luggage
headed for the elevator that had been the scene of the
crime, "the investigation will be slowed."

MacKenzie was watching the elevator doors creak open. "I
hope my men got everything in there," he murmured.
"What?" He turned his attention back to Judith and Renie.
"Oh, indeed, everything—lab work, forensics, the works. I
don't expect we'll have the inquest until next week. Rotten
luck, but at least there aren't a lot of survivors clamoring
for a verdict."

Judith dug into the Oriental carpet with her red wedge-
heeled shoes. "Now just a minute, Detective MacKenzie.
You can't mean that we have to stick around for an entire
week?"

MacKenzie looked like a cloud of gloom had attempted
to pass over him, got caught on his hat, and settled atop

his head. He sighed deeply. "We can't keep you against your will, of course. But as a courtesy, we'd certainly prefer that you stay in Port Royal. Even if you don't, you'll probably have to come back later."

Judith and Renie exchanged frustrated glances. "If we do, we do," Judith finally conceded. "But I have to be home tomorrow night."

MacKenzie shrugged, making the raincoat ripple like dirty bathwater. "Go ahead. We'll try to have the statements ready for you by then. They've got to be processed before the inquest is held. Otherwise, you'll have to come back Thursday to sign them."

"Thursday!" Judith all but reeled. "That's Thanksgiving!"

MacKenzie regarded her with the merest hint of amusement in his eyes. "Not here, it isn't. Excuse me," he said, turning to Doris who was hoisting a telephone receiver in his direction, "the one officer on duty down at headquarters must be trying to call me. Maybe he's lonesome."

MacKenzie lumbered off to the desk, leaving the cousins simmering in front of the Nubian lamp. "That's ridiculous," fumed Renie. "I'll have Bill call our lawyer! I'll call the American consulate! I'll call my mother!"

"Go ahead," remarked Judith, trying to damp down her ire. "Aunt Deb could talk them out of anything. Except it would take her until Christmas to do it. I've got a better idea."

"What?" asked Renie, following her cousin's sudden pivot toward the elevator.

But Judith didn't answer. She stood by the button, her face set and her eyes gleaming.

"Oh, no," breathed Renie as the car descended to the first floor. "You mustn't!" They got in, along with an older couple wearing matching tams and clashing tweeds. Judith still didn't reply. "You can't," said Renie in a desperate voice. "You wouldn't!" But of course she knew that Judith would.

Five minutes later, Judith's voice was covering the one hundred twenty miles of telephone line that led from the cousins' suite at the Clovia back home to the Metropolitan Homicide Division and the office of Detective Joe Flynn.

SEVEN

RENIE HAD ARGUED, all the way down the hall and into the hotel room. But Judith had already heard it all. From herself. Yes, Joe might think the call was a ploy to put pressure on him. Yes, Joe might perceive her request as a devious means of resuming contact before his annulment was granted. Yes, playing Damsel in Distress was a repugnant role to Judith. And yes, yes, yes, if Gertrude found out that her daughter had asked Joe for help, the Thanksgiving turkey wouldn't be the only thing that would get roasted at Hillside Manor. As for Renie, Judith knew she wasn't against the possibility of resuming the romance—she just didn't want to see her cousin headed for any more heartbreak. Judith wasn't keen on that, either.

To her mixed reaction of relief and anxiety, Joe was in his office. Only the briefest of pauses indicated he was surprised to hear from Judith.

"Jude-girl," he said in that smooth, casual voice that could melt metal, "how've you been?"

For openers, Judith wanted to tell him to drop the

hated nickname, but didn't wish to get the conversation
off to a rocky start. Besides, the sound of his voice brought
back a rush of memories: of dancing on the car deck of
the first ferryboat at dawn; of drinking Dom Perignon and
tossing caviar-covered crackers to the fish in the city
aquarium; of playing gin rummy on a raft in high summer
and getting burned to a crisp; of pillbox hats and
the Simple Sheath Dress and a standing appointment for
a weekly shampoo and set. But most of all, of Joe himself,
charming, tender, passionate, romantic, and attentive beyond belief. He had been too good to be true. Literally.

"I'm fine," said Judith. "I'm in Canada. With Renie.
We seem to have gotten mixed up in a murder."

"Jeez!" The hiss slithered along the telephone wire. "You
two always were mixed up, but this makes your second murder this year. Have you found a new hobby or is it just pure
dumb luck?"

In the wake of his initial shock, Judith could hear the
amusement in Joe's voice. She could picture him, sitting
at his desk, with his tasteful tie loosened, his loafer-clad
feet up, a wry grin on his round, faintly ruddy face. Carefully, she explained the situation, including taking tea with
Bob-o, the cocktail party with Maria and Max, the grisly
discovery in the elevator, and the unexpected police strike.

"What that means," she emphasized as Renie watched
her like a hawk, "is that we may not be able to sign our
statements and get out of here in time to fix Thanksgiving
dinner. To expedite matters, I'd like you to do a little
homework for me. I know it's a bother, but I can't do it
from this end, and probably neither can the police. At
least not when they're so shorthanded."

Joe was silent for a moment. Judith could picture his
high forehead creased, a hand ruffling the red hair with its
hints of gray. "To be honest, Jude-girl, I'm off duty. I
only came in this morning to pick up my paycheck. Incredible as it may seem, I took the whole week off for
Thanksgiving."

Judith gritted her teeth and avoided looking at Renie. If

Joe was separated from his wife, where was he going to spend the holiday? With his children? Friends? Another woman? Judith fought down a sense of rising panic and concentrated on the task at hand. "This would only involve a phone call, Joe."

He sighed. "Where to?"

"London."

"London? Hey, forget it! How could I justify a call on the city's line to London?"

"Call from home," she said tersely, wondering where home might be for Joe these days. "I'll reimburse you."

Joe sucked in his breath. Probably his stomach, too, thought Judith nastily, remembering the hint of a paunch Joe had acquired over the years. "Who do I call?"

"Where's your brother, Paul, these days?"

Joe sighed again. "London. He's been posted at the embassy there for almost five years. I didn't think I'd mentioned it to you. How did you know?"

"I have my methods," said Judith, employing her most mysterious tone, and wondering how Joe could have forgotten that Paul Aloysius Flynn's picture and history had been spread all over the *Times* the previous summer in a feature about a local boy who had made good in the diplomatic corps. Paul at the Court of St. James, Paul with the Queen, Paul at Ascot, Paul at St. Paul's—it had all been there in glowing black and white. But knowing the sibling rivalry that had always prevailed among all four of the Flynn brothers, Judith wasn't too surprised that Joe chose not to remember Paul's moment in the sun.

"Okay, here's what I want you to ask him to find out," said Judith, scanning the brief notes she'd made on the Clovia's stationery. "Anything about a Robin O'Rourke, born November 11, 1918, and probably an actor or some kind of stage performer. Also, what became of his wife, name unknown, and his daughter, Helen. Where he worked and when he emigrated to Canada. See if there are any connections with him and the following people . . ."

"Hold it," rumbled Joe. "Let me get this all down."

He paused. Judith could picture him scribbling frantically. "We've already got a trip to the Vital Statistics at Somerset House, the *London Times,* and whatever the English versions of the stage and screen actors guilds may be. Paul has other things to do as charge d'affaires than chase after wild geese."

"He also has a staff," Judith replied coldly.

The small grumbling noise at the other end of the line indicated that Joe was capitulating. "You don't care how you spend your tax dollars, do you?"

"Ha!" snorted Judith. "If I didn't give them something to do, they'd all be sitting on their fat duffs eating plaice and chips and ogling Princess Di's legs. And that's just the women."

"Okay, okay." Joe sighed with resignation. "This goes against my principles, but I wouldn't want your mother to explode." He paused very briefly. "Actually, I would, but I'll call Paul anyway. Paul," he repeated, making the name sound like a communicable disease.

"Great," said Judith breezily, and bit her lips to keep from smiling with pleasure over the telephone contact with Joe. She gave Renie a thumbs-up sign. "How soon can you get back to me?"

"It's going on midnight in London," said Joe. "I probably can't reach Paul until morning. I'll be lucky if he calls me back by Thursday."

Judith's thumb turned down, eliciting a frown from Renie. "Tomorrow, Joe. By noon."

Joe uttered something obscene under his breath. "That's impossible, Jude-girl. Even my brother can't work miracles."

"He can work the angles," said Judith.

There was the sound of a creaking chair in the background, clashing on Judith's end with the Heat Pixies who were dancing in the Clovia's pipes. "I can't promise," said Joe. "Give me your number up there."

Judith did. "I wouldn't ask you to do this if it weren't important. Our so-called vacation is already in tatters. Now

Renie and I don't want to screw up the family's Thanksgiving dinner, too.''

Joe's voice turned wistful. "How many are coming?"

"There'll be fourteen of us. Unless you count Mike's girlfriend, Kristin, as two people. She's big. Last spring we used her for a Maypole."

"Has Mike finished college?" Joe asked, his voice again normal.

"Not yet. He's turning college into a career. Of course he's only twenty-two. He'll be home tomorrow. That's another reason I want to get back on time. I haven't seen him since August."

"August," said Joe in a musing voice. "That's when I saw you last, at Nordquist's, buying Mike's birthday present, right?"

"Right," said Judith dryly, making a face at Renie who was flipping through the yellow pages of the Port Royal telephone directory.

"When is his birthday?" Joe inquired.

"August. Why do you ask?" She and Renie locked gazes.

"Oh—just curious," Joe remarked, even more casual than usual. "Mine's August eighth."

"I know," said Judith. "So's Mike's."

"It is?" Joe sounded more startled than surprised.

"Yeah. Hey, I've got to go, I've charged this to my credit card and it's prime time. Call me tomorrow. I'll be here in the room right around noon."

Joe's sigh was audible. "Okay. But I may not have heard back from Paul by then."

"Yes, you will," said Judith briskly. " 'Bye." She started to take the receiver away from her ear, then put it back. "Thanks, Joe."

"Sure, Jude-girl. Just remember, if you catch the murderer, I don't have any jurisdiction up there." Joe hung up before Judith did.

Observing that Renie had at least a dozen questions, probably none of which had to do with the investigation,

Judith waited for her cousin to pounce. But instead of asking about Joe, Renie tapped the phone book's open page. "It's under Concessionaires, not Popcorn."

"Huh?" Judith didn't have the faintest idea what her cousin was talking about.

"Somebody had to provide that crummy popcorn to Bob-o. Isn't it possible that whoever did might know something about him? He's been peddling the stuff for years."

Judith nodded with approval. "You're right. Who'd you find?"

"Several. Let's just start with the first one. It's called Ascot Unlimited."

Renie did the calling. Ascot Unlimited served big events, such as horse races, rock concerts, and professional sports. Their very proper British receptionist informed Renie that individual vendors, such as Bob-o, probably purchased their wares from either Port Royal Amusements or Bundles of Fun. The former knew Bob-o by reputation only; the latter wanted to know when the popcorn cart would be returned.

"After the funeral," Renie informed the grating male voice at the other end, restraining herself from telling Bundles of Fun that Bob-o's corpse would be transported on the wagon instead of in a hearse. "We're trying to track down his heirs," she lied, wishing that Judith had handled the call. "Would you know of anyone—maybe some of his friends? I assume he had a backup when he got sick or went on vacation."

"Vacation?" The grating voice sounded nonplussed. "Never took one. Never got sick, or if he did, nobody substituted for him. Sorry, I can't help you."

Disappointed, Renie was about to ring off when Bundles of Fun spoke again: "Wait—there was some fellow who came in with him once, a year or so ago, to help straighten out an invoice. Bob-o's mistake, not ours. I remember that because the chap was not the type I'd figure for a friend of Bob-o's. I thought at first he was an irate customer, bent on suing us. And Bob-o.''

"Do you remember his name?" Renie sounded faintly breathless.

"No. He didn't give it." There was a pause; Renie waited with her eyes on Judith's expectant face. "Distinguished chap, silver hair, moustache, clothes right out of Savile Row. But not an Englishman. Probably Canadian or American.''

Renie mouthed the single syllable to Judith: "Max." She spoke again into the receiver. "Why did he come with Bob-o?" she asked.

"Moral support, I guess. Bob-o was upset. Hey, there's the other phone, you want to hold or what?''

Renie opted for hanging up. She thanked Bundles of Fun, then relayed her slim pickings to Judith.

"Assuming that was Max," said Judith, "he knew Bob-o from somewhere. But of course we can't be sure.''

"We could take a picture of Max to Bundles of Fun," suggested Renie.

"We could also talk to Maria. She's holding back." Judith drew her feet up onto the sofa and frowned in concentration. "There's got to be a connection between this crew and Bob-o. My guess is that Max and Maria—and who knows how many of the others—knew Bob-o in London, before he emigrated to Canada. But which one of them is going to talk? Maria? Evelyn? Spud? We're stuck until we hear back from Joe.''

"There's always the library," Renie suggested, somewhat dubiously.

"We don't have time to go through old English newspapers on microfilm." Judith rested her feet on the handsome marble-topped coffee table. "Something's bothering me.''

"Me, too," said Renie. "It's my stomach. Lunchtime draws nigh.''

Judith gave Renie a baleful glance. "Later. I'm talking

about something else, something I saw. Or didn't see. If only I could . . .''

A knock at the door broke into Judith's musings. Renie got up to answer it. Maria, wearing beige wool draped from neck to hem, and carrying her sable coat over her arm, sailed across the threshold.

"My dears," she exclaimed, "I feel I owe you an apology for my ramblings last night. I was quite unhinged. Would you join me for lunch at Ernesto's?"

"Of course!" responded Renie, all smiles.

Judith gave her cousin a sidelong warning glance. "We don't want to impose, Maria. You have your friends here."

But Maria was waving an imperious hand. "I insist. As I told you, they aren't my friends so much as Max's. He's off watching the Dickens gala rehearsal. Desiree's playing the Ghost of Christmas Past. Evelyn and Spud are downtown somewhere, Birdwell is lunching with a fellow critic from Montreal, and I don't know where Alabama is. As for Mildred . . .'' She made a dour face, her fine eyebrows coming together. "I don't much care. I'm not overfond of Mildred's company."

Judith gave in, restoring Renie's waning exuberance. "Okay, but we'll go Dutch. You can tell us all about life as a firebird, a swan, a—"

"Duck," Renie broke in. "Ernesto's has the most terrific duck cooked in Barolo wine with pappardelle."

Maria gave Renie a thin smile. "I prefer the smoked chicken and tagliatelle. Shall we go?"

They went. Ernesto's was about a mile away by cab, a replica of an Italian villa in one of Port Royal's older, refurbished neighborhoods. Cypress trees stood like sentries outside the espaliered walls, while the splashing fountain in the courtyard featured a band of chubby cherubim. Inside, all was stately Renaissance splendor, fit for a doge, or a Medici pope. Judith admired the statuary, the frescoes, the pilasters, the waiters. Renie buried her pug nose in the menu and sighed a lot.

For the first hour, Maria duly regaled them with anecdotes from her career. It struck Judith as a rehearsed performance, culled from interviews Maria had given over the years, and ran the gamut from the hilarious to the poignant to the spectacular and back again. The cousins made appropriate comments at suitable intervals, and were both generally entertained and enlightened. As the meal concluded—all three women having opted for the Oyster Tortelli Special despite professed predilections—Judith regarded her old school chum with what she hoped was the proper amount of awe:

"It must have been difficult to give up dancing. You were very young to retire."

Maria's high forehead creased slightly. "We can't all be Dame Margot Fonteyn and go on forever. It's grueling, demanding work, requiring endless rehearsal and topnotch conditioning. No other performers, including athletes, exist so much at their bodies' whims. I simply didn't have the stamina to keep going." Her long lashes, which Judith had decided were false, dipped above the high cheekbones. "Besides, I met Max." She was looking not at the cousins, but at the remnants of her lunch. As Judith had suspected, Maria didn't exactly belong to the Clean Plate Club.

"At least you were able to stay in the theater world," remarked Judith as their soulful-eyed waiter poured more coffee. "Max has certainly been involved in a number of varied projects." Judith really had no idea, but was hazarding a logical guess.

"Oh, yes." Maria brightened, resuming eye contact. "New works, especially Alabama's, the classics, musicals, revues, even an ice-skating show that toured all over the world. A half-dozen films, too, and a production of Wagner's Ring Cycle in Buenos Aires." She uttered her tinkling laugh. "Everything *but* ballet, actually."

Having been lucky once, Judith winced inwardly as she rolled the verbal dice a second time: "It was in the revues that he met Robin O'Rourke, right?"

Maria's jaw didn't quite drop, but she definitely evinced

surprise. "Who?" She fumbled with her napkin, and Judith felt a pang of real remorse. Maria, after all, was a friend, not a foe. Unless, Judith reasoned, she was also a murderess.

"You know—Bob-o." Judith sensed Renie's questioning gaze, but kept her own on Maria. "He had your picture in his apartment. I assumed you and Max both knew him from somewhere other than his popcorn stand."

The restaurant, which had been quite noisy during the lunch hour, had grown comparatively silent. Most of the other patrons had left within the last ten minutes, isolating Judith, Renie, and Maria in a sea of quiet. Maria was glancing about in a furtive manner, her thin fingers fretting at the drape on her dress. At last, she drew herself up, lifted her chin, composed her face, and stared straight at Judith. "My dear, you must be confused. I can't imagine how you know anything about the contents of that poor man's apartment, but I'd never seen him before in my life. Why on earth would I—or Max—be acquainted with a popcorn vendor?" The notion suddenly seemed to strike her as uproarious. She flung her head back, exposing her long throat in a lean, graceful arc. Judith swore she could have counted the vocal cords inside Maria's larynx.

Maria let the laughter die down naturally, then looked at her expensive Swiss watch and gasped. "Oh! It's almost two o'clock! I have a hair appointment!" Maria reached for the check, waving aside the cousins' feeble protest. "Please, I told you, it was my treat." She flipped a credit card out of her purse, then signaled to the waiter who appeared as if by magic. "My dear," she said, putting a hand on Judith's arm, "you could always make me laugh! Remember the time we skipped Mrs. Wigmore's French class to smoke behind the Beanery? You told her we'd had to call an ambulance for a man with a heart attack! Such marvelous fiction! So typical of your inventive mind!"

"Inventive?" Judith murmured. "It was true. The principal fell flat on his flute when he caught us. We'd accidentally set the Beanery on fire."

Ignoring Judith's demurral, Maria deftly signed her name, added a generous tip, and removed her customer's copy. "I must dash." She was on her feet, allowing the waiter to help her slip on her sable. "A cab, please. Gold Top." She gave the cousins her most dazzling smile. "We must have drinks before Max and I fly out tomorrow night. *Ciao.*"

Judith and Renie watched her fur-clad figure float across the restaurant. Neither cousin spoke until Maria had disappeared into the gilt and marble foyer. It was Renie who broke the uneasy silence:

"Hair appointment, my foot. She just winds that mane up and sticks a bunch of pins in it." When Judith didn't respond, Renie continued in a less volatile tone. "Okay, okay, she dyes it and needs a touch-up. Or conditioning treatments. Or—hey, coz, wake up!" Renie snapped her fingers under Judith's nose.

Judith shook herself, then returned Renie's snap. "That's it. The Spider and the Bear!"

Renie goggled. "Huh?"

"Remember—yesterday, through the breezeway in the parking garage? I saw Bob-o's silhouette looking like a big black bug. He was talking to someone. I thought of a bear. But it wasn't."

"Probably not," remarked Renie dryly. "So few of them stay at the Clovia."

Judith overlooked her cousin's flippancy. "It was Maria, in that sable coat. She's lying through her capped teeth, of course. Come on." Judith was on her feet, grappling with her jacket and handbag.

"Where?" asked Renie, brushing Parmesan cheese off her beige slacks.

"The public library," replied Judith, over her shoulder. "Which one is closest?"

Renie was practically running between the tables to catch up with her long-legged cousin. "Three blocks from the hotel. We went right by it when we were shopping yesterday. But you said we couldn't waste time doing homework.''

"A basic search," said Judith as they emerged into the street and discovered it was pouring rain. "That's all. Let me use my slightly rusty but never forgotten librarian's skills."

"Let me use a bus," retorted Renie. "Run, coz, that's a Number 4 Prince Albert stopping right across the street."

The cousins darted between cars, evoking curses from three British Columbians, two Albertans, and an Oregonian. Accustomed to the less civilized Metro drivers at home, Judith and Renie were amazed to discover that the turbaned and bearded young man at the wheel not only waited for them, but flashed a brilliant white smile as they got on the bus. Seven minutes and a dollar twenty-five apiece later, they were in front of the Prince Albert Branch of the Port Royal Public Library.

"We'll start with Max," whispered Judith, finding her way to the periodical section virtually by instinct, and selecting a vacant computer monitor. Around them at other screens, tables, and shelves were a varied lot of local residents, including a statuesque blond matron in a loden coat, a middle-aged Tlingit wearing a beaded parka over his business suit, a dainty Japanese girl taking copious notes, and a grizzled old man in a watch cap who had fallen asleep over his copy of the *Jerusalem Post*. Judith keyed in Max's name and waited for results. A long list of articles, mostly in theater magazines, scrolled down the screen. "This one. *Theatre World,* May 14, 1988. Write it down," she ordered Renie. "Let's try Maria." In less than ten minutes, they also had articles on Desiree, Alabama, Spud, and Birdwell. As an afterthought, Judith noted down a background piece on Jonathan Castle and Clea Rome.

"Why them?" Renie asked as they moved into the stacks. "They're in Hong Kong."

"But they're part of the Sacred Eight. I'd hate to leave

anybody out.'' Judith handed Renie the appropriate issue
of *Theatre World,* then took *Dance Today* for herself. ''Just
an overview,'' she reminded Renie in hushed tones as they
sat down next to a couple of long-haired young men who
had the look and smell of grad students about them. Judith
read; Renie read. Both took notes. They followed the same
procedure for Desiree, Alabama, and Spud, then for the
absent Jonathan and Clea. Their search for Birdwell, however, had left them empty-handed. ''Maybe,'' murmured
Judith when they had finished with their notes, ''we should
have tried 'D' instead of 'S' for de Smoot.''

She was right about the second time, but ended up just
as frustrated. ''How come all four of the issues with articles on Birdwell are checked out?'' Judith asked, more
of herself than of Renie.

''Maybe it's his fan club.''

''It is,'' said Judith, pointing toward the lobby. ''There
goes Mildred.''

Renie gaped at the faintly clandestine figure who was
scurrying out of the library. ''Where did she come from?
And why?''

''She sure didn't want us to see her,'' murmured Judith.
''She must have been sneaking around the stacks, avoiding
us.'' Her lips pursed in disapproval. ''She's not only a
sneak, but a thief.''

''What are you talking about?'' Renie gave her cousin
a puzzled look.

''Mildred's not a resident. She can't check out materials
from a Port Royal library. Neither can we, which is why
we're taking notes.'' Judith frowned, then grabbed Renie's
arm. ''She left by the main entrance. Let's go talk to the
librarian at the desk, quick.'' Noting Renie's still baffled
expression, Judith explained in rapid, low tones. ''See
those gates we came through? That's a security device. It
picks up any items that aren't checked out and automatically locks the gates. There isn't a detector at the Heraldsgate Hill branch, but we had one at Thurlow.''

''No wonder,'' remarked Renie. ''Your patrons out there

would have stolen talking books from the blind. I was always surprised anybody in that neighborhood could read.''

"We had a lot of picture books," Judith said. "Scratch-'n'-Sniff, too. Real popular with the drug addicts." She paused, approaching the desk with her professional librarian's manner intact. The pale young man in the lambswool sweater looked up and smiled diffidently.

"Excuse me," Judith said with her most winning smile, "didn't we meet at the North American Library Congress in '87 in St. Paul?"

Renie rolled her eyes, knowing that Judith had never been further afield on business than the semiannual workshops held downtown at the main branch. But five minutes later, Judith and the Prince Albert librarian, whose name was Ian, were chatting like old chums.

" . . . Not collecting fines from children under sixteen may encourage them to read, but it doesn't stimulate responsibility," Judith was saying. "By the way, I must be suffering from an overactive imagination today, but didn't I see an old friend leave a few minutes ago? Her name is Mildred Grimm."

Ian's narrow face grew quizzical. "Grimm? Let me see . . ." He fiddled with his computer. "No, nobody by that name among the last dozen or so patrons."

"Oh, that's right!" Judith clamped a hand to her cheek in chagrin. "She got married last year. And she dropped the Mildred. Let me think, what was it? Uh, um . . ."

"The woman who just went out was named . . ." Ian peered at the monitor. "Here it is . . ." He looked up in alarm as he noted that the line behind Judith and Renie had grown five deep. "Excuse me, I'll have to help these people, then we can talk some more."

Judith put up a friendly hand. "That's fine, we've got to run. What did you say her name was?"

Ian turned away from the stack of sci-fi novels proffered by a baldheaded man in a dark blue coverall. "Oh—sorry you have to leave. The name . . . Wittelstein, Gerda Wittelstein.'' He gave Judith his diffident smile. ''Come again.''

''Love to,'' said Judith, as she and Renie made for the door. ''Maybe I'll run into good old Gerda.''

EIGHT

JUDITH AND RENIE hurried through the rain, typical native Pacific Northwesterners who didn't own an umbrella between them. The rain, after all, was too frequent, usually too light, and always too unpredictable. Umbrellas were only something to lose on the bus. Indeed, for those savvy but effete transplants, it wasn't necessary to ever actually buy an umbrella—they simple went down to the lost and found at Metro headquarters and claimed one as their own.

All the same, the cousins weren't keen on getting drenched in the uncommon downpour that was falling over Port Royal. Pulling up in unison at the door of a bake shop, they slipped inside to the accompanying aroma of hot coffee and fresh bread.

"So how did Mildred get Mrs. Wittelstein's library card?" asked Renie, settling into a white metal chair at a round white table.

"It seems to me as if everybody has been calling on Mrs. Wittelstein for one reason or another," Judith replied, shaking raindrops from her salt-and-pepper hair.

"But why steal the card just to get articles on Birdwell? If Mildred's trying to suppress something, those magazines must be in every branch of the Port Royal library system."

"We're only guessing she took them," Renie pointed out as a ponytailed waitress in a frilly pink apron came to take their order. "You should have asked your old pal Ian."

But Judith shook her head, dispersing more raindrops onto the white table top. "All that he could tell from the computer was that she'd checked out four periodicals. It wouldn't say what they were. The real question about Ian is why didn't he realize that Mildred wasn't Mrs. Wittelstein? Mildred may seem like a mouse, but our Gerda isn't the kind of patron you forget. I suspect Mrs. Wittelstein doesn't go to the library very often. Judging from her apartment, she considers *The Inquirer* real deep stuff."

The waitress reappeared, placing steaming mugs in front of each cousin. Renie sprinkled nutmeg on her mocha and delved into her enormous purse. "Okay, here we go. This is what I got on Max." She put on her red-rimmed glasses, the scratched lenses making Judith cringe as always. "Born May 23, 1930, Toronto, to Gilbert and Dorothy (nee Damrosch) Rothside. One sister, Suzanne, born 1933, and a half-sister, Estelle, born 1921." Renie glanced up over her glasses. "Hmmm. Must have been a second marriage for Dad or Mom." She returned to her notes. "Educated, University of Toronto, apparently did not graduate. Worked in New York theater, 1952 on, also in London. Protege of Dame Carmela Finch. Began producing own plays in 1961. Married Desiree Sinclair, 1964, divorced, 1972. Married Maria Filonov, 1977. Thence follows a list of his successes, awards, and so on. Given addresses in both New York and London. No kids. No scandal. No help." She pulled a face at Judith and put the card aside.

Judith was frowning at her own notes. "Nothing of interest on Maria, either. Parents, Victor and Mary Lou Filonov, maiden name, Little. That early stuff is all old news to us, anyway. To Paris to study ballet, 1960, debut, 1962, Covent Garden. The rest of it we heard today at lunch.'' She sipped at her latte and scanned the scribblings she'd made on Spud. "He was born in Ogden, Utah, joined the National Guard, married Evelyn Novotny in 1963, two kids. He's directed plays all over the place, including London, I might add. Other than that, zero. They live in New York," she added as an afterthought.

"Here's Alabama," said Renie without much enthusiasm. "The only really interesting thing about him is that his real name is Beauregard Longstreet Smith. He joined the army after he got out of the University of Alabama, was stationed in Germany, and discharged in 1960. He went to New York, had his first hit play, *Dixie Biscuits,* and went over to London with it in '66 where he got married.''

Judith's brow puckered. "To Desiree? That can't be right."

"No," replied Renie. "Actually, maybe this part *is* interesting. By comparison. He married one Helen Brookes." Her turned-up nose wrinkled. "Helen—that was Bob-o's daughter's name. What do you think?"

Judith considered briefly. "I think it's a fairly common name. Plus her last name wouldn't have been Brookes. Let's pass on that for now."

Renie gave a short nod. "Okay. That first marriage was fast work, since it took place the same year that he arrived in England. Then Alabama tied the knot with Desiree in 1976."

"But divorced when?" Judith's question was academic, her eyes on the waitress who was making a spectacular confection with coffee, milk, some kind of syrup, and six inches of whipped cream.

"Didn't say," replied Renie, giving Judith a quizzical look. "Odd, maybe?"

Judith shrugged. "Maybe. Maybe just sloppy record keeping."

Putting Alabama's card aside, Renie summed up the

biographical data: "He and Desiree have homes in New York and Aspen. No kids."

"Don't doubt it." Judith rested her chin on both hands and began to read from the notes on Desiree in a semi-mumbling manner. "Born San Jose, 1943 is year given with a question mark, to New York, 1961, Broadway debut in something I never heard of in '62, married Max in '64, divorced, married 'Bama, blah-blah." She yawned. "I think we wasted a lot of time."

"Maybe we should have looked up Bob-o," remarked Renie, gazing with longing at the bakery case.

"I did," said Judith. "Nothing. I hope Paul has better luck." She glanced at the small menu in its plastic case on the table and calculated their bill in her head. "Put down three bucks Canadian. Let's go back to the hotel. I could use a real drink about now. It's almost time to call Mother."

"Mothers," corrected Renie. "Assuming I can get through to mine. It's a wonder her ear hasn't permanently adhered to the receiver. Oh—didn't you want to hear about the Castle-Rome lash-up?"

"Not really," said Judith, but dutifully sat at attention. "Shoot."

"Clea Rome is a native of Chicago, real name, Romanoukis, born 1960. Got her start as lead female singer with group called Stiff as a Board. Many gold and platinum records, six films, fabulous concert tours. Married Jonathan Castle, 1981. One child, a boy." She paused to see Judith's nod of acknowledgment. "Jonathan Castle, real name, John Holmes, born 1959 in Lebanon. Must have been a government issue," Renie noted, adjusting her battered glasses. "Diplomatic corps or the American University, maybe. Where was I? To New York, 1977—the rest is on Jonathan's successful stage and screen career," she admitted. "There's not even a description of his searing dark eyes and rough-hewn lean features and athlete's magnificent body."

Judith reclined in the chair and let out a purring noise

that might have come from Sweetums, had that particular animal possessed any typical feline traits. "What a pity they couldn't be here. I would love to see Jonathan in the . . . flesh." She let the last word out on a slither of sound.

"Jeez," breathed Renie, looking askance. "Maybe I should call the chancery when we get home and give the archbishop a nudge. You've been a widow too long."

But Judith was already sitting up straight and looking very businesslike. "A momentary lapse. Face it, coz, you have absolutely zip."

"Afraid so," conceded Renie, getting up.

Judith followed suit. "Maybe we missed something."

"Like what?" inquired Renie, as they girded themselves to face the rain.

"I don't know." Judith bit her lip, casting a helpless glance into the window of the Prince Albert bookstore. "Cleveland, for one thing." She pointed to a large coffee table-sized book on the Great Lakes. "Didn't Desiree say that Mildred was from Cleveland? So why's Mildred's mother living in a little burg like Sweet Home, Oregon?"

"It's not exactly a burg anymore," said Renie. "Don't you remember our dads' cousin, Mabel Frable? She's lived there forever. My mother still exchanges Christmas cards with her, and she constantly complains about how Sweet Home has grown. I think it's up to almost seven thousand by now."

"Mabel Frable would complain about going to heaven on a riverboat," remarked Judith. "Her letters make Birdwell seem like Pollyanna."

Renie tilted her head in assent. "Yeah, but the fact is, Sweet Home isn't precisely a village."

"Still, it's a long way from Cleveland," mused Judith, avoiding a large puddle. "I'd like to know why she came West."

"To help augment the population and drive Mabel Frable nuts?" offered Renie.

"And that part about Alabama's first wife—how come

no mention of a divorce? The other pieces told about Max splitting from Desiree, and vice versa.''

''Gee, coz, they were different articles from different magazines written by different writers,'' countered Renie. ''You can't expect uniformity.''

The cousins were crossing Prince Albert Street, a block from the hotel. Through the blur of rain, the Clovia looked sad, like a genteel old lady beset with family troubles. At least the police pickets were gone, though the familiar patrol car was once again at the curb across the street on Empress Drive.

''MacKenzie?'' Judith arched her eyebrows at Renie.

''Maybe he's brought our statement to sign.'' The cousins took heed of the pedestrian signal and crossed the wet pavement. Though not yet four o'clock, it was growing dark, and most of the cars had their lights on. ''Maria was certainly optimistic about flying out of here tomorrow night,'' Renie noted.

''Blowing smoke,'' said Judith, but wondered if any of the sacred Eight was actually under suspicion. As far as Judith knew, only she and Renie had admitted to an acquaintanceship with Bob-o. The thought made Judith feel as gloomy as the heavy black clouds that hung low over Prince Albert Bay.

Smelling not unlike a pair of sheep in their wet wool clothing, the cousins climbed the half-dozen stairs and were grateful for the warm, dry haven of the lobby. At least two dozen people were crowded onto the velvet sofas and high-backed armchairs, taking tea and nibbling small sandwiches.

''Damn,'' breathed Renie. ''I forgot to tell you about high tea. You have to make a reservation.''

''I'll survive, '' said Judith, pulling at Renie's sleeve. ''I don't see MacKenzie. Let's ask Doris.''

Behind the desk, Doris was registering a young sun-tanned couple from New Zealand. She summoned the aged Chinese bellman to help with their luggage. His smile was beatific, his shoulders stooped.

"That's Lui," Renie whispered as he chugged off toward the elevator looking not unlike a two-legged packmule.

"Poor old guy," said Judith. "That's a tough job at his age."

Renie snorted. "You kidding? He owns the place. He only does the bellman bit to keep an eye on the customers. And the help."

Judith overcame her surprise at Renie's pronouncement to return to Doris's conspiratorial smile. "Is Detective MacKenzie around?" she asked.

"He was here again after lunch," Doris said, her face puckered in disapproval. "He certainly keeps any information to himself, though he did say he thought Bob-o had been shot with a certain kind of gun."

Judith braced herself against the desk. "What certain kind?"

Doris looked vague, her bony fingers fiddling with the waistband of her Clan Gordon tartan skirt. "I don't remember. A .36? Or was it a .38? I don't know the least thing about firearms. But I do wish the police would stop prowling about. It makes the guests nervous."

"It should make them feel safer," said Judith. "At least they've got enough manpower to keep a car staked outside."

"Hrmpf!" Doris's bow-shaped mouth turned down even further. "That MacKenzie has a man with a search warrant, going through some of the rooms. It'll take him forever, our guests will be wild, and I'll bet my next paycheck he won't find anything."

Judith didn't feel like arguing the point. She wondered which rooms were being searched. Theirs, probably, she thought with a new wave of gloom.

Renie obviously was pondering the same question: "What floors is he doing?" she asked.

Doris shook her head. "I wouldn't know. He has one of our master keys. I think he started out looking for French Separatists. Or the IRA." She sniffed with disdain at police methods, or, it occurred to Judith, possibly the Quebeçois and the Irish.

Judith, however, decided to steer the conversation in a slightly different direction. "Did anyone see Bob-o come in last night?"

Doris rested her elbows on the deck and leaned closer. Judith and Renie bent their heads. "I didn't, but Sybil did." She nodded at the dumpy blond who was filling registration cards in the office just behind the desk area. "He ambled in here looking all at sea. 'Confused,' was how she put it. Sybil thought about stopping him—it crossed her mind he might be claiming a guest had short-changed him. He was never any good at figures, I'm told. Rest his soul," she added hastily. "Anyway, he went over to the elevator and poked the button and got in."

"Alone?" queried Judith, aware that a party of two older couples had just entered the lobby from the parking garage, towing their suitcases on leashes.

"Yes. Up he went." She turned mournful. "But he never came down. At least not the same way."

Judith glanced at the quartet behind her and Renie. Each couple was wearing matching caps and jackets, one pair in blue, the other in red. "Could we talk to Sybil for just a minute?" Judith inquired hopefully.

Doris looked dubious, then apparently remembered how helpful the cousins had been the previous evening, and shrugged. "Go ahead. Step through here." She clicked open the waist-high door in the desk, meanwhile smiling graciously at the new arrivals. Judith and Renie scooted inside and went to the open office door.

Sybil was no more than twenty, and her pasty skin looked as if she hadn't been outdoors in years. Judith tee-tered on the brink of telling a monstrous lie about some official connection with the case, but decided on semi-candor.

"I'm in the hostelry business myself," she said after introductions had been made. "Incredible as it may seem, we had a murder at my establishment earlier this year.

Naturally, I'm in shock over what happened last night. I understand you saw Bob-o come into the lobby."

Sybil's pale blue eyes had grown very wide. It didn't seem to occur to her that Judith's explanation and question were a non sequitur. "Oh, I did, and that's a fact!" Her nasal voice had traces of an English accent. "All fumbling and bumbling he was, with none of his usual patter. He went to the elevator, and I told myself, 'Syb, old girl, you'd better stop that man. He's going to cause trouble.' But the phone rang just then, and I had to answer it. He got into the elevator and went up." She shook her head, the picture of tragedy. "How could I guess what trouble there would be!" Sybil was clearly enjoying her role as a witness.

"Did you notice where the elevator stopped?" Renie asked.

Sybil turned vaguely dejected. "No. The phone call was for a reservation and I had to write the information down in the book."

"Did you hear the shot?" inquired Judith.

Sybil brightened a bit. "I must have done. Of course I thought it was the crackers."

"When? How long after Bob-o went up did you hear the noise?" Judith was leaning on an old wooden filing cabinet, suddenly aware of how much her feet hurt.

"Oh—not that long. Maybe a minute or two." Sybil nodded once, confirming the estimate in her own mind. "It was about five minutes after seven. I remember that because I was due for my dinner break at seven, but Doris had gone to the loo." She seemed very pleased with herself for being so precise.

"Did you tell all this to Detective MacKenzie?" queried Judith, shifting her weight from one tired foot to the other.

"Of course." Sybil's chins went up proudly, a portrait in civic duty. "He was amazed at how much I'd observed."

"He should be," agreed Judith, trying to envision the

dour Angus MacKenzie in a state of amazement. "You did very well."

Renie, who had been idly toying with a small totem pole that had been sitting on Sybil's desk, looked up. "Were other people trying to get the elevator while it was stopped?"

Sybil's doughy forehead furrowed. "No—not at first. Well, yes," she corrected herself, apparently not having been put to the test on this question until now. "Mr. Frobisher was there." She apparently didn't notice the look of surprise which flitted over both cousins' faces. "No, no—that was just before Bob-o came in. Then afterward, maybe five minutes or so, the Marchants in 302 and the Brewsters in 210 came along. I went to dinner then. And you called Doris just after I left."

Judith and Renie exchanged swift glances. "I suppose you mentioned Mr. Frobisher to Detective MacKenzie," said Judith in a casual voice.

Sybil's face scrunched up in the effort of recollection. "No—I guess that's because Mr. Frobisher was down here before the . . . accident."

Obviously, the Clovia staff had been counseled to soften the terms of the tragedy. But Judith was more interested in substance than semantics. "What was Mr. Frobisher doing?" she inquired, hoping she still sounded casual.

"Doing?" Sybil looked vaguely puzzled. "Nothing. That is, he came down the hall from the Hepburn Street entrance and went to the elevator."

"Was he wearing a coat?" Renie asked, not casual at all.

Again, Sybil's face screwed up. "Um . . . I don't think so. Truly, I don't remember. Oh, dear." Failure settled around here like an albatross.

"Never mind," soothed Judith, "you've been splendid. Thanks for your time. You've helped us enormously."

Sybil perked up and gave the cousins a toothy smile. "I just can't believe," she said, with only minimal success at toning down her excitement, "I was the last person to see poor Bob-o alive!"

Judith gave the girl a wry glance. "Except, of course, for the murderer."

Sybil's pudgy hand flew to her cheek. "Oh! Well, yes."

Judith and Renie offered more thanks, then hurried out through the desk area and waited for Doris to unlock the little door. She looked up from the reservation book and once again gave them her conspiratorial smile.

"Wait," said Doris. She bent down in a swish of plaid and brought out a huge floral arrangement of gold, bronze, and white chrysanthemums. Renie moved to give her a hand, but Doris obviously had been dying to make the presentation herself. "These are for you, Mrs. Mc-Monigle. You must have quite an admirer!"

"What. . . ?" Judith all but staggered under the flowers while Renie extricated the small gift card.

"I hope Sybil was helpful," said Doris as the phone rang.

"She was great," replied Judith, unable to see over the towering bouquet. "The card," she hissed, letting Renie steer her toward the now infamous elevator. "What does it say?"

Renie deliberately waited to reply, hoping to send Judith into a frenzy of impatience. The elevator arrived, disclosing two cheerful priests. Judith stumbled over the threshold, which hadn't quite meshed with the lobby floor.

"Listen, you . . ." Judith began as the doors creaked shut.

"It says," interrupted Renie in a slightly soupy voice, " 'Mum's the word. Joe.' "

Judith propped herself up against the back of the car, her upper torso obliterated by the huge arrangement. She sighed heavily. "Now what the hell does that mean?"

"Knowing Joe," said Renie, glad that Judith had her hands full, "It means trouble."

"What time is it?" Judith asked as they entered their suite.

"Four-twenty," replied Renie, helping her cousin set the flowers on the coffee table. "Yikes!" She spun around the room, then switched on a light. "What's happened?"

Judith stopped gazing at the arrangement and tried to quit thinking of Joe. "What? Oh, good grief!"

The sitting room didn't qualify as a shambles, but the sofa and chair cushions were all awry, both drawers on the matching end tables were pulled out, and the escritoire had been opened.

"The police," breathed Judith, but there was a question mark in her voice.

Renie also looked uncertain. Both cousins jumped as they heard a noise emanating from the vicinity of Renie's bedroom. They stared at each other, then tiptoed to the half-closed door. All was silent; even the Heat Pixies seemed to be resting. Judith grabbed the fireplace poker and stepped into the bedroom.

It was empty, and in semi-darkness, with only the light from the sitting room casting a spectral aura over the furnishings. Judith peered in every corner, noting that Renie's suitcase had been rifled and the bureau drawers had been emptied. She started toward the bathroom which connected the two bedrooms, then decided to check out the closet first. Renie yanked her thumb in the direction of Judith's room, then slipped back out through the door, presumably to cut off the intruder's rear exit.

The closet revealed only Renie's limited travel wardrobe on wooden hangers, two pairs of shoes, and some extra bedding provided by the hotel. Judith paused in the middle of the room, heard nothing except the overloud thumping of her heart, and progressed to the bathroom. Cautiously, she opened the door. It was dark, and she momentarily forgot where the light switch was located. Something stirred not four feet away. Judith gripped the poker and swung.

The other person had lunged away. The poker glanced off the wall. Judith reached out frantically with her other hand, and shuddered when she made contact. Her victim was in her grasp. Unfortunately, Judith was also in the grasp of her victim. The two grappled briefly, then abruptly stopped.

"Coz!" squeaked Renie.

"Coz!" shrieked Judith.

The cousins let go of each other. Renie turned on the light. Judith laughed. "You look sheepish."

"You *smell* sheepish," said Renie. "You damned near brained me with that poker."

"I missed by a mile." Judith surveyed the wall where the poker had struck. A three-inch long gash showed up in the Clovia's plaster. "Shoot," sighed Judith. "I've defaced a historical landmark."

Renie was about to respond when the cousins both heard another noise, this time very faint—and very near. Their eyes darted to the bathtub where the shower curtain was pulled shut. With the poker again held aloft, Judith stood at one end of the tub while Renie guarded the other. Renie yanked at the curtain, revealing a cowering Mildred Grimm.

"Well, Mildred, first you show up half-naked in the middle of the night, then you come to take a shower with your clothes on. What gives?" asked Judith, putting the poker down.

"You'd never understand," whined Mildred, gingerly climbing over the mahogany surround.

"Could we try?" asked Judith, keeping her exasperation at bay.

Mildred stepped out of her low-heeled pumps, which

apparently had gotten wet in the tub. "You wouldn't believe me," she said, not looking at either cousin.

"You'd be surprised what we'd believe about now," remarked Judith, as the trio emerged from the bathroom, went out through Renie's bedroom, and into the sitting room. "We presume this handiwork is yours, not the police's?" Judith made a sweeping gesture with one hand while replacing the poker with the other.

"Yes." Mildred drooped, a pitiful thing in her baggy blue sweater and pleated skirt. "I'm sorry, I would have put everything back if I'd had time."

Renie was already straightening the sofa cushions. "Sit down, we'll have a drink, we'll talk. What were you looking for, Mildred? More library cards?"

Whatever color Mildred possessed drained away. She collapsed onto the sofa like a rag doll. "How did you know?" she gasped.

"We were there," said Judith, closing the drawers on the end tables.

"Yes." Mildred sighed. "I saw you. But I didn't think you saw me."

Renie was at the phone. "What will you have, Mildred?"

Mildred opened her mouth, started to shake her head, then reconsidered. "A martini. Very dry. With a twist."

"Drat." Renie replaced the receiver. "No dial tone. I'll run downstairs and give the bar our order." She was gone before Judith could say "scotch."

With only one cousin confronting her, Mildred seemed to revive a bit. "I tell you, it's not believable."

"Let me decide," said Judith, sitting in the armchair opposite Mildred. "You owe us an explanation. You broke into our room, you ransacked our belongings. We could have you arrested."

"I know." Mildred's face crumpled again. "But that will probably happen anyway. Only on a more awful charge."

"Of what?" asked Judith, but the catch in her voice told Mildred she already knew.

The close-set blue eyes welled up with tears. "Murder. Bob-o was killed with my gun."

NINE

JUDITH HOPED IT wouldn't take forever for Renie to get the drinks up to Suite 804. A stiff scotch had never sounded better. Ordinarily, weeks could go by without Judith feeling the need for a drink. But this wasn't one of them.

"Okay, Mildred, now give me this very carefully. You own a gun?"

Mildred nodded. "I bought it for my mother so she could protect herself after that break-in. She agreed to go with me and get fingerprinted and do everything that was necessary to obtain a handgun in Oregon. I'd only planned on staying two weeks, but there's a new law down there that requires a fifteen-day waiting period, so I had to stay over an extra day. Then, after I got it for her, she refused to use it. She wouldn't even have it in the house." Mildred stared at Judith, as if her hostess couldn't possibly understand the contrary nature of the older generation.

Judith, of course, could—and often did, given Gertrude's particular brand of orneriness. "That makes perfect sense. Go on."

Mildred looked faintly relieved. "I'd spent almost four hundred dollars for the blasted thing, and even though handguns aren't legal in New York, it occurred to me that someday I might need one. It's a very violent city, you know."

"So I've heard," said Judith dryly.

The irony was lost on Mildred, who was absorbed in her own troubles. "I also knew it wasn't lawful to bring the gun into Canada, but what could I do? The customs men didn't even ask me if I had one—I guess I don't look the type." She stared sadly at the folded hands in her lap, as if regretting all the things in life for which she had not been suited. "The next thing I knew, it was gone."

"Gone?" Judith gaped at Mildred. "When did you discover that?"

"About an hour ago. I'd come back from the library, and that woman at the desk—Donna?"

"Doris," offered Judith.

Mildred nodded faintly. "Doris. She said that the police had told her the popcorn vendor was killed with a .38 caliber revolver. Well, she didn't exactly put it that way, but I knew what she meant. That's what I've got, a LadySmith with a three-inch barrel. I bought hollow-point bullets for it."

"Great," breathed Judith, wincing at the mere idea.

"I had it in my suitcase, in a box of . . ." She paused and actually flushed. ". . . sanitary napkins. I thought a customs man would be too embarrassed to look there."

"I should hope so," concurred Judith primly, inwardly marveling at Mildred's naivete.

"Naturally, when Doris told me about the weapon used to murder that poor old man, I came up to my room to make sure my revolver was still there. But it wasn't." She swallowed hard, her stockinged feet pawing anxiously at the thick pile of the carpet. "I can only guess that the killer stole it and used it to shoot Bob-o."

Judith was silent for a moment. "Who knew you had a gun?" she finally asked.

Mildred was dabbing at her eyes with a rumpled Kleenex. "No one. I was so nervous about having it, I started to ask about using the hotel safe, but I got terribly flustered and changed the subject. I pretended I bought Krugerrands in Oregon. I could hardly admit I'd smuggled a handgun into British Columbia, could I?" She blew her nose, as if to underscore the statement.

"True," agreed Judith, wondering what was taking Renie so long at the bar. "The question is, what happened to the gun?"

"That's what I was trying to find out. I started with Max and Maria's suite, then yours."

"Uh—how did you get in?" Judith inquired.

"I had a key to the Rothsides', in case I needed to get anything for Max." She flushed again, the color adding immeasurably to her appearance. If ever, Judith reflected, a woman was in dire need of a makeover, it was Mildred Grimm. "As for this room," Mildred went on contritely, "I told that nice little Chinese bellman a terrible fib. I said I visited you earlier today and had left my purse here. He let me in. I'm so sorry."

"That's okay," sighed Judith. "No real harm done. But what about Mrs. Wittelstein's card?"

"Oh, that." Mildred's color deepened. "I called on her this afternoon to offer my condolences. After all, she seems to be the only friend Bob-o had. I borrowed the card so I could use the library. If we're going to have to stay here a few extra days, I wanted some reading material to help pass the time." The blue eyes that gazed at Judith held a hint of challenge.

Judith decided to let the lame excuse pass as a breathless Renie burst through the door, announcing that drinks were on the way. They were, in fact, almost on her heels. Room service, in the form of a much younger, taller version of Lui, arrived with a tray bearing one dry martini, one scotch on the rocks, and one rye, water back. Renie signed the bill, forked over a tip, and plopped down on the other end of the sofa to listen without comment to a rehash of Mildred's story. At the conclusion, Renie had a question:

"When did your mother move from Cleveland, Mildred?"

Mildred evinced mild surprise. "It was in 1957, the same year I went to New York. My father died in 1955. He was a sheet-metal worker and had a sudden heart attack on the job. Mother remarried a man from Oregon two years later. Pappy—that's what I always called my stepfather—passed away four years ago on the Fourth of July." She paused, cocking her head at Renie like a curious wren. "Why do you ask?"

Renie shrugged. "I was just curious. Judith and I have a distant cousin in Sweet Home on our fathers' side of the family. Mabel Frable. I thought you or your mother might know her."

But Mildred shook her head. "I don't think I do. I try to get out to Oregon at least twice a year, but I don't do much visiting. I just spend my time taking care of things for Mother. It's been a real trial keeping her in her own home since Pappy died. I'd like to get her to move to New York so she could live with me."

"Don't!" Judith blurted, then swiftly recanted. "I mean, old folks should stay independent as long as they can." She glanced at her watch. "Holy cats, it's after five! I've got to call my own mother!"

"Me, too," said Renie, springing to her feet. "I'll go downstairs and do it. There's a pay phone in the hall by the Hepburn Street entrance."

"Don't bother," said Judith. "You know Gertrude— she'll only stay on the line long enough to insult and upbraid me five or six times."

Renie sat back down, but now Mildred had gotten up. "I really must go," she said, looking a bit more composed. The dry martini apparently had done its job. "I can't tell you how sorry I am to have caused such trouble. When they arrest me, I'll send you a formal apology from prison."

Judith stood up to see their uninvited guest to the door. "Don't worry about it. If the police don't find the gun, they'll never connect you with the crime. And even if they do come up with it, that doesn't prove a thing."

Mildred, however, remained unconvinced. Still begging forgiveness, she departed the suite with the air of a victim headed for the firing squad.

"True or false?" Renie inquired after Mildred was gone.

Judith shrugged and picked up the phone. "Who knows? It may all have been a ruse to cover the fact that she actually did kill Bob-o. Still," she added, dialing her home phone number, "I feel sorry for her."

"You would," murmured Renie under her breath.

The phone rang. And rang. Judith counted to eleven before Gertrude's raspy voice broke into the line.

"Where were you, Mother? Outside playing fetch with Sweetums?"

"Your hairball of a cat got hit by a truck," retorted Gertrude with an evil chortle. "The truck's totaled."

"Funny, funny Mother," muttered Judith. "You will have your little jokes. Are you doing okay without us?"

"Hunh," snorted Gertrude. "I had one of my spells today. Had to chew two packages of Tums. I almost called Dr. Clapp."

"Feeling that miserable, huh?" Judith gave Renie a knowing look. "How much of Arlene's lasagne did you eat last night?"

There was a pause. "Enough. It sure was a cut above yours. She even cooks the noodles."

"Pasta," corrected Judith absently. "How do you feel now?" She winced at the question.

"Not so hot. Deb's driving me nuts with her phone calls. That woman could talk the bark off the trees. When are you two dumbbells coming home?"

"Tomorrow night, around eight. Just like we planned." Judith and Renie exchanged grimaces. "Mike will probably get there before I do. You take it easy, okay?"

"Easy? What's easy about running this big house all by myself? What's easy about all these phone calls from Deb and your goofy customers? What's easy about being *old?*"

"Not a damned thing," agreed Judith. "But you're tough as a two-dollar steak, which, I might add, is how you got to be so old in the first place."

Gertrude turned away from the phone and cussed. "Disgusting cat. He just ate the hibiscus plant you sent me. Why did you waste your money on that anyway?"

"What? I didn't send you any plant."

"Well then, who did?" Gertrude waited for an answer, didn't get one, and growled into Judith's ear: "Never mind, it's ruined anyway. I got to go, Arlene's making sauerkraut and wienies with Knöpfle noodles. Hers beats yours six ways to Sunday." The phone banged in Judith's ear.

"Dear Mother," sighed Judith, relinquishing the phone to Renie. "She's as full of sentiment and good cheer as usual. I'll go soak in the tub for an hour or so while you call yours."

"Wait—don't you want to hear what I found out?" asked Renie, looking smug.

Judith pivoted in mid-step. "About what?"

Renie smirked. "I took advantage of Mildred's presence here to return the favor. You didn't really think I couldn't get through to room service, did you? Ta-da!" She had reached into her slacks and pulled out a large key on a small ring. "One of the Clovia's master keys. I stole it from under the desk while I was supposedly trying to help Doris with your floral tribute from Joe. Clever, huh?"

Judith's long mouth curved into a broad smile. "Brilliant! I always knew you could be a first-rate crook if you tried. Well?"

"Her mother's name is Myrtle Grimm Little, Mrs. George Little. I found a carry permit made out to the old dear tucked way inside Mildred's wallet. That's why I wasn't too surprised when I heard about the gun. I also peeked in her bankbook. Mildred makes a lot of deposits, many of them small, maybe dividend checks or such. On the first of each month, she puts anywhere from $2,500 to $3,000 into savings. I'd guess that's her salary from Max. But on the tenth, she deposits $2,000. It doesn't vary, and she's been doing it every month since the beginning of that passbook which dates back to May of '88.''

"An annuity?" Judith remarked dubiously.

"Could be," replied Renie. "Could be something else. I don't think a sheet-metal worker would leave an estate that would pay an annuity like that every month."

"Blackmail." Judith sighed and sank down further into the sofa cushions. "Mildred isn't just an old gray mare, she's a real dark horse."

Renie agreed. "A mixed bag in more ways than one." She finished off the dregs of her rye, then took a sip of water. "I also found those magazines from the library. I didn't have time to give them much of a look, but a couple of things sprang to my eye. Birdwell is from Blue Earth, Minnesota, was a Rhodes Scholar, and was married early on for less than a year to someone named Sylvia Finch-Pitkins." She gazed at Judith, waiting for a reaction.

There was none, at first. "So? I'm not surprised Birdwell got bounced so fast. The woman was probably a living saint to have put up with him that long."

"Finch-Pitkins," repeated Renie. "As in Dame Carmela Finch?"

Enlightenment dawned on Judith. "Aha! Max's patroness. But how do you know Sylvia and Carmela are related?"

"Because Carmela married Gilbert Pitkins. He was a well-known designer in the English theater between the wars, and I did a paper on him for a class at the university. They had a couple of kids. I'll bet one of them was named Sylvia, and had the regrettable misfortune to marry Birdwell, if briefly."

Judith considered Renie's thesis. "You may be right. But as far as this case is concerned, so what?"

"I don't know," Renie admitted. "If memory serves worth a hoot, Dame Carmela had retired from the stage by the late 1950s. But she was still active somehow, both in New York and London. I suppose she was playing mentor to people like Max. Maybe her daughter Sylvia's marriage shows the ties between the Sacred Eight early on.''

"Which I find strange in itself," remarked Judith. "Maria, the Smiths, the Frobishers, Birdwell, and Mildred are all about the same age. Even Max isn't that much older. But Jonathan Castle and Clea Rome are a lot younger, practically from another era. I wonder how they got into the clique?"

"Max has produced a couple of Jonathan's films," said Renie. "Maybe he's worked with Clea, too."

Judith tipped her head to one side. "He's worked with a lot of people, but they don't all belong to the Sacred Eight."

"Max may be the type who enjoys having younger people around him. He's never had any kids of his own."

"Jonathan and Clea aren't exactly kids," noted Judith.

"True," conceded Renie, once again digging into her slacks. "I also found this."

Judith looked into Renie's palm. It was an earring, shaped like a spaceship. The cousins locked gazes. "Maria," breathed Judith.

"It was under the bed. Maria must have lost it there after we left the Rothside suite," said Renie. "The trouble is, I can't remember if she was wearing these earrings when she came to our table at the Prince Albert Cafe."

Judith gnawed on her thumb in the effort of concentration. "Damn, neither can I. Maybe the fact that we don't remember means she wasn't. If she wasn't wearing them later, then she must have gone to Mildred's room after we left the cocktail party but before we went to dinner."

"Meaning she could have gone there to get the gun and shoot Bob-o." Renie rubbed at her little chin. "That wouldn't give her much time. And how did she know about the revolver?"

"How did any of them know? If Mildred were really clever, she should have told us that they all knew." Judith pressed her lips together in a tight line. "There is a kind of logic in this somewhere, but I can't figure it out until I take a bath."

"Okay," said Renie on a sigh of surrender. "Time to call Mumsies. Maybe I should make our dinner reservation first. How about Yokohama's? It's excellent, and has a wonderful view of the downtown harbor."

"Hold it." Judith stood by the mantelpiece and wagged a finger. "We have less than twenty-four hours to figure out this mare's nest. Put your stomach on hold, coz. We can't afford to lose a couple of hours guzzling sake and chomping on tempura."

Renie looked cross, but for once didn't put up much of a fight. She, too, wanted to get home for Thanksgiving. As Judith turned away, Renie was picking up the Clovia's room service menu, which seemed to have a soothing effect.

"Attagirl," said Judith with encouragement, and marched off to the bathroom.

Twenty minutes later, she emerged much refreshed, wearing her bathrobe and with her hair wrapped up in a towel. Renie was still talking to Aunt Deb.

"Yes, of course we're being careful . . . No, we aren't going anywhere after dark . . . Yes, I'm wearing my rain bonnet . . . No, nobody's gotten fresh . . ."

Judith leaned against the doorway, arms folded across her breast, an ironic expression on her face. It was feast or famine, she was thinking, as far as their mothers were concerned. The two women who had married the Grover brothers couldn't have been more dissimilar on the surface. Yet each had produced only one daughter, been widowed comparatively young, and despite their apparent differences, were actually quite attached to one another. As for their offspring, Judith and Renie had grown up more like sisters than cousins. Better than sisters, they often joked, because as children they could send each other home when they had a fight. Absence might not make the heart grow any fonder, but somehow it healed the wounds

more quickly. Almost a half century of being both family
and friends, Judith mused, watching Renie sit Indian-style
with her shoulders hunched over the phone.

". . . No, we haven't run into any problems up here . . ."
Renie made a droll face at Judith. Obviously, the murder of
an obscure popcorn vendor wouldn't cause any stir in the
media across the border. "Of course I love you, Mom . . .
Sure, I'll tell her . . . Yes, she loves you, too—you're her
favorite aunt . . . Certainly Aunt Gertrude will be glad to
hear from you. Again. Good night, Mom. Yes . . . okay . . .
sure. Good night." With a heavy sigh, Renie put down the
phone.

"I'm having the pheasant," she said, tossing the menu
at Judith. "What about you?"

Judith perused the Clovia's offerings. "Poached
salmon," she announced. "Let's get a couple more drinks
and a spinach salad."

Renie duly placed the order, then sat with her chin on
her fist and her eyes on the telephone. "Mom gave me
Mabel Frable's phone number. Shall I call?"

"We already know why Mrs. Grimm left Cleveland.
Forget it. Our phone bills are going to cost more than the
rest of the trip." Judith walked over to the window and
looked out. The rain had let up slightly, but the wind was
now blowing in from the west, ruffling the waters of the
bay and making the lights on the anchored ships dance
like fireflies. Traffic was still heavy on Empress Drive, and
the pavement was a sleek ribbon of amber and ebony.
Across the street, the police car remained in place. "Gee,"
remarked Judith, "MacKenzie's minion must still be making his search. Maybe he found something."

"That's more than we did," replied Renie, punching in
the area code for Oregon. "Despite our digging at the
library and my illegal search of Mildred's room, I still feel
at a loss. I'm calling Mabel."

Judith started to say something, but Renie held up a
hand. "Cousin Mabel, this is Serena, Cliff Grover's
daughter. No, no, nobody died. We're all fine." She grit-

ted her teeth at the unintentional lie. "I've met some people from Sweet Home, and I thought you might know them. What? No, I didn't realize that two of the mills had been closed. That's a shame." Renie rolled her eyes at Judith. "The spotted owl? Yes, it's quite a controversial issue. Both the conservationists and the loggers have good arguments. No, you're right, I've never tried to eat a spotted owl, either. But I think my dad did once."

Deciding that the conversation was going downhill fast, Judith went back into the bedroom and changed into black flannel slacks and a gold cable-knit sweater. Renie was right: Almost an entire day had gone by, and they were no closer to finding Bob-o's killer than they were when they had found Bob-o.

Turning on her portable hair dryer, Judith tried to build a link between the victim and the murderer. Bob-o was from London. All of the Sacred Eight had spent time there. Birdwell had been a Rhodes Scholar. As a world-class critic, he'd no doubt been a frequent visitor to the London theater scene, and had even been married to an Englishwoman. As for Evelyn, she'd no doubt accompanied Spud on his directorial duties abroad. And Mildred, of course, would have tagged along with Max as his dutiful assistant. If Bob-o had indeed been some kind of entertainer, any and all of the Sacred Eight could have known him in some capacity.

Yet Bob-o appeared quite harmless. The usual motives of gain and jealousy seemed unlikely. Therefore, Judith reasoned as she shut off the hair dryer, he had known something, probably from long ago. Then why wait all these years to kill him? Perhaps the murderer and Bob-o hadn't seen each other since London. That, in theory, would rule out Max and Maria who had been in Port Royal the previous year. But maybe they hadn't learned by then what it was that Bob-o knew. Certainly Maria had been unnerved by something, unless she was generally unstable. Judith remembered her as a bit high-strung, but a seemingly sound young girl.

Outside, the wind howled around the Clovia, scattering the crimson ivy leaves and stripping the horse chestnuts along the Esplanade. There were no revelers shooting off their crackers on this stormy November night. The windows rattled in their casements; Judith felt a draft blow past her cheek. She applied lipstick and mascara, then rejoined Renie in the sitting room.

"Jackpot," said Renie, with a smile of triumph.

Judith saw the new tray with drinks. "Bless that son of a Lui," she said.

"Grandson," corrected Renie. "That's Brian. I didn't mean the drinks, I meant Mabel. Once we got past the sagging economy, the loss of funding for the schools, the property tax hike, and the ominous courting of California mini-industries, she dug into her satchel of scandal and picked out a plum."

Judith sat in the armchair, scotch in hand, feet up next to Joe's floral arrangement. "Such as?"

"Back in 1959, the year of the drought and the demise of Mabel's poodle, Charles and Diane Holmes, married almost ten years and unable to have children, adopted a baby boy. The town was all agog, since everybody knew the kid was illegitimate." Renie paused to see how her information was registering with Judith.

"They don't make bastards like they used to," commented Judith, with a shake of her head. "I mean they do, even more so, but nobody much cares. Except my mother."

Renie looked over the rims of her crooked glasses. "Shut up. This is hot stuff. The mother of the baby, a mere teenager, had moved in with her Uncle George and his new wife. She stayed with them until she had the baby, and then let the poor childless pair adopt it, seeing as how her aunt and uncle were already middle-aged and had grown children of their own by their first spouses. Mabel couldn't remember the girl's name, but if I tell you that her uncle was George Little, can you guess?"

Judith stared vacantly, then clapped a hand to her head,

spilling some of her drink on the rug. "Maria! Her mother's maiden name was Mary Lou Little! How did we miss that?"

"Easy enough. It's a common name," said Renie. "But you should have noticed the part about Maria going to Paris. You both got out of high school in June of '59. The magazine piece said she went abroad to study in 1960."

Judith nodded. "That's right, and that's where we all thought she had gone right after graduation. But she didn't," Judith added wonderingly. "She went to Sweet Home instead." Her black eyes widened as she gazed at Renie. "Good grief, that baby must have been Spud's! No wonder she threw up in geometry class! She was pregnant!"

"You got it. Maria Filonov, prima ballerina, and Kent Frobisher, Tony award–winning director, are the parents of some young man in Sweet Home, Oregon." Renie paused, her pug nose twitching.

"What's wrong?" inquired Judith, also feeling some sort of qualm.

"Huh?" Renie shook herself. "Nothing, I guess. Do you suppose Spud knows?"

A knock at the door prevented Judith from answering. Renie was on her feet. "Dinner," she breathed. "Let me at it!"

It was not room service, but Maria. "I tried to call you, but your line has been busy for the last hour," she said with the hint of reproach in her voice. "I wanted to ask you to have a drink in the bar with us."

Judith indicated her glass. "We've got some. Any more and we'll both put lampshades on our heads. Have a seat, we were just, ah . . ." She glanced at Renie. "We were just talking about old times."

Carefully arranging her burnt-orange taffeta skirt, Maria sat down next to Renie. "I can't stay, my dears. I'd so hoped you could join us for a bit. Max hasn't really gotten acquainted. He's been gone all afternoon at the King

Charles II Theatre. The rehearsal didn't get over until after five o'clock.''

Judith got up, came over to the sofa, and squeezed in on the other side of Maria. "I'm sorry about that. He seems like a nice guy.'' She bit her lip, then went on speaking. "Forgive me, but I'm about to upset you. Your chances of getting out of here tomorrow are as slim as ours unless everybody stops playing games.'' Judith saw the look of alarm in the other woman's eyes, but plunged ahead. "How long has Mildred been blackmailing you about your illegitimate son?''

Hemmed in between the cousins, Maria couldn't have fled if she'd tried. Her nostrils flared, her gray eyes grew enormous, and her hands shook. The protest she had begun to form died on the tip of her tongue.

"How did you know?'' she asked in a hollow voice.

"It wasn't too difficult,'' said Judith, not unkindly. "Mildred's stepfather was your Uncle George. You went down to Oregon to stay with him and Mildred's mother to have your baby. Somewhere along the line, Mildred found out. She'd probably always been jealous of you after you married Max, seeing as how she's the classic dutiful dogsbody who has no doubt been in love with him forever. So she got her revenge by putting the squeeze on you to the tune of two grand a month. Right?''

"My God!'' Maria gripped her pearl and topaz necklace. "I can't believe it! You're uncanny!''

"No,'' replied Judith. "Renie and I just happen to have a lot of relatives in a lot of different places. And I always was good at library research.''

Renie was proffering the remains of her rye. "Take this, Maria. We're fresh out of smelling salts.''

But Maria waved the glass away. "No, no. Thank you.'' She took a series of deep breaths, then gave Judith a pained looked. "It was about to happen all over again,'' she said. "That's what I was going to tell you last night.''

"What was going to happen?'' inquired Judith, deciding she could get off the sofa and resume her seat in the armchair.

"The demands. More blackmail." Maria licked at dry lips. "A note was left at the desk Sunday, telling me someone had a secret. There was no signature, just a crude drawing of a bird. Nobody at the desk—they had the weekend help on—noticed who it was. I didn't want to tell Max. Then Monday morning, another note came. Even though it was addressed to me, that Doris woman gave it to Max. It mentioned a secret again and said I'd have to meet with this person. But it didn't say who or where or when. Max didn't tell me about it until we were leaving for dinner. He assured me that it must be a prank, and not to worry. I was so upset about that poor man being murdered that I decided to let Max take care of any problems. He always does," she said in that childlike tone.

"But Max doesn't know about the child?" asked Judith.

Maria shook her head. "No. I could never tell him such a thing. You see," she said, the long lashes sweeping the high cheekbones, "when we were first married, he wanted a family. But I didn't. Not then. I just wasn't emotionally able to cope with a baby. I told him I couldn't have children." She turned her ashen face to each cousin. "It was the most awful lie. But then I couldn't see how to get out of it. And as time went by, he seemed to get over the idea."

Compassion welled up in Judith's breast, though Renie was looking more cynical. "We all can think up the strangest ways to hurt ourselves," Judith said, almost to herself. She knew from bitter experience: Her heedless marriage on the rebound from Joe had brought over eighteen years of misery. "Well." Breaking out of her brief reverie, Judith became brisk. "How was the second note delivered?"

"Doris said it had been slipped under the door, probably very early." Maria was gazing at the floral arrangement and shaking her head slowly. "Nothing has come today, though."

And nothing probably would, thought Judith. She was certain that the notes had come from Bob-o. The drawing of the bird, which could have signified a robin, pointed to that. Or, she reasoned, someone else had wanted to pin the blame for the missives on the popcorn vendor.

"Oh!" exclaimed Maria. "My earring!" She reached out to pick up the spaceshiplike bauble on the coffee table. "Wherever did you find it?"

"Under the bed," replied Judith, semi-truthfully. "Where did you lose it?"

Maria was looking puzzled. "I took them off before we went to dinner. They're quite heavy and they hurt. I thought I put them on my dressing table. But this morning, this one was gone." Her forehead creased as she looked at Judith. "Do you suppose a maid picked it up and then dropped it in here?"

Judith considered clarifying the situation, but decided against it. "Maybe. I suppose the Clovia can have light-fingered help like any other hotel." Seeing Renie start to protest, Judith tightened her lips to silence her cousin. "The main thing is that you recovered it."

With some effort, Maria stood up. "I must get back to the bar. Max will think something has happened to me." She gave a lame little laugh. "It has. It did." She reached a thin hand out to Judith who had also stood up. "My dear, I don't know what to say! I can't bind you to keep my secret, and yet . . ."

"Does Spud know?" Renie asked bluntly.

Two spots of color showed up on Maria's high cheekbones just below the dashes of blush. "No. My parents wouldn't let me tell him. That's why I went away so soon after graduation. And he was moving to Nebraska with his family about that same time. He had his football scholarship and I had been accepted at the academy in Paris. It seemed the best way to handle the matter. At the time." Her voice took on a wistful note.

"It must have been difficult later, though," said Judith, taking Maria's hand and giving it a squeeze, "seeing each

other in the theater, and all that Sacred Eight together-
ness."

"It was, at first. But I was married to Max by then."
She smiled tremulously. "I love Max very much, you see.
What I felt for Spud was what we used to call puppy love."

Judith let go of Maria's fingers. "Don't worry about
your secret as far as we're concerned. We could use the
money, but we're not much good at blackmail. Frankly, if
I were you, I'd tell Max and get Mildred off your back.
You could have her arrested, you know."

Maria cringed. "I couldn't! It would break Max's
heart!" She recovered some of her pose and again attempted a smile. "Thank you for being so kind about all
this. Perhaps I'll see you tomorrow before we leave."

It was only after the rustle of taffeta and the closing of
the door that it occurred to Judith that Maria had been
unclear about what would break Max's heart—revealing
the existence of an illegitimate child, or sending Mildred
to prison. She said as much to Renie.

"You're right, coz," Renie agreed. "Mildred is a real
piece of work. And Maria is living in a fool's paradise if
she thinks she's leaving on schedule."

Another knock sounded at the door, and this time it was
dinner, served on a small trolley with covered silver dishes
and a red carnation in a white porcelain vase. The cousins
pushed Joe's floral extravaganza to one side and allowed
Brian to serve them on the coffee table.

"Not bad," remarked Renie, digging in.

"Not bad? You just ate the carnation." She saw Renie's
startled look, and laughed. "I'm kidding, coz. But I
wouldn't put it past you."

Again, there was a rapping on the door. Judith and Renie
stared at each other. Judith got up, wondering which mem-
ber of their cast of characters was calling on them now.
To her surprise, it was not one of the Sacred Eight, but
Angus MacKenzie, looking wet, windblown, and out of
sorts.

"I'm interrupting dinner, it seems," he said in a voice

that made the intrusion sound like a capital crime. "My sergeant just went to get his. I'm taking over the search." He produced his warrant with an air of apology.

"Go ahead," sighed Judith, refraining from mentioning that they'd already been searched once in the past couple of hours. "But why us?"

MacKenzie had taken off his hat and was poking about in the escritoire. "The only way we could convince the management that we didn't intend to insult any of their guests was to insult all of them. A lot of good it's done us, I might add. Six Americans are threatening to sue, and one of the Aussies has called the Canadian ambassador in Canberra." He ambled about the room, pulling out drawers, looking behind and under the furniture, shaking the drapes. At last his gaze came to rest on the big bouquet of chrysanthemums. "Pretty. Somebody's birthday?"

"No," Renie answered before Judith could. "Just one of Judith's admirers among the homicide squad down home. They always send her flowers when she finds a dead body."

MacKenzie looked askance before wandering off into Renie's bedroom; Judith glowered at her cousin. "Big mouth," breathed Judith, spearing a shrimp out of the salad.

Renie lifted one shoulder in an indifferent manner. "It's sort of true, isn't it? As true as a lot of the stuff you tell people, anyway."

MacKenzie returned, looking long-faced and empty-handed. It struck Judith that his search had been perfunctory. "Thank you, ladies. I'll be on my way. Your dinners look good." He spoke with longing.

"Have a roll," offered Judith, handing him a small wire basket. "How's the strike coming?"

MacKenzie accepted the *petit pain*, but didn't bother to butter it. "Nothing. They won't even sit down to talk about talks until tomorrow."

Judith sighed. "I don't suppose you're on the track of the killer yet?"

"No." MacKenzie chewed lugubriously. "We ought to be turning up some heirs, if there are any." His doleful eyes rested on Renie. "What do you think, Mrs. Grover?"

"Huh?" Renie had been caught with her mouth full.

"We were just trying to help," said Judith. "you *are* shorthanded, after all, and we want to go home."

"So you've said." MacKenzie was looking quite stern. "But you're interfering. That won't do."

"It was harmless," insisted Judith. "And, I might add, we weren't the only ones."

"So I hear," said MacKenzie, a gleam of amusement returning to his eyes. "Mrs. Wittelstein has had quite a raft of visitors. Everybody seems to want to go home. The only difference between you and the others is that you, Mrs. Jones, actually posed as a relative."

"I could have posed as a model, but my legs are too skinny." Renie looked up from her cream of mushroom soup long enough to take in the severity of MacKenzie's charge. "So what? It was only an act to get information out of his landlady."

"Really." MacKenzie had put his hat back on and shoved his hands in his pockets. The skeptical note in his voice didn't get past the cousins, who were now both regarding him quizzically. "It wouldn't have been an attempt to inherit that million dollars in his savings account, would it, eh?"

Judith and Renie gaped at the detective. It was Judith who finally recovered sufficiently to ask a strangled question: "Bob-o was rich?"

MacKenzie nodded. "Rich—and eccentric. Or maybe just tight-fisted. It's not just we Scots who are a saving people. It seems he preferred to live the way he did, and push that popcorn wagon up and down the Esplanade. It gave him something to do. Actually, there's over a million dollars in his account at the Bank of Newfoundland. There may be more elsewhere. We haven't had the manpower to go beyond making one phone call," concluded the detective on a melancholy note.

"Where'd the money come from?" Judith inquired, unable to believe that anyone could get wealthy wearing a bird suit.

MacKenzie shrugged. "It was deposited at regular intervals from a bank in New York. We're looking into it. When we have time," he added mournfully. He expelled a deep breath, then shambled toward the door. "Please, ladies, behave yourselves. Amateur detectives are not better than no detectives. Trust me." On that note, he took his leave.

Judith and Renie regarded each other with amazement. "So money may be a motive after all," Judith murmured.

"But there aren't any heirs," Renie pointed out. "His daughter died young."

Tapping her fork against the edge of the coffee table, Judith seemed sunk in thought. "So we're told," she said at last. "But what's the truth? And heirs or not, where did Bob-o get all that money?"

"More blackmail?" suggested Renie.

Judith gave a derisive laugh. "I don't know," she replied musingly, "but a million bucks is an awful lot of popcorn."

TEN

THE PHONE RANG, startling both cousins. Judith picked it up, and a broad smile spread over her face. It was Joe. Renie stopped stuffing spinach into her mouth long enough to let out a little groan.

"What's the death count up to by now?" Joe asked by way of greeting. "I'm surprised I got through. Your line was busy for over an hour a while ago."

"Yeah, well, we're busy people," replied Judith, her eyes fixed on the flowers. "We've been crank-calling the Mounties."

"I've got some news for you," said Joe. "Paul called me back about five, our time. That's the middle of the night in London, so I hope you appreciate this."

"You didn't wait to call him until morning?" inquired Judith, surprised.

"No, I decided it would be more fun to annoy him. Of course he had to show off, so he got some poor junior diplomat to run all over London annoying other people." Joe didn't bother to keep the irritation out of his voice. "Okay," he went on, all business, "you got a fax machine at the hotel?"

"A fax machine?" Judith glanced at Renie, who shrugged, "I don't know. Let me check." She pulled out the plastic card from under the telephone and scanned the directory of services. "I'll be darned, they do. Here's the number."

Joe took it down. "It should be there in about ten minutes. I don't know how much help this stuff will provide, though. I take it you haven't cracked the case on your own?"

"We're working on it," replied Judith. "Did Paul—or his flunky—find out anything juicy?"

"You'll be seeing it all shortly. Hey, Jude-girl, I've got to run. I'm meeting a friend at Mick O'Flaherty's for dinner. Let me know how this all turns out." Joe hung up.

"The son of a bitch," muttered Judith who had turned very red in the face. "I hate him!"

"Huh?" said Renie, breaking open her third *petit pain*. "What now?"

"That big creep was in such a rush to get off the phone that he couldn't even talk about the case! He had a dinner date! At Mick O'Flaherty's! Damn his rotten Irish hide!"

Renie raised her eyebrows. "Mick's? Or Joe's?"

"Never mind," fumed Judith, in one of her rare pouts. "He's scum, that's what. My mother is right."

"I guess you didn't even get a chance to thank him for the flowers, huh?" Renie was giving Judith a sly little smile.

"What?" Judith stared at the huge arrangement, then assumed a prim expression. "No, I didn't. This thing is probably just a joke."

"About a hundred-and-fifty-dollar joke, from the looks of it. Who's his dinner date?" inquired Renie in a more serious vein.

"Who knows? Some . . . friend." Judith's pout lessened a bit. "To be honest, he didn't say it was a woman. But I know it was," she added hastily.

"You don't know any such thing, you twit," declared Renie, licking salad dressing off her fingers. "The guy knocks himself out for you calling London, puts himself on the line with his brother, sends you flowers that are worth a day's wages to a lot of folks, tries to get through to this stupid phone and can't because we're yakking with our mothers and Mabel Frable, then goes off with Woody Price or some other guy he knows to get a bite to eat. Jeeeez!" Renie would have thrown up her hands, had she not been ripping a leg off her roast pheasant.

The phone rang again. A chastened Judith answered it, half hoping it was Joe calling back. But it was Doris, informing her that there was a fax message at the desk. Should Brian bring it up?

Judith hesitated, considering the margin for a disaster en route. But despite what she had said in deception to Maria about the Clovia's staff, she basically trusted them, if only because Renie did. "That would be great," she told Doris, automatically reaching for her purse to find a tip. "Thanks."

Five minutes later, the cousins had the fax in hand. "You read," said Renie. "I'm eating."

Judith complied, though she'd just discovered that the poached salmon was delicious. "Okay, here we go— Bob-o was born . . . we know all that, it's a match. Son of Sean and Katharine O'Rourke, Irish music hall performers. Robin made his debut at the age of three as a toadstool in Carlisle." She stopped, scanning the list of youthful credits that appeared to have been garnered in the company of his parents. "He played the Palladium for the first time in 1936, doing a comic bird imitation routine. In 1939, he married a dancer named Estelle Roth. He served in the Royal Air Force from 1940 to 1944." Judith glanced up from the fax. "Flew without a plane, no doubt. Where was I? Hey, wait a minute!"

"What?" asked Renie, polishing off a wing.

Judith dug through her purse for the notes they'd made that afternoon at the library. "Here—Max's half-sister was named Estelle. She was born in England in 1921. What do you bet she shortened her name from Rothside to Roth, and went on the stage?"

Renie's brown eyes widened. "Good grief! That would mean that Bob-o and Max were brothers-in-law! Or half-brothers-in-law," she amended, trying to sort out the relationship. "Max's connection with Bob-o is clear enough. Which also ties him in with Maria."

"They're all connected somehow," asserted Judith, still studying their earlier notes. "I saw Maria talking to Bob-o on the street. Since she's not my idea of a junk food freak, I should have assumed she had other business with him. That was a lot of guff about her not knowing Bob-o. If he—or whoever sent those notes—didn't sign anything but the bird, then how would she know it was meant to be him unless she also knew his first name was Robin?"

"What about Birdwell?" Renie asked on a sudden inspiration.

Judith lifted her curved eyebrows. "Birdwell? I never thought of him. Somehow, it doesn't sound like his style. But we can't rule him out."

"MacKenzie said that Bob-o's money came from a New York bank," said Renie, polishing off the last morsel of pheasant. "Could that mean Max?"

"It could." Judith digressed from the fax long enough to eat some of her salmon before it got completely cold. "But why? And how? Max and Maria are well-off, but I doubt that they're fabulously rich. Let's face it, she retired thirteen years ago, and I suspect that one of the reasons Max has gone into other ventures is because there simply isn't that much money to be made in the theater these days."

"The American stage has been moribund for over two decades," said Renie. "Bill says one of the biggest problems is that too many of the younger playwrights concentrate on social issues which don't make good drama. Just the other day, he was saying that if Shakespeare had been born four hundred years later, he'd have gone straight to Hollywood, not to—''

"Hell in a Hand-cart," said Judith, cutting short Renie's latest recital of Bill's interpretation of social and cultural issues. "Sorry, coz, that's the name of a revue Bob-o was in after he got out of the service. Estelle was killed in May 1941, the raid in which Parliament was hit. Their daughter, Helen, was born in January of that same year."

Unoffended by her cousin's interruption, Renie chewed her asparagus and made an observation: "If Bob-o wasn't demobbed until 1944, someone else must have taken care of the child. Got any candidates?"

"Not in this crew," replied Judith after a pause to reflect. "None of them were in London then. Or would have been old enough if they were. The only outsider would be Carmela Finch, and I don't see that grande dame of the stage playing nanny to Bob-o's baby."

"A lot of people in England did a lot of unusual—and selfless—things during the war," Renie pointed out. "What about Max's other sister?"

Judith again consulted her notes. "Suzanne? She would have been only a kid. Besides, she was born in Toronto, same as Max. I don't suppose his parents are still alive," Judith added doubtfully.

"They could be," said Renie. "We could check a Toronto phone directory. There's one in the lobby."

Judith tucked the suggestion in the back of her brain. "Okay, let's see—more revues, a tour to Australia and New Zealand in '46 and '47, more music hall appearances in London and other cities in the U.K., also some TV work in the early fifties." She went silent for a few moments, reading through the fax. "His credits are listed in fairly minute detail, lots of those blasted bird imitations, including one of a kiwi that must have been a scream. No doubt he picked up that idea in New Zealand. Ah! Here we are! Oh, coz, I think we've hit paydirt!"

Renie actually flew off the sofa to land on the floor next to Judith's chair. "What is it?"

"In 1974," Judith read slowly, a faint tremor betraying the excitement in her voice, "his daughter, Helen O'Rourke Brookes Smith died in a tragic fall at the Mayfair flat she shared with her husband—the noted American playwright, Alabama Smith! Eureka!"

"Wow!" Renie grabbed a corner of the fax to see for herself, but forgot she wasn't wearing her glasses. "This is terrific! Hey, that's right, the article on Alabama said he was married first to somebody named Helen. She must have had a first husband named Brookes. We shouldn't have been so disinterested."

"We were interested, we just couldn't make it fit." Judith's black eyes were riveted to the fax. "Listen, it gets better. Joe has included something that Paul must have said off the record—'Judith: Here's a bit of information that might be of help. At the time of Helen's death, Robin O'Rourke suspected foul play, but nothing was ever proved, and the case was subsequently closed several years ago. However, this item may be worth noting in view of your current situation.' " Judith glanced up from the page. "Gee, that Joe sure can write the most romantic notes!"

"Screw Joe," said Renie, then frantically waved her hands. "No, no, I didn't mean that. Just get on with the fax."

"That's about it," said Judith, trying to get rid of several disturbing images that had suddenly surfaced and had absolutely nothing to do with the murder case. "Within six months, Bob-o had retired from the stage, and in early 1975, he emigrated to Canada."

The cousins were both very quiet for a long time. At last, Renie got up from the floor and returned to her place on the sofa. She poured coffee from a silver carafe into two matching Royal Worcester cups and passed one to Judith. "Except for Alabama, there's no other mention of the Sacred Eight, is there?"

"That's enough, especially if we think Max is Bob-o's brother-in-law. That ties in Maria, Mildred, and Desiree." Seeing Renie's brow cloud over, Judith tapped at the fax. "Desiree was married to Max and then to Alabama. The only ones who aren't directly connected are the Frobishers and Birdwell."

"So why have they all been so stubborn about admitting they knew Bob-o?" inquired Renie.

"Probably because he got himself killed," reasoned Judith, deciding that even cold, the Clovia's poached salmon was a treat. "Why get involved if you don't have to? They're ten thousand miles and fifteen years away from their association with him. Every one of them—with the possible exception of Mildred—is in the public limelight. They don't need a scandal like that if they can avoid it."

"If that was her picture at Bob-o's, Helen was very beautiful," Renie mused. "I can see why Alabama married her. Of course Desiree is a real knockout, too." She stirred sugar into her coffee, and turned an inquiring gaze on Judith: "When did Alabama marry Desiree?"

Judith didn't need to check their notes; she'd already thought of that particular question. "On January 2, 1976. A decent interval, I might add." Putting the covers back on their plates and tidying the tray, Judith was vaguely aware of a noise somewhere that had nothing to do with the wind. "We need to get somebody in this crew to talk to us."

"Spud?"

"He talks a lot, but I'm not sure he says much." Judith removed the coffee carafe, the cups, and the sugar from the tray, then carried the remnants of their dinner to the door to put outside for room service to collect. "I'd opt for Evelyn. She's indebted to us for not squealing on her about the visit to Mrs. Wittelstein."

Just as Judith opened the door, a shrill scream pierced the peace of the Clovia's corridor. Across the hall, Birdwell de Smoot was hopping up and down like an outraged pigeon, venting his ire on Angus MacKenzie.

"You have no idea who you're dealing with! I have privileged information in my possession! Newspapers all over the world are sitting on edge, awaiting my latest piece on underground theater in the Western Provinces! My readers can't be contained!''

Judith didn't hear MacKenzie's low reply, but she saw the long-suffering expression on his face. She was torn between staying put and sneaking back into the room when Birdwell swiveled about and shot a finger in her direction.

''Aha! A witness! Will you come forward and note how this odious policeman is abusing me? He just spat on my head!''

Judith, who had now been joined by a curious Renie, ankled over to the two men. ''Hi, Mr. de Smoot.'' She nodded at MacKenzie, giving him a swift look of commiseration. ''What's the trouble?''

Angus MacKenzie started to open his mouth and make a reply, but Birdwell sprang between Judith and the detective. ''Trouble! He's ransacked my suite! He's gone through my most private papers! He may even have *smoked!*''

''Now, now,'' interjected MacKenzie, ''I never smoke in the line of duty. See here, Mr. de Smoot, I have a warrant, and I assure you, everything is in place. We're through with this floor now, and if you don't mind, I'll be on my way. If you have any complaints, please call this number.'' He handed the still enraged Birdwell a card. ''Don't expect anyone to answer, of course. They're on strike, too.'' Doffing his hat to Judith and Renie, he ambled over to the elevator.

''Savage,'' muttered Birdwell, cramming the card in the pocket of his dinner jacket. ''I should know better than to ever go farther west than Philadelphia!''

''What about Blue Earth?'' blurted Judith.

Birdwell actually jumped. ''What? Are you from Blue Earth?''

''No, but Cousin Sue's husband's brother's first wife was from Frost, Minnesota. It's just down the road, as I recall. Near East Chain.'' Judith smiled pleasantly.

Birdwell was simmering down, wiping his forehead with

a handkerchief. "Well, yes, very close to the state line. I haven't been back in years."

"You and Sylvia didn't live there, I take it?" said Judith at her most casual.

Birdwell gulped and gaped. "What? How do you know Sylvia?"

"Uh . . ." Judith was caught slightly off-guard. She cast a desperate glance at Renie. "I don't. My cousin knew her father, Gilbert. Renie's a designer."

"Well." Birdwell brightened. "I knew you must be connected with the theater somehow. What have you done lately, Mrs. . . . er, ah . . ."

"Jones," supplied Renie, with visions of booting Judith dancing in her head. "I haven't been involved in the theater for some time," she said. "I'm strictly corporate these days."

"Oh." Birdwell looked disappointed. "But you knew Sylvia?" he asked suspiciously.

Judith came to the rescue. "She knew *of* Sylvia, right, coz? You actually knew Gilbert when you were married to Mr. Grover of Cornwall."

Renie looked faintly dizzy. "Yeah, oh, that's right, we were thick as thieves."

Birdwell's little eyes narrowed. "And a child bride. Gilbert Pitkins died in 1951, Mrs. Jones."

"I thought he seemed awfully quiet," said Renie, with a weak grin. "I suspect we're talking about two different people," she went on in a vain attempt at salvaging some shred of integrity. "Do you mean the Gilbert Pitkins who painted billboards?"

Birdwell gave Renie a withering glance. The cousins' game appeared to be up: Birdwell de Smoot stood with his hands on his hips, shiny patent leather shoes set at angles, lips pursed in a disparaging attitude. "If you must pry, at least do so with some amount of intelligence. Why are you asking me about Sylvia?"

Having maneuvered Birdwell from high dudgeon to low-down candor, Judith opted for the truth: "We've been researching everybody on this floor. We found out you were married to Dame Carmela Finch's daughter. Who, of course, was also the daughter of Gilbert Pitkins.''

"Or did he do movie posters?'' mused Renie, refusing to give up the game.

"We also discovered that Max was Dame Carmela's protégé. We wondered if that was how you came to know Max.'' Judith spread her hands in an appealing gesture.

Birdwell's round face tightened and his eyes narrowed behind his spectacles. "The first time I met Max was in court,'' he said abruptly. "Dame Carmela left him all her money. She had cut Sylvia out of her will.''

Judith's eyes widened. "Why did she do that?''

Bitterness consumed the little man. "Why? Because Sylvia married me. That's why.''

Birdwell's frank admission left Judith and Renie momentarily speechless. Across the hall, the elevator groaned to a halt, and Max got out. He exhibited his charming smile and doffed his fedora. "The Clovia has a well-appointed conference room on the main floor,'' he said with a twinkle. "Or is this a social gathering?''

"A chance encounter,'' mumbled Birdwell, doing his best to hide his pain. "I was just going out.''

Max, suave as ever in a charcoal double-breasted pin-stripe suite, inclined his head. "So are we. That is, Maria is waiting in the bar. I came up to get our coats. We're going to dine at Les Jongleurs.'' He turned to Judith and Renie. "I'm sorry you couldn't join us downstairs. We've been watching the storm over the bay, and reminiscing about all the spectacular port cities we've visited over the years. Copenhagen is my favorite, but Maria prefers Marseilles.''

"I prefer Marseilles, too,'' declared Birdwell with unwonted fervor. "That's the trouble, Max, you and Maria have very little in common.''

Though Max's left eyebrow lifted slightly, his aplomb appeared otherwise unruffled. "Oh, I don't know. We seem to share a great many interests, actually. It's the differences that add spice to our lives.''

"Twaddle," snapped Birdwell, then apparently thought better of further baiting Max. "I must go. I'm already late." He swerved on his two-inch heels, heading for Suite 805, then stopped and turned back toward his own room. "I forgot my overcoat. You're right, it's blustery out there. Rotten weather, utterly unpredictable. I wish I were in Rio." He stomped into his suite and banged the door shut.

Max looked bemused. "Poor old Birdie. I'm sorry he's so unhappy. Perhaps that's what makes him such a perceptive critic."

"At least," allowed Judith, "It gives him a forum to vent his spleen." She caught Max's shrewd glance, hesitated, and plunged into murky waters. "It sounds to me as if he has a crush on Maria."

Max uttered a sigh of resignation. "He has indeed, dating back to the first time he saw her dance in London. Birdwell has a habit of falling for the wrong woman. I never met his first wife, even though I knew her mother very well. But since that marriage was short-lived, I have to assume it was a mismatch." He made a face of mild dismay. "My word, I'm gossiping like a garrulous old woman! Forgive me, I think murder must have the effect of loosening one's tongue."

Judith assumed her blandest expression. She noticed that Max hadn't mentioned either Dame Carmela or Sylvia by name, an indication of his inherent discretion. "We're all a bit on edge," she said, and, on an impulse both calculated and reluctant, put out her hand. "I must offer my condolences, Mr. Rothside. I didn't realize at first that Robin O'Rourke was your brother-in-law."

For just an instant, Max's face froze and his grip on Judith's fingers tightened. Then he bent his head, gave a rueful little smile, and sighed. "I felt it was best that no one knew. For Maria's sake, of course. She's such a sensitive person."

Judith slowly withdrew her hand. "Oh. You mean that Maria didn't realize you and Bob-o were related?"

"That's right," said Max. "That is, she didn't know Bob-o was Robin. He had moved to Canada by the time we were married. I wrote to him early on, but he never answered, so I stopped." His handsome features assumed an aura of regret. "He preferred cutting all ties after he left England. And of course Estelle—my half-sister—had been dead for years." His fine slate-blue eyes studied Judith a little too closely. "I must confess I'm intrigued—how did you know about the relationship?"

For the briefest of instants, Judith could have sworn she saw a glint of fear in Max Rothside's face. His reaction prompted her to tell an outright, bald-faced, no-nonsense lie: "Bob-o told us. We had tea with him yesterday afternoon."

Under the tan that Max had no doubt acquired in Palm Beach, Mazatlán or the Greek Isles, he went quite pale. But otherwise, he showed no other sign of dismay. "How fascinating! He wasn't much for company. Or so I'm told." The smile was now forced. "I suppose he regaled you with his entire stage career?"

"Oh, yes," replied Judith cheerfully. "He talked about everything and everybody. Especially Larry and Viv." That much, Judith thought as a salve to her conscience, was true.

"Well, of course! There was a fateful coupling." Max looked ruminative. "Unfortunately, I never met Vivien, but I worked with Larry twice. Marvelous actor. Wonderful man." He paused, adjusting the already perfect knot of his maroon and silver tie. "No doubt he resurrected all sorts of old scandals and amusing backstage scuttlebutt."

Judith chuckled, while Renie shifted rather awkwardly in place. "From Albee to Zeffirelli," said Judith. "There was no stopping him. I just wish we'd had the chance to go back for more."

Max's smile now seemed stuck. "I'm sure you do. My, my!" He glanced at his watch. "Almost eight o'clock!

Maria must be drumming her nails. It's been a pleasure."
He made a courtly bow, and swung around to head for
Suite 800 at the end of the hall.

Judith and Renie watched him go inside and close the
door. "We sure make the Rothsides time conscious," remarked Renie. "They can't seem to get away from us fast
enough. By the way," she added, suddenly serious, "are
you sure you did the smart thing by implying that Bob-o
told all? What if Max is the murderer?"

The cousins were back on the threshold of their own
suite. "I know I took a chance," Judith admitted as she
started to shut the door. "Even if Max is innocent, he
may spread the word among the others. But dammit, coz,
we've got to take some kind of risk to flush out the killer
so we can get home!"

Renie shivered. "That's the trouble, you're more afraid
of your mother than you are of a murderer! Meanwhile,
we could end up dead as dodos!"

Judith, who was still at the door, motioned for Renie to
be quiet, and peered out through the small slit. "Ah—as
I thought." Carefully, she closed the door all the way and
clicked the latch. "Birdwell was going toward Mildred's
room at first, then made up that excuse, and went back to
his own. He and Ms. Grimm just headed for the elevator.
She's wearing pink chiffon."

"Gag," remarked Renie, flopping back down on the
sofa. "You mean Birdwell didn't want Max to know?"

"So it would seem," replied Judith, just as the phone
rang. She picked it up to hear Evelyn on the other end.
Her voice was devoid of its usual crispness. She was, however, characteristically direct:

"Have you seen Spud?"

Judith reflected briefly. "I haven't seen him since the
two of you came in for breakfast." She paused, then, when
Evelyn didn't respond, switched to a less casual tone. "Is
he missing?"

"No. He taped an interview this afternoon at CLIP-TV.
I thought he'd be back a long time ago, but they must have

run into some problems.'' The slight quaver in Evelyn's voice betrayed her anxiety. "It occurred to me he might have stopped to talk to you about the old days."

Judith eyed Renie, who looked as if she were about to explode with curiosity. "He'll probably show up any minute." She gestured at Renie to contain herself. "By the way, Evelyn, I've got some names for him from our class. He's been listed as 'Address Unknown' for the last three ten-year reunions. Shall I bring these contacts over?"

Evelyn said yes, but without enthusiasm, then hung up. Getting her fat little address book out of her purse, Judith explained to Renie about the missing Spud. Renie's reaction was anticlimactic:

"Big deal. He probably stopped for drinks with the TV crew."

"Spud doesn't drink," Judith reminded her cousin. "Okay, okay," she continued before Renie could respond. "So he could sip some pop while the others got loaded. You may be right, but wherever he is, it's worrying Evelyn. That means she's vulnerable right now, and I'm off to take advantage of her."

"Crass," remarked Renie, springing to her feet. "You aren't going to be that opportunistic without me."

But Judith fended Renie off with her purse. "Not this time, coz. I had good luck going one-on-one with Mildred. I might do the same with Evelyn. No offense, but as a team, we may be a little overwhelming."

Renie was torn between incredulity and hurt. "Us? Rot. We're about as intimidating as lint."

"All the same, let me go alone. In all modesty, I'm told I have a knack for getting people to open up. You're the one who told me." She picked up the Clovia's menu. "I'll do what I do best, you do ditto. Order dessert."

Suite 801 was a medley of English country decor. A green and gray Brussels-weave carpet, a Delft urn on a pedestal, two deep burgundy club chairs, a plate rail lined with Wedgwood, Royal Doulton, and even a matching pair of Staffordshire botanical designs gave the room an elegant yet homey look. Judith couldn't help but wonder how the various pieces of china and objects d'art had survived Spud's occupancy.

Evelyn apparently had been passing the time with work. The Regency desk was littered with a large looseleaf binder, a yellow legal-sized tablet, a Rolodex, and a stack of papers.

"Have a seat," offered Evelyn, looking tense and lean in a lavender cashmere sweater and white wool slacks. "Have you been searched yet?"

"Of course," said Judith, sitting in the mate to Evelyn's club chair. "You, too, I gather?"

"Oh, yes." Evelyn grimaced. "The policeman didn't find anything. What are they looking for? The gun?"

"I suppose so," Judith replied noncommittally.

"Preposterous," scoffed Evelyn. "It's probably out in the bay. They'll find it washed up in Empress Park six weeks from now."

Judith was flipping through her address book. The room smelled of sandalwood, and looked out onto the high-rise apartments and condos of Prince Albert Bay. A forest of buildings, a shimmer of lights rose out of the rain. For a brief instant, Judith let go of everything but the magic enchantment of the city at night. All those windows, she thought to herself, and all those lives, caught up behind glass and concrete. Human nature fascinated her in all its complexities and simplicities. She could almost hear the voices, quarreling, giggling, pleading, bantering. No matter how similar, Canada and the United States were two separate countries, yet to Judith, people were people, regardless of national origin. She was captivated by the notion, momentarily swept away by the common bond of the human race.

"Kay Kramer Norville and Ron Patricelli are the alumni chairmen for our class," she said, shaking off her contemplative mood. She wrote down the names, addresses and phone numbers on the back of one of her Hillside Manor business cards. "Have Spud drop one of them a line. I know they'd love to hear from him." Judith spoke the truth, but didn't personally care if Kay or Ron ever heard from anybody. Judith hadn't gone to any of the reunions, having been too ashamed to own up to the kind of life she had created for herself.

"Thanks," said Evelyn absently, putting the card to one side. "To be honest, I don't think Spud has very fond memories of high school. He hardly ever talks about it."

"He's being modest," said Judith in her most conversational tone. "Spud was quite a football hero. Plenty of girls thought he was Hot Stuff." The statement was something of an exaggeration: While Spud's athletic prowess had been undeniable, he had been known to most of Judith's female chums as "Old Bucket-Head."

Evelyn was watching both the door and the eighteenth-century faux marble clock on the mantel. "Spud never talked about his girlfriends much, either. There were a couple in Lincoln he used to mention, but I never gathered he got very serious." She crossed and uncrossed her legs, trying to get comfortable. "Maybe I should call CLIP."

"Go ahead," said Judith. "I'm in no hurry. It looks like we're stuck here for the duration."

Evelyn arched her straight brown brows. "I hope not. I called home tonight and the kids will be in tomorrow before dinnertime. We've got an afternoon flight."

Judith sadly shook her head. "That's too bad. You'll never make it."

"Of course we will!" Evelyn had become quite heated, her hazel eyes snapping. "The police can't detain us! We're leaving, and that's that!"

"Good luck," said Judith with irony, then she leaned forward in the club chair. "Evelyn, I don't want to sound like a pretentious fool, but I think I may be on to something as far as finding out who the killer is." She paused; Evelyn's skeptical expression indicated she thought Judith was a pretentious fool.

But Judith was as undaunted as she was devious. "What happened to Helen Smith?"

Evelyn receded into the chair, her face sagging. "Helen! I hadn't thought about her in years!" She closed her eyes briefly, hands gripping the brass-studded chair arms. "Helen," she repeated in a faraway voice. "So you know about Helen? How on earth did you find out?"

Judith shrugged. "Renie and I have friends who have relatives in strange places. Were you in London when Helen died?"

Evelyn took a cigarette out of a gold case and flicked on a small silver lighter. "Yes. Spud was directing Desiree in *Blithe Spirit*. She was very good, by the way. Of course he deserves much of the credit." Cigarette smoke mingled with the sandalwood. "Helen's death was a terrible tragedy. She fell down a flight of stairs and broke her neck."

Judith looked properly dismayed. "I gather that sort of unhinged Bob-o?"

"Of course. He'd lost his wife in the war, Helen had been through one bad marriage, and then there was this awful accident." Evelyn's mouth set in a tight, thin line. "She was drunk, you know."

"I didn't, actually," replied Judith in surprise. "Was she alone?"

"Allegedly." Evelyn's face hardened. "If so, it was a rare occasion."

"Oh." Judith digested Evelyn's words. "Helen sounds like a problem."

Evelyn inhaled, exhaled, and slumped a bit in the chair. "She was, but to be fair, she'd had a rough time. She never knew her mother, Robin was in the service, a couple of old maiden aunts—no relation, really, just family friends—raised her out in the country, Devon, I think, and even after the war, she was sort of sent from pillar to post. Robin's career didn't leave him much time for fathering. Then there was an early marriage to a real swine, some sort of musician who was a drug addict as well as a drinker. That's what got Helen started." She sighed and stubbed out her cigarette. "I suppose you're wondering why none of us admitted we knew Bob-o?"

"True," conceded Judith. "Unless you just didn't like his popcorn."

Evelyn gave Judith a dour look. "I can only speak for Spud and me." She glanced at the clock again. "Where is that man?" Her body was tensed for any sound coming from the hall, but there was nothing, except for the wind blowing at the windows and among the Clovia's chimneys. "We had no idea who Bob-o was until his real name was given on the news last night. Even then, we weren't sure it was the same Robin O'Rourke. Max told all of us the first thing this morning."

Judith tried to detect the lie in Evelyn's voice, but couldn't be sure. "Why did you go to see Mrs. Wittelstein?"

Evelyn actually laughed, if bitterly. "We all agreed that we didn't want to get mixed up in any scandal. I was delegated to go to the Tudor Arms to look through Robin's apartment and see if there was anything that might implicate any of us. But as you know, I couldn't get in."

Judith was puzzled. "Why did you want us to keep your visit a secret from Spud?"

Evelyn ran a hand through her short, neat hair. To Judith's amazement, it fell back into place, as if on command. "Spud didn't want me to do it. He was afraid I might get into trouble somehow. He's very protective of me. And vice versa. It's the way we work together."

With a pang, Judith thought it was a very nice way. Fleetingly, she wondered what such a marital arrangement would be like. "How did Desiree get into the act?"

"Simple. Spud asked her to take my place. She loved the idea, playing yet another part. Desiree went as the Comfort Lady from St. Willibrord's Anglican Church. She wore black crepe and put her hair in a bun. I went over there anyway because I know Desiree—she probably gave a wonderful performance, but forgot what she was there for. She tends to get wrapped up in her roles." Evelyn turned wry. "Not that it mattered—she couldn't get in, either." She lighted another cigarette and opened the phone book.

"I don't suppose," Judith said musingly, "that there was any doubt about Helen's death being an accident?"

Evelyn looked up from the yellow pages. "What?" Her hazel eyes widened. "Oh, no. I told you, she was drunk. Alcohol is a killer in more ways than one."

"Were any of the other members of the Sacred Eight in London at the time?" Judith asked, wistfully thinking that Evelyn's cigarette smelled wonderful.

"We weren't the Sacred Eight back then. Jonathan and Clea hadn't arrived on the scene yet. But yes, the rest of us were all there, as a matter of fact. Even, if you'll excuse the expression, Birdwell." She stopped speaking at the same time she finished dialing. After what appeared to be three separate parties coming on the line, her face fell. Evelyn put the phone down and stared at Judith with hollow eyes. "Spud left CLIP-TV just before five. *Where the hell is my husband?*"

ELEVEN

JUDITH HAD DECIDED not to press Evelyn further. There were still a lot of unanswered questions: Spud's appearance in the lobby just before Bob-o was shot, the inclusion of Jonathan Castle and Clea Rome in the Sacred Eight, Birdwell's bitterness toward Max, and the stash of money Bob-o had left behind would all have to wait for a more propitious moment. Evelyn's mood had deteriorated from anxious to frantic. She was on the verge of calling the police when Judith left her, though it was dubious if they had the personnel available to search for a husband who was a mere three hours late.

Still, Judith felt she'd made some sort of progress. At least she knew why Evelyn and Desiree had gone to the Tudor Arms. Her suspicions about the Sacred Eight's reluctance to admit to any connections with Bob-o had been confirmed. She had to assume that Evelyn—and perhaps Spud—didn't know about Maria's illegitmate baby.

She was at the door of Suite 804 when the elevator opened. Spud emerged, whistling.

"Spud!" exclaimed Judith. "Evelyn's having a fit! Where have you been?" She had no right to ask, but the words tumbled out all the same.

"Gosh, nowhere special," said Spud, colliding with the fire extinguisher on the wall. "I was just chewing the fat with some of the TV folks." He looked at his big wristwatch. "Wow! It's after eight! Ev must be starved! I'd better hustle the little woman off to dinner pronto."

Spud wheeled around, somehow tripping over his own feet, but managing to stay upright. Judith watched him head down the hall to 801 and call out a hearty greeting as he hurtled through the door. Oddly enough, Judith shared Evelyn's imagined relief. Though perhaps it wasn't so odd, she told herself as she entered her own room: In a sense, all of them were in this mess together. The only outsider was the murderer, and at this point, Judith had no idea whose face hid behind the killer's clever mask.

Renie was lying on the sofa, an empty plate on her stomach and a guest copy of a travel book propped up in front of her. "You were right. I did dessert beautifully."

"Let me guess," interrupted Judith, fingering her chin. "Bailey's Irish Cream cheesecake?"

Renie reared up, knocking the plate onto the carpet. "How'd you know?"

"You've got some of the remains in your hair." She sank down in the armchair, propping her tired feet up on the coffee table. Renie was frantically wielding a brush through her unruly chestnut curls. "Spud has returned," Judith said.

"Good," responded Renie, bending down to retrieve the plate. "So has Desiree."

"What?"

Renie looked smug. "You aren't the only one who can have exciting adventures while on vacation in a foreign land. I went out to get my cheesecake from Brian, and there was Alabama, looking like U. S. Grant was at his heels. Being the considerate sort, I asked him what was wrong. He demurred a bit, then said his wife was very late getting back from her rehearsal." Renie arched her eyebrows at Judith.

"Well!" Judith tipped her head to one side. "It may be a coincidence, of course."

The look the cousins exchanged revealed they didn't believe it was anything of the sort. However, they would have been willing to dismiss the extramarital peccadilloes of Spud and Desiree, had war not broken out in the suite next door. The Clovia's best efforts at soundproofing could not prevent Desiree's high-pitched and highly trained screeches from carrying through the wall. A crash, a thud, and a thunderous stream of epithets from Alabama followed.

Judith and Renie froze in place. Somehow, Judith managed to speak without moving her lips: "Should we call the desk?"

"We can't call the cops. At least the hotel isn't on strike. Yes," mouthed Renie as Desiree shrieked again.

"Maybe," said Judith in a more natural manner, "we should call on the Smiths."

Renie shuddered as something heavy bounced off the wall. "Forget it. This is a job for hotel security." She picked up the phone and dialed.

"I didn't know they had any," said Judith, wincing at Alabama's stormy voice.

"It's actually Lui." Renie turned from her cousin to speak into the phone. "Doris? Oh, Sybil? Who? Hello, Elaine. This is Mrs. Jones in 804. There's a bit of a commotion next door in 803. Could you send someone up? We'd hate to have another accident," she added ominously.

The screaming, shouting and crashing stopped just as Renie replaced the receiver. The cousins sat very still, waiting for a resumption of hostilities. Nothing happened. "Rats," breathed Renie. "We've avoided an Accident, but we've created an Incident."

"That's okay," soothed Judith. "Whoever comes up can at least verify that Desiree and Alabama are still alive.'' She spoke the words all too seriously, then went to the door and peeked outside. Brian was just arriving. He winked at Judith and went down the hall to 803. Judith ducked back inside, but left the door open a crack. Two minutes passed before Brian returned, looking unperturbed.

"It's cool," he said, brushing back his dark hair. "Mr. and Mrs. Smith are alive and well, but I'm afraid we'll have to assess them a damage fee."

"Serves them right," said Judith with approval, remembering the shattered Roseville vase an irate orthodontist had pitched at his wife when she'd exceeded their credit card limit during a stay at Hillside Manor. "As long as you're here, how about getting us a couple of Irish coffees?"

Brian grinned. "Sure. Chill out. It's that kind of night. Be right back." He buzzed for the elevator, which hadn't yet budged from the eighth floor.

Judith sat down to file a full report with Renie, going backward. From Brian's assessment of Suite 803, she moved up to the conversation with Evelyn. Renie was mildly impressed.

"So where does it take us?" Renie queried. "Are we to assume that one of the Sacred Eight—or however many there were then—did in Helen? And Bob-o knew who it was, so the killer finally knocked him off, too?"

"Maybe." Judith was frowning. "Alabama was married to Helen at the time. She was a faithless wench, thus making him the logical suspect."

Renie shook her head. "Alabama has a habit of marrying faithless wenches. It seems to me he yells and carries on, but doesn't do much damage. To the wenches, that is."

"He was going to throw Birdwell out the window," Judith reminded Renie.

"Who wouldn't?" retorted Renie. "Anyway, Birdwell is no wench." She got up as a knock sounded on the door.

Brian entered with two Irish coffees, their whipped cream toppings looking like small mountains.

"By the way, Mrs. Jones, I finally had time to check out that Toronto directory you called about. No Rothsides listed. Sorry."

"I guess they checked out. Permanently." Renie looked faintly aggrieved. She glanced at Judith. "While you were gone, I asked Brian to look up Max's parents in the phone book. No luck."

Judith shrugged. "Not everybody lives as long as our relatives."

"My Uncle Hui is a hundred and four," said Brian.

"Hui?" echoed Renie. "Where's Dui?"

"Calgary. Have a nice night."

"So," said Judith, after Brian had left with a grin on his face and another tip in his pocket, "we can't rule out Alabama just because he didn't murder Desiree tonight. We also can't dismiss Desiree, since she became the next Mrs. Smith about a year later. Then we have Spud, who may have been carrying on with Desiree even then. He was directing her in a play at the time."

"Why would he kill Helen?" Renie asked reasonably. She lapped at her whipped cream like a cat.

Judith looked stumped. "You're right, that doesn't wash. Alabama and Desiree might have a plausible motive. As for Max, Helen was his niece. He might have stood to gain by her death somehow. Or he wanted to silence her." She shook her head. "Neither idea fits Max very well. And he wasn't married to Maria then, so I don't see how she'd figure into the picture."

"Jonathan and Clea are out of it," said Renie. "They were just kids in 1974. What about that million bucks? That's a motive any murderer could sink his or her teeth into."

A pensive Judith gazed at the huge spray of chrysanthemums. "Bob-o probably left it all to Tootle. But then again, maybe not." Her black eyes strayed to Renie. "Let's just suppose he was very fond of one of the Sacred

Eight. He might have chosen one as his heir. Or maybe more than one.''

"But which? Max, maybe?'' asked Renie, stirring her Irish coffee with a slim glass stick. "Then Bob-o would have to have made out a will. How long before the police find it, or a lawyer speaks up?''

"Good question,'' mused Judith. "Bob-o didn't strike me as a legalistic type. If he never spent any of the money, I doubt if he'd bother to dispose of it properly. What happens then? Some third cousin twice removed in Ireland who never heard of him gets it all and moves to Beverly Hills?''

Renie looked perplexed. "It sounds as if we're back to Helen. Maybe Birdwell was nuts about her. Maybe Helen was blackmailing Mildred. Maybe Evelyn found Helen's alcohol addiction so appalling that she threw her down a flight of stairs. Maybe Max was ashamed of her. Maybe I ought to shut up.''

"We're still missing something.'' Judith sighed, taking a sip of Irish coffee. "The whole case is a jumble. It doesn't make any sense.''

Outside, the wind was still howling. Inside, the Heat Pixies had renewed their dance. Judith gritted her teeth. "How do you rake up alibis from so far back? Even if we could, how do you disprove them?''

"We can't give up,'' Renie asserted, but her voice sounded flat. "While you were with Evelyn, I tried to clear my brain by reading up on tourist treats in the Western States and Provinces.'' She tapped the guidebook next to her on the sofa. "It didn't work. Somehow, the torpedo trips in Yreka, California and the world's largest strawberry shortcake in Lebanon, Oregon, didn't inspire me.''

"Don't forget the Milton-Freewater Pea Festival,'' remarked Judith. "Do you remember the year we drove down there with our folks, and your dad pulled up in Wallula to—'' She stopped abruptly, leaned forward in the chair, and raised her voice above the clamor of the radiators. "What did you say?''

"Huh?" Renie looked up from her glass with the shamrock embedded in the stem. "I didn't say anything. That was the Heat Pixies."

"No, before that." Judith looked slightly agitated. "About . . . shortcake."

Renie lifted one shoulder. "Well, I like it a lot, but last year the berries didn't have as much flavor as—"

"Shut up!" Renie and the Heat Pixies were getting on Judith's nerves. "About the town, dopey. What did you call it?"

Semi-offended, Renie wrinkled her pug nose. "You should pay closer attention. The home of the largest strawberry shortcake in the world is Lebanon, Oregon. Yikes!" She sat up like a rocket. "Where's that map?" Her fingers raced through the pages of the guidebook. "Jeez, I can't believe it! Lebanon is right next to Sweet Home!"

The Heat Pixies had taken a break. In the relative silence, the cousins stared at each other.

"Are you sure, coz," said Judith slowly, "that Jonathan Castle was born in Lebanon the country, or Lebanon the Oregon town? Your glasses, after all, are a disgrace."

Renie turned indignant. "I can see just fine. How the hell do you think I produce such brilliant design concepts?"

"Sheer dumb luck," snapped Judith. "Think. Which was it?"

Renie shook herself. "I don't need to. Jonathan Castle's real name was John Holmes. Oh!" She gave herself a slap on the cheek. "I get it—Holmes, as in H-O-M-E-S, equals Castle!"

Judith clasped her hands together. "John Holmes, the baby Maria gave away, is really Jonathan Castle. Well, well!" She finished off the Irish coffee and chewed on her thumb. "Our problem is that we keep missing these connections. Too many people involved, I guess, to catch everything the first time around." She paused as the Heat Pixies picked up the tempo. "The next question is, does Maria know Jonathan Castle is her son? Does Jonathan

know that Maria is his mother? And what about Spud?''
She was all but shouting now, trying to drown out the din
emanating from the radiators.

''There is a resemblance,'' yelled Renie. ''Jonathan has
Maria's coloring and bone structure.''

''And what?'' But Judith figured it out before Renie
could repeat the remark. ''He's got Spud's build, too. I
wonder if Joe knows anybody in Hong Kong?''

''King Kong?'' Renie looked flummoxed. ''What's he
got to do with it?''

''I said . . .'' Judith put her hands over her ears. ''I
can't stand this!'' she shrieked. ''I'm getting a headache!
Let's go down to the lobby.''

Renie didn't try to argue. But even as she stood up, she
snapped her fingers. ''Wait.''

Puzzled, Judith watched Renie mouth something to herself and point around the room as if she were counting.
Then she reached into her purse, pulled out the master key
she'd pinched from the hotel desk, and signaled for Judith
to follow her out of the room. Blessed quiet reigned in the
hall.

''Last year we stayed in Room 502,'' Renie explained.
''The Heat Pixies were driving Bill absolutely nuts. In
fact, he thought some of the noise was coming from outside, so he opened the window to check. Nothing, it was
just the radiators, but he got so mad, he cussed and swore
and pounded on some sort of pipe that ran along the outer
wall. The clanking stopped.'' Renie gave Judith an ingenuous look.

''Why not try our own windows?'' Judith asked as a
chunky maid emerged from the freight elevator with a fresh
set of towels, a mop, and a broom. She gave the cousins
a weary smile, then proceeded down the hall to Desiree
and Alabama's suite.

With the maid's arrival, Renie had stuffed the master
key in her pocket. ''My window's stuck. I'll bet yours is,
too. Last night I wanted some fresh air and I couldn't
budge the blasted thing.''

At Renie's lead, they had progressed the few yards down the hall to Birdwell's room. "Okay, so why are we breaking into this particular suite?"

"For obvious reasons," Renie replied, first knocking to make sure no one was inside, then taking a quick look along the corridor. "One, because we can, and we ought to check Birdwell out while he's at dinner. Two, he's in the room directly above the one Bill and I stayed in last year. Maybe we can find the pipe and put out the Heat Pixies' lights."

Birdwell de Smoot's lodgings were as avant-garde as their occupant was orthodox. White-on-white, leather, chrome, and glass dazzled the eye. Judith was thankful that he, not they, had ended up in Suite 802.

"What's Mildred's like?" inquired Judith, gazing at the ultimate mating of form and function.

"Late Victorian. Lots of frills and heavy oak. It looks like Grandma Grover's attic before you remodeled it." She went to the window, where the sash opened easily. "You detect while I correct," said Renie, picking up a steel paperweight before reaching out into the rain and wind.

The Heat Pixies weren't as loud in Birdwell's room, their dance more attuned to Guy Lombardo than Mötley Crüe. Renie began feeling for the pipe. Judith, meanwhile, searched in vain for any sign of Birdwell's personality in the sitting room. The bedroom wasn't much help, either. His briefcase revealed assorted reviews written by him and other critics, several play programs, two spiral notebooks, and a half-dozen business letters. The only surprise, though Judith found it a mild one, was a signed photograph of Maria at the bottom of his empty suitcase. She was costumed as Giselle, and had written, "To my severest—and sweetest—critic. Love, Maria." Judith smiled faintly, put the picture back, and turned to the bureau. Neatly stacked white underwear and several pairs of socks, all black, rested innocently along with a few toilet articles. The closet was equally devoid of interest. In the gleaming white and chrome bathroom, she found only the usual shaving kit, three bottles of prescription pills—two for stomach disorders, one for allergies—and a toothbrush. Judith felt gypped.

She emerged from the bedroom to find Renie standing by the window. She still held the paperweight in one hand; in her other, she cradled a gun.

"What on earth. . . ?" Judith began.

Renie gulped. "It was stuck in the ivy." She gave her cousin a dazed look. "My fingerprints are now all over it. Do you think it's loaded?"

Judith stepped closer. "Probably." She stared at the gleaming weapon, the steel tinged with blue, the grip richly veined and deeply grooved. "It says 'LadySmith, .38 S. & W. Special CTG.' Whatever that means," Judith added lamely. "Put that sucker down before you blow my feet off."

Renie complied. "What do we do now? Call Mac-Kenzie?"

Judith considered. "I'll go get a shopping bag. We'll carry the gun in it back to our room and phone him from there."

Judith was gone less than three minutes. Renie's gaze was still fixed on the gun as if she expected it to fire on its own. The Heat Pixies were relentless.

"I didn't subdue them," Renie confessed. "I don't have Bill's knack."

"Maybe he just got lucky," said Judith, using a Kleenex to pick up the gun from the leather divan where Renie had set it. Gently, Judith put the weapon into the Prince Albert Bay Outback shopping bag she'd gotten along with a pair of Dingo boots to give Mike for Christmas. "Let's get out of here."

Safely back in Suite 804, Judith called police headquarters. It took almost as long for the receptionist to answer as it had for Gertrude. MacKenzie wasn't in. They'd page him. Maybe.

Renie looked at her watch. It was almost nine o'clock.

"Should we go through Maria and Max's room before they get back?"

Judith shook her head. "We don't want to miss MacKenzie's call. Besides, if the police didn't find anything, I doubt that we will. Except for a very nice picture of Maria and a fond inscription, Birdwell was a bust."

Forced to agree, Renie sank back onto the sofa. Only then did both cousins realize that the Heat Pixies had stopped their deafening clatter.

"Birdwell," declared Judith after considerable mulling, "may be one person Mildred would confide in about the gun."

"If he took it," objected Renie, "why would he ditch it outside his own room?"

"Where else? He didn't have much time. By the way, did you notice you didn't have any trouble opening his window?"

"No. I mean, yes, of course." Renie nodded in understanding. "I see what you mean—mine was stuck, and it took two of us to get Alabama and Desiree's all the way up. Maybe somebody—such as Birdwell—took care to see that his window worked easily. And quickly."

This time, the knock at the door was a sharp rat-tat-tat. "MacKenzie?" breathed Judith, but looked doubtful even as she rose to let their caller in.

Desiree Sinclair Smith wore a stunning forest-green dinner suit with padded shoulders, a stand-up collar, and a slim tulip-shaped shirt. Small gold buttons marched down from the hint of cleavage to the exposed knee. Maria could make men's heads turn; Desiree was the kind who could make men lose them. Judith was impressed in spite of herself.

"You're a real pair of morons," Desiree announced, sailing over the threshold with Alabama riding her wake like a dinghy following a yacht. "Are you the ones who turned us in to Charlie Chan's number-one grandson?"

"You were kind of loud," replied Judith.

"So were you." Desiree waited for Alabama to close

the door. "That's why we reported you. I hope you get blackballed!"

"Nobody's talked to us about it," put in Renie. "Of course," she added a bit vaguely, "we were out for a while."

Desiree sidled up to Renie, wagging a finger within an inch of her nose. "Listen, sweetie, you're lucky you're not out for the count! Nobody complains about Desiree Sinclair and Alabama Smith!" The tip of Desiree's finger almost made contact with Renie.

Incensed, Renie emitted a growling sound and made as if to take a bite out of Desiree. With a yelp, Desiree jumped back, raising a hand to swing at Renie. Alabama stopped her just in time.

"Calm down, darlin'. We don't want any more trouble." His voice had grown careless in its effort to eradicate his Southern accent. "Let's be frank here. We couldn't understand most of what you two were sayin', but it sounded like maybe you had some pretty crazy ideas about poor Maria."

"Invasion of privacy!" shouted Renie, still feisty. "What did you do, hold a glass against the wall?"

It was Judith's turn to intervene. She put a hand on Renie's shoulder and smiled politely at their most recent uninvited guests. "Forgive my cousin. The Heat Pixies have damaged her brain." Ignoring the blank look on the faces of both Smiths, she continued: "As a matter of fact, we were talking about Maria. Spud, too. And Jonathan Castle." She deliberately waited for a reaction.

But Desiree merely gave a toss of her copper mane. "From what we could hear—without any stupid glass"— she shot Renie a nasty look—"you said something about Jonny being Maria's love child. That's utter nonsense! You ought to be sued for slander!"

Judith let go of Renie, and made a hospitable gesture with one hand. "Have a seat. Let's all calm down and talk this out. I know," she went on as the Smiths perched warily on the sofa, "you aren't as anxious to leave Port Royal as the rest of us."

"I'm not," Desiree replied in a less heated tone. "I've got to play to do. But Alabama has to be in Minneapolis Friday."

"Okay," said Judith quietly from the armchair. She noted with relief that Renie had hauled over a footstool and seemed under control. "Renie and I have been doing some research. We may be wrong. In fact, whatever we've come up with about Maria—and Jonathan Castle—may be irrelevant." Judith had to admit to herself that Desiree and Alabama's defense of Maria seemed genuine. It was, she reasoned, possible that they didn't know about that shameful incident of over thirty years ago. But the pair could answer some other questions. "How," she asked pointedly, "did Helen die?"

Desiree gasped; Alabama sagged. Neither of them spoke for a long time.

"You *have* done your homework," Desiree said at last, her husky voice even huskier than usual.

Alabama was getting a grip on his emotions—and his accent. "It was a terrible tragedy. I suspect she'd had a few drinks. I don't know, I wasn't there. I'd spent the afternoon at Boodle's with Max and some financial backers from the City. When I came home, I found her in the foyer, at the bottom of the stairs." His face registered pain, and he looked away. "She'd been dead for some time."

"I'm sorry." Judith was: Unless Alabama was as good an actor as he was a writer, his grief seemed all too real. "Did you call the police?"

He shifted a bit on the sofa, turning to Desiree. "Did I? No, I called for an ambulance. I don't think it ever occurred to me to call the police."

"Did Robin call them in later?" asked Judith, hating herself for opening up old wounds.

Alabama was still looking at Desiree, as if she were

holding up cue cards. "I don't think so. But I don't remember."

"He might have," said Desiree with a shrug. "Helen's death sent him right off his head. It's a wonder he didn't call Number 10 Downing Street."

Renie, who was still regarding Desiree with a certain amount of mistrust, posed a question:

"Was Bob-o always a little loony?"

This time it was Desiree who looked to Alabama for the answer. "I'd call him . . . what?" Alabama was searching for the right word, a sign of his craft. "Not crazy, not eccentric . . . a rugged individualist, except not particularly rugged. If you've seen my play, *Southern Comfort Station*, you'll recognize the type. I modeled the ticketmaster after Robin."

"But," put in Desiree, not wanting to be upstaged, "he wasn't really nuts until Helen died, right?"

Alabama nodded sagely. "That's true. Just as the ticketmaster doesn't go insane until his Creole mistress falls down the one-holer."

"I missed that one at the rep," murmured Renie. "I had croup."

"I was working nights that season at the Meat & Mingle," mumbled Judith.

Alabama tried not to look affronted. "It's a very deep work," he remarked.

"It sounds like it." Judith turned brisk. "Was Helen part of Max's . . . uh, cadre?"

Alabama evinced surprise. "Helen? Oh, no. She wasn't involved in the theater, except by association. Robin was very firm about keeping his daughter out of show business. Two generations of O'Rourkes on the boards were enough, he used to say. Helen never really worked at all, except for a bit of modeling. She was," he went on with an apprehensive glance at his present wife, "very attractive."

"I only met her once," Desiree said, as if a single encounter was insufficient to validate Alabama's opinion.

"So," said Judith, on a sudden inspiration, "if Helen

didn't work, she couldn't have had much money of her own. Bob-o's wealth must have come from his stage career.''

Alabama fingered his short beard. "Wealth? Robin made a decent living, but he certainly wasn't wealthy. I'm sure he would have used up all his savings by now if it hadn't been for—'' He caught himself, along with a jab in the ribs from Desiree.

"Hey, hot grits, it's getting late,'' said his wife, standing up on her four-inch sling-heeled pumps. "Let's go eat. I've got rehearsal in the morning.''

Following Desiree's lead, Judith, Renie, and Alabama all rose and went to the door. "Well, now,'' drawled Alabama, once more the Southern good ol' boy, "Ah guess we aired ouah differences. Just remembah, don't go believin' everything you heah about people. 'Specially Maria.'' The smile in the beard was a trifle wolflike.

"In other words,'' said Desiree, "don't be a couple of chumps. St. Maria of the Thundering Thighs is as pure as the driven snow. And don't give me that old line about how she drifted. It's not her style.''

So saying, Desiree made her exit, Alabama once again bringing up the rear. Judith closed the door behind them and gazed at Renie. "They don't know about Maria and Spud. They do know about Bob-o's stash.''

"Why is everybody so protective of Maria?'' demanded Renie. "She may be your old pal, but she'd drive me batty in about three days. Too artificial.''

Judith measured Renie's words. "Artificial, yes. Phony, no. Maria has been living a lie for thirty years. It shows.'' She headed for her bedroom. "Get your coat. We're going out.''

"What?'' cried Renie. "It's almost ten o'clock! There's a gale out there! Are you nuts?''

But Judith had already left the room. Renie shrugged and went to fetch her raincoat. Moments later, they were at the elevator, waiting for the car to struggle up from the first floor where it had presumably just let off Desiree and Alabama.

"What about MacKenzie?" Renie asked. "I thought you didn't want to miss his call."

"We won't be gone more than ten minutes," replied Judith. "We're not going far."

The elevator arrived, the cousins stepped in, and the cables played their now familiar refrain. "Remember, we said there must a photo of Desiree in Bob-o's apartment?" Judith paused as Renie nodded. "Yet neither of us recalls seeing it. I think we would have remembered it in retrospect after we met Desiree. If it had been there."

"I'm confused," admitted Renie, as they got out of the elevator on the main floor. A gap-toothed brunette, presumably Elaine, was behind the desk, consulting with the suntanned couple from New Zealand. A handful of guests milled around the lobby, chatting and looking at the display of picture postcards. By the main entrance, Desiree and Alabama were waiting for a taxi. Judith and Renie ducked out through the Hepburn Street exit.

"Let me clarify," said Judith as the wind whipped through her hair and made her slacks flap at her legs. "Bob-o had pictures of everybody, or so it seemed. It's possible that he excluded Desiree, because she married Alabama, and thus took Helen's place. But somehow I don't think that's so. In fact, I don't know why, but in the back of my mind, I have this feeling that . . ." She faltered, shaking her head. "It's weird, I wish I could think of what's making me think this way."

"Me, too," said Renie, scooting along beside Judith. They were at the curb, waiting for a pizza deliveryman to pass. Across Empress Drive, the horse chestnuts along the Esplanade swayed in the wind. Whitecaps ruffled the bay's inky waters, while a stately freighter moved slowly toward the mouth of the inner harbor.

Keeping her head down against the rain and wind, Judith forged onward, toward the alley that ran behind the Tudor Arms. Renie squeaked in protest at her cousin:

"We'll never get into Bob-o's apartment! It's padlocked! The turkey skewers are useless!"

"I don't want to get in," responded Judith as they entered the darkened alley. The footing was slippery, and Judith slowed her pace. Just before they reached the dumpster, she peered about, looking for the Siamese cat. He was nowhere to be seen. "Give me a hand," said Judith, grappling with the heavy lid of the dumpster.

"Oh, great, now we're scavengers!" moaned Renie. "I'll ruin my clothes!"

"You get more garbage on them when you eat than you will here," retorted Judith. "Lift, coz! My arms are killing me!"

With a mighty heave, the cousins pushed up the dumpster's lid. Renie was too short to look inside, but Judith took out her little flashlight and shined it over the jumbled contents. The wind was even sharper in the alley than it had been on the street, the narrow space between the buildings creating the effect of a funnel. Renie edged closer to the apartment house, trying to avoid the rain.

"Find anything?" she asked in a feeble voice as her cousin rummaged selectively through the trash.

Judith didn't answer. A horn honked out on Prince Albert Street. Upstairs in the Tudor Arms, someone was playing rock music with the volume up. An old newspaper blew through the alley, sticking to a discarded tricycle. Judith kept searching.

"You'll get a disease," Renie announced ominously. "And I'll get pneumonia. Who then will fix the turkey dressing?"

"Mother," said Judith, and immediately let out a little cry of triumph. "Here it is!" Carefully, she plucked a mangled glossy photograph from the dumpster. "Look," urged Judith, focusing the flashlight on the picture, "it's Desiree!"

It was, a typical studio glamour pose from at least fifteen years earlier, all masses of hair and pouty lips and exaggerated eyes. There was no inscription.

"Congratulations," said Renie. "Let's go back. I'm soaked, frozen, and possibly dead."

Judith was ready to comply, but not until she had pocketed the flashlight, put the photo inside her purse, and replaced the dumpster lid. The cousins were just turning around to head out of the alley when they saw a tall figure outlined against the night. They stopped abruptly, instinct bringing them close together. A passing car on Prince Albert Street highlighted the man just enough so that the cousins could see he was holding something. It was a gun, and it was pointed straight at Judith and Renie.

TWELVE

THE COUSINS GRIPPED each other by the arms. Judith heard her heart thudding; Renie felt her knees turn to water. Neither could speak, let alone scream. The figure advanced at a leisurely pace. The cousins each thought of flight, but knew it was futile. Their teeth were chattering when they saw the gun being lowered, and heard the familiar voice call out:

"I warned you not to meddle. Do you want to get yourselves killed?" It was Angus MacKenzie, without his hat.

Or, Judith noted as relief swept over her, at least he wasn't wearing it. Instead, he held the battered headgear in the hand that didn't cradle the gun. "My hat blew off," he said, apologetic as ever. "I chased it for almost a block." With resolution, he jammed it back on his head, then carefully put the gun inside his coat.

"All right," he continued on a note of resignation, "what in the name of all that's crazy are you two doing here tonight?"

Judith was the first to recover her voice. "Uh—going

through the dumpster because room service didn't deliver? Um—looking for the Siamese cat?'' She saw no change of expression on MacKenzie's stolid face. ''How about collecting Canadian souvenirs?''

MacKenzie let out a heavy sigh. ''Come along, I was just on my way to see you. Then my hat blew off. I thought you were a couple of burglars.'' He was moving at a much brisker pace than usual, one hand holding his hat fast to his head. ''Though God knows, even burglars have more sense than to come out on a night like this,'' he added in a vexed voice.

''Do you always pull your weapon so fast?'' demanded Renie, her temper regained along with her nerve. ''You could get yourself into a lot of trouble doing that down home.''

MacKenzie gave her a dour look as they crossed the street. ''Except for practicing at the range, that's the first time I've drawn my gun in four years. But I'm not usually the only policeman in the vicinity. And, as you may recall, we had a homicide here last night. There's a murderer lurking about somewhere.''

They were approaching the entrance to the Clovia. The lights in the lobby had grown dim. Renie peered at her watch. ''It's after ten o'clock. We'll have to let ourselves in.''

But Brian was heading for the door, his grin fading a bit at the sight of MacKenzie. ''Hey, man, what's going down?''

''We're going up,'' MacKenzie replied with nonchalance. ''You don't shut off the elevators after ten, do you?'' He kept moving, with Judith and Renie trailing behind. Brian exchanged puzzled looks with Doris, who was locking up the cash drawer at the desk.

The trio made the ascent to the eighth floor in silence. Both cousins still needed some time to recuperate after their fright in the alley. It wasn't until they were inside Suite 804, had removed their coats, and sat down that MacKenzie asked why Judith had called him.

"Because of this," she said, reaching for the Outback shop's sack. It all but danced out of her grasp. "Damn!" she cried. "It's gone!"

"What's gone?" MacKenzie was as stoic as ever.

Judith and Renie were looking at each other with dismay. "The gun," Judith finally replied, waving the empty shopping bag at the policeman. "We found a .38 caliber LadySmith outside Birdwell's window. It was caught in the ivy."

A flicker of incredulity passed over MacKenzie's long face. "I am . . . amazed. I think." He spoke very slowly. Cradling his battered hat in his lap, he smoothed his moustache and stared up at the ceiling. "Let me see . . . You were somehow in Mr. de Smoot's room, and for some reason, you were mucking about in the ivy on the hotel's outer wall, and you happened to find a gun." The ceiling seemed to fascinate him. "Yes, that's amazing."

"It probably sounds kind of goofy," Renie allowed, "but it really wasn't. We can explain . . ."

At last, MacKenzie broke off his contemplation of the hotel ceiling, and shifted his gaze first to Judith, then to Renie. "Go right ahead. I can't wait to hear it."

Renie seemed to be appealing to Judith to bail her out. Judith tried to ignore her cousin, but finally capitulated. "It started with the Heat Pixies," she said. "They were giving me a headache."

MacKenzie tipped his head to one side. "Really? The Heat Pixies, eh? Well, now! Go on." He wore the expression of an Oxford don who had inadvertently wandered into a kindergarten classroom. Or a lunatic asylum.

Judith pushed forward. "The Heat Pixies are what we call the horrible noises the radiators make," she explained in her most reasonable voice. "Renie had a theory—actually, it's her husband's—about banging on a pipe that runs down the back side of the hotel. We went into Birdwell's room to see if we could find it, and found the gun instead." She lifted up both her palms, as if she'd just outlined the simplest of incidents.

To MacKenzie's credit—or perhaps Judith's—he looked thoughtful, rather than skeptical. "It would probably be best for me not to ask how you got into Mr. de Smoot's room. I'm assuming, of course, that he wasn't there, having seen him return with Miss Grimm just as I pulled up a few minutes ago. For the moment, we shall let that part pass. Would you tell me again what kind of gun you found?"

Judith repeated what she'd already said, along with a description of the weapon. She was on the verge of telling MacKenzie that Mildred Grimm owned such a handgun, but decided against it. The revelation would certainly get Mildred in trouble, while not necessarily advancing the investigation. And to be honest, Judith told herself, she wasn't absolutely positive that the revolver they had found was the same one which had been stolen from Mildred.

"I don't suppose," said MacKenzie gloomily, "that you took down the gun's serial number?"

"I don't suppose we saw it," confessed Judith. Renie started to open her mouth, caught Judith's warning glance, and shed her shoes instead.

"Don't move," MacKenzie commanded, cautiously getting up from the armchair. He started with the carpet, moved on to the furniture, and then went into each of the bedrooms. "It looks about the same as when I was here earlier," he observed upon his return to the sitting room. "The carpet and the shopping bag would be the give-aways. I wonder if I can get a man up here to check for footprints or fingerprints." His soulful gaze rested on the phone.

Miraculously, there was an evidence specialist on duty, having been called in to assist with a grisly killing at the harbor. "Drunks," said MacKenzie in disgust. "Why couldn't they have waited until the strike was over?"

His remark spurred Judith into unloading the story of Helen O'Rourke Brookes Smith. This time, MacKenzie listened with rapt attention. Indeed, when Judith had finished, he beamed his approval. "Now that's very good,

Mrs. McMonigle. Hold it, don't move, you might ruin the evidence. I'm afraid you'll both have to just sit there until my man arrives.'' MacKenzie himself was being very careful not to disturb anything in the room, his big feet set close together, his shambling body held upright in the armchair like an icon on a throne. ''That's the kind of thing we're missing from this case. We simply don't have the resources to get information out of Scotland Yard. Tomorrow, maybe. We'll contact London and see what we can find out. I must say, this is very promising.''

Judith and Renie both felt partially exonerated, even a little exhilarated. The mood was broken only by the arrival of Jasper Jarwoski, a fussy young man with blond hair that curled over his collar and fell in his eyes. He brought along several plastic sacks and a little machine that worked like a vacuum cleaner. Through rimless glasses, he scanned the sitting room.

''Thick pile in the carpet.'' Jarwoski gave a dejected shake of his head. ''The shopping bag won't give good prints.'' He made a disapproving face. ''Too much upholstery,'' he continued in a disheartened manner, ''and not enough smooth surfaces. I don't like this much at all.'' Despite the complaints, Jarwoski went to work. In less than fifteen minutes, he was done.

''I'll have the results in a couple of hours,'' he told MacKenzie. ''I should be home in bed, you know. *Sir.*''

''So should we all,'' responded MacKenzie in his indolent manner. ''Any preliminary conclusions?''

Jarwoski glanced around. ''Only the obvious. Whoever came in here wiped his or her feet off very carefully first. Otherwise, there would be more than three sets of damp patches on the carpet.''

MacKenzie nodded. ''Good point. Carry on.''

The harried Jarwoski nodded in salute at his superior, mumbled something to Judith and Renie, and was gone. ''You can move now,'' said the detective, getting up to stretch. ''By the way, you've never explained what you were doing in the alley.'' His eyes narrowed slightly at the cousins.

"Oh, that.'' Judith gave him her idea about Desiree's picture, her theory no less garbled than when she had presented it for Renie's consideration. Delving into her purse, she produced the photograph. "As I told Renie, I'm not so concerned about the picture itself, but about why it bothered me. I can even understand how it ended up in the dumpster.''

"You can, eh?'' MacKenzie was skeptical.

"Sure,'' replied Judith. "Desiree didn't want to be connected with Bob-o. So she, or Alabama, pitched the photo in the garbage.''

MacKenzie digested her idea. "That's fine as far as it goes. But when?''

"When?'' Judith went blank. "Oh! I see—was the picture removed before or after Bob-o was killed. Hmmm.'' She put her chin on her fist and thought hard. "I'm sure we didn't see it when we were there in the afternoon,'' she said at last. She frowned, then turned a disturbed face to the detective. "This was all very cleverly planned, wasn't it?''

"It seems so,'' said MacKenzie.

Judith thought some more, and suddenly gave a little jump. "The crescent! That's it! Or part of it,'' she added on a more subdued note.

MacKenzie, as well as Renie, was looking mystified. "What crescent?'' he inquired.

Judith turned to Renie. "Do you remember yesterday afternoon when we were coming back from Bob-o's, I picked a bit of glitter in the shape of a little moon off my slacks?'' Not waiting for Renie's response, she hurried on: "I'll bet you anything, it got stuck there at Bob-o's. And I think I know where it came from—originally. What about you, coz?''

Renie looked as if she were trying to figure it out, but failed to come up with an answer. Judith rushed to her rescue. "Desiree's closet. All those fancy costumes with spangles and bangles and shining stars and silver moons. Well?''

Renie might not have figured out what Judith had meant at first, but she wasn't buying the theory wholesale. "Are you trying to tell us that Desiree runs around Port Royal dressed like Glinda from *The Wizard of Oz* and nobody notices? Come on!''

Judith felt the air go out of her balloon. "Oh." She slumped against the back of the sofa. "Okay," she said, a trifle defensively, "so I got carried away. But I still like the basic concept.''

MacKenzie was ambling toward the door. "You've done very well. I commend you. As a reward, I'll have your statements ready to sign in the morning." He gave them his uneven smile. "You'll be free to go then.''

Renie grinned from ear to ear. Judith, to her own surprise as well as that of her cousin and the detective, didn't react with jubilation. "That's great," she said in a flat voice. Aware of the two puzzled sets of eyes resting on her, she forced a happy face. "I'm glad. Honest.''

"I expected you would be," said MacKenzie, looking unconvinced. "I'll admit, I'd rather everyone stayed around for a few days, but officially, we can't stop any of you. For the last time, please don't take any more chances." He pointed to the dead-bolt lock. "Use this tonight. Don't forget," the detective added in warning, "somebody has a key to this room. Whoever it is now also has a gun.''

MacKenzie's warning had a sobering effect on Judith and Renie. After his departure, the cousins sat down on the sofa, mulling over the evening's events. The wind had died down, and the rain had dwindled to a drizzle. It appeared that the storm was moving inland, toward the mountains.

"Why," asked Renie, "did you refuse to rat on Mildred?''

"Why," countered Judith, "could you find her mother's handgun registration when the police couldn't?''

Renie pondered. "You think they did find it, and MacKenzie's not saying?"

"Could be. The point is, it was there for the finding. Plus, we can't swear in court that the gun we found belongs to Mildred." Judith felt her eyelids beginning to droop, along with her brain. "The real question is, how did anyone know we found the blasted gun? Unless somebody was doing a random search of our room and came across it."

"I don't know why the Clovia didn't put us all up dormitory-style," said Renie through a yawn. "It would have been a lot easier than sneaking in and out of each other's suites like a bunch of cat burglars."

"We know Mildred has a master key," said Judith. "You've got one, too. How many are there?"

Renie shook her head. "I don't remember. I think there was one more left. But the police already had one."

"That is a question we can't ask Doris, given our own guilt," lamented Judith with a rueful expression.

"I'm beat," Renie announced. "I'm going to take a bath and go to bed. You must be worn out, too. You sure didn't seem very excited about going home."

Judith evaded her cousin's gaze. "Of course I am. I was just surprised that MacKenzie planned on having those statements ready by morning." She glanced at the time. "I'm going to watch the eleven o'clock news. We missed it last night."

Renie raised a hand in a feeble wave, then trundled off into her bedroom. Judith turned on the television set, making sure she tuned in a Canadian rather than an American station. The hundred and twenty miles between the two major cities allowed viewers on both sides of the border to watch the local and national news broadcasts of their choice.

CLIP-TV led off with the police strike, featuring interviews with Port Royal's commissioner, the head of the local law enforcement guild, and a spokeswoman for the city. The bottom line was that no progress had been made.

Half dozing, Judith watched reports on a warehouse fire in a Port Royal suburb, a scam that had fleeced almost a million dollars from a dozen senior citizens, and a storm-induced two-hour traffic jam on the St. George Bridge.

At last, the apple-cheeked anchorwoman and her square-jawed partner zeroed in on Bob-o: "Lack of available personnel has slowed the murder investigation of one of Port Royal's best-known characters, Bob-o, the Prince Albert Bay popcorn vendor," reported the chipper blond anchorwoman. "The long-time fixture on Empress Drive, whose real name was Robin O'Rourke, was found shot to death early last evening in the elevator of the Hotel Clovia." A pan of the Esplanade, followed by an exterior of the hotel, appeared on the screen. "Homicide Detective Angus MacKenzie said today that police are doing their best under trying circumstances."

The camera had caught MacKenzie at his most doleful. "The strike hampers us in several ways," he said, sounding even more lugubrious on videotape than in person. "However, it's just a matter of time before we catch the killer. Nobody can get away with murder in a respectable hotel like the Clovia."

MacKenzie's image was replaced by the well-scrubbed anchors. "Gavin," said the blond, turning to her compatriot, "do the police feel this was a random killing or is there a personal element here?"

Gavin set his square jaw and looked sincere. "From what I'm hearing, it's definitely a maniac, possibly with drug connections. Everyone I've talked to is convinced the police are dealing with a wild card killer."

"It's certainly someone with a lot of nerve," declared Gavin's vis-à-vis, turning to face the camera head-on. "Residents of Prince Albert Bay may not be sleeping quite as soundly as usual tonight, but tomorrow they'll be able to take their minds off their troubles by going to the Empress Park Zoo to welcome the new panda from . . ."

Judith clicked off the TV. She didn't believe that MacKenzie—or anyone else in an official capacity—was feeding stories of a drug-crazed maniac to the media. It struck her as odd that there had been no mention of the various celebrities staying at the Clovia. The Sacred Eight's members were getting their wish to avoid scandal. Or else, it suddenly occurred to Judith, Spud had been doing his bit to blow smoke at the TV station. He had, after all, been at CLIP that afternoon to tape his interview.

Finding Renie once again struggling with the window, Judith expostulated her most recent theory. "Might be," said Renie, moving over so that Judith could help. Several groans and many pushes later, the window edged up a good six inches. Renie was satisfied, if limp. "I don't like sleeping in a closed room. Do you want help with yours?"

Judith hesitated. She shared Renie's sentiments about fresh air. The previous night, she had been too preoccupied with Bob-o's death to think about opening windows. But now it sounded like a good idea. The cousins were more fortunate in Judith's bedroom: Although the sash resisted initially, they achieved success on their second try.

"It's stopped raining," Judith said in surprise. Off in the distance, they could hear the mournful notes of a foghorn. The storm had definitely passed.

Renie stood at the casement, looking out. "Coz," she said quietly, "why are you upset about going home tomorrow?"

Judith let out a long sigh. There was never any point in trying to keep anything from Renie. "I hate unfinished business. I hate things that don't make sense. I hate being fooled by a cold-blooded killer." Her voice had begun to rise, fervor building like water in a boiling kettle. "Most of all, I hate being a chump!"

"Look," said Renie calmly, "once upon a time you had a murder fall in your lap. You had—what? Eight suspects right there under your roof. You were very clever, and you figured it all out. But let's face it, you can't expect lightning to strike twice. You're in a strange city, a foreign country. You're out of your element. Give it up, coz. Get some sleep, okay?"

Every so often, the old childhood habit of deferring to Renie's two years of seniority surfaced. Judith heard the compassion in her cousin's voice. She knew Renie was not only concerned, but that she was probably right.

"Okay," agreed Judith wearily. "I'll turn in my badge."

"Just turn in." Renie gave Judith's shoulder a pat. "It's going on midnight. If we bag all this murder stuff, we can go downtown tomorrow and shop and have lunch and shop some more and then head home around five. How about dinner along the way at Pie-Oh-My!?"

"Sounds good," said Judith, with a wan smile. She watched Renie troop off through the connecting bathroom. Judith began to undress. Renie made sense. It was absurd, even arrogant, to suppose that she could track down Bob-o's killer. It was possibly irrelevant, now that they could sign their statements and go home. Her mother was waiting, Mike was on his way, the rest of the family was looking forward to the big holiday dinner. As for Joe, he was . . .

Judith paused, standing barefooted in her flannel nightgown. Joe was somewhere. She knew not the address or the situation, only that he was back home, a hundred and twenty miles away. Judith climbed into bed, hugged the pillow, and fell into a dreamless sleep.

THIRTEEN

HER FIRST SENSATION was of dampness, then of murky light, and finally of an odd sound close to her ear. She rolled over and let out a small shriek. A seagull stood on the windowsill, begging eyes trained on Judith.

"Beat it!" she grumbled. "I don't do room service for birds!"

The gull lifted one claw, pecked under its wing, and settled in on the sill. Judith sat up in bed. Outside, the fog had rolled in, thick and gray. She couldn't see across the street. Another foghorn, much closer than the one she'd heard last night, echoed over the bay.

Judith got up, waving her glitzy paperback in a menacing manner. "Scoot! Go away! How would you like to meet Sweetums?"

The gull eyed Judith with disdain, then flapped its wings and flew off into the fog. Judith felt vaguely penitent. It occurred to her that the seagulls and other birds that resided in the neighborhood had no doubt dined frequently on Bob-o's popcorn, especially those bags tossed away by disgusted customers. That meal ticket

was canceled. The avian inhabitants would have to look
elsewhere for sustenance. But not necessarily to Judith.
Quieting her conscience, she headed for the bathroom,
noting that it was almost eight-thirty. She'd take a shower, and
then rouse Renie.

The warm waters cascading over her body brought Judith fully awake. She let out another little cry, shut off the
faucets, grabbed a big fleecy towel, and flew into Renie's
room.

"Coz!" she shouted, shaking the inert bundle that was
Renie, "I've got it! Wake up!"

Renie burrowed further down under the covers. Judith
shook her again. "Get with it for once! Come on, I've all
but solved the murder!"

"Drmpdud," mumbled Renie, pulling the sheet over
her head.

"Drop dead yourself," retorted Judith, accustomed to
Renie's early morning mutterings. "Get your tail in gear."

"G'fkyrzf." Renie was putting the pillow over her head.

Judith yanked it away. "I will not. You're going to
smother."

In a tangle of bedclothes, Renie began to emerge,
though her eyes were still shut. "Wzrg?" she asked.

"Nothing's wrong," replied Judith, impatiently. "I've
finally figured out what I've been trying to remember. It
was that damned seagull."

"Seagull?" Renie's eyes had opened. "What seagull?"

"There was one in the window just now. It made me
think of Bob-o and Tootle. Go splash water on your face.
I'll order breakfast."

Judith had said the magic word. Renie struggled out of
bed, staggering toward the bathroom. Back in her own
bedroom, Judith toweled off and got dressed. Five minutes
later, she was calling room service. Doris answered.

"Gee, Doris, don't you ever get any time off?" inquired Judith, thinking of her own long hours as general
factotum of Hillside Manor.

"Usually, yes," Doris answered crossly. "But this

hasn't been your average week. I had to come in last night to straighten out the payroll. We've still got the press prowling around, annoying our guests. Did you see the hotel on the news last night? Imagine, the Clovia mixed up in such a mess!''

Judith commiserated, but Doris wasn't done yet with her litany of complaints: ''Now we find out the airport is closed because of the fog! I've already had about two dozen people screaming at me as if it were my fault!''

Judith could guess who some of them might be. She sympathized some more, then put in her breakfast order. Sounding somewhat mollified by Judith's understanding manner, Doris promised that Brian would be up in twenty minutes.

''Where's breakfast?'' asked Renie, emerging from the bathroom in her purple robe.

''It's coming,'' Judith assured her. ''Have a seat. I'll give you my brainstorm.'' She was slightly put off by Renie's vacant stare, but Judith plunged ahead anyway: ''Do you remember all those goofy rhymes Tootle recited?''

''Tootle who?'' muttered Renie, still staring.

Exasperated, Judith gave her cousin a little poke. ''It's going on nine o'clock. Try waking up an hour early for once. This is important.''

Slowly, Renie came into focus. ''Parakeets don't recite,'' she said, sounding more like herself. ''They repeat.''

''Right,'' agreed Judith, relieved that Renie had decided to join the Land of the Living. ''Ergo, Tootle was mouthing stuff he'd heard, probably from Bob-o. One of the things Tootle said was something about 'Don't forget your key.' That could mean somebody else had access to Bob-o's apartment.''

Growing ever more alert, Renie mulled over the idea. ''That's true. Mrs. Wittelstein, maybe. But where does it get us? I thought we were going to forget about playing sleuth.''

Judith waved her hand at Renie. ''We can't. Not now.

We're too close. But you're right, that rhyme isn't much help. The other one is more illuminating. Help me remember how it went—'Polly put the kettle on, wearin' o' the green.' What's next?"

"It wasn't Polly, it was Daddy." Renie definitely did not look pleased with Judith's re-immersion into the murder case. "Where's breakfast?"

"Parakeets don't have lips," declared Judith. "Tootle probably meant to say Polly." She hesitated, then shook her head. "You're right, Daddy would make more sense because then it was something about Mummy and biscuits and not keeping clean. Have you got it yet?" Judith leaned forward eagerly.

"I don't even have a lousy cup of coffee," Renie exclaimed. "No," she said through clenched teeth. "I haven't got it. And I don't much care."

Judith was taken aback, but not yet defeated. "The references are to a girlfriend. If 'Daddy' is Bob-o, then 'Mummy' must be his . . ." She sought the right word. ". . . mate? Ducks and drakes, remember!"

Renie yawned. "So what?"

"It's all part of my theory," said Judith, growing irked by her cousin's indifference. "Never mind, just don't come crying to me when the police find the gun this time and your fingerprints are the only ones that show up. I hope you'll like that thin gruel they serve in prison for the holidays."

Apprehension crept into Renie's eyes. "That's silly. MacKenzie knows I found the gun. We told him so. Of course my prints are on it."

Judith emitted a small snort. "MacKenzie thought our entire story was a fable. He's a cop, he deals in facts. If the bullet that killed Bob-o matches that .38, and your prints are on the gun, you can bet your Bally boots they'll haul you in."

Renie's disinterest had given way to the instinct for survival. "Damn! Why did I ever ask you to come up to Port Royal with me? The worst thing that's ever happened when we've stayed at the Clovia was the time Bill was taking a nap and the headboard fell on him! Okay, run this nutty idea of yours by me again. So far all we have is Bob-o making tea for some woman who could be Mrs. Wittelstein who could be a homicidal maniac but I doubt it. This deduction does not a conviction make.''

Judith was still undaunted. ''The part about wearing green—Desiree does, a lot.''

Renie rolled her eyes. ''Desiree and Bob-o making out like minks? How about the Pope and Cher?''

''I don't mean Desiree and Bob-o were lovers. Desiree no doubt had other things on her mind if she called on him.'' Judith was about to elucidate when Brian arrived with breakfast. ''Wow, we may have people sleeping in the lobby tonight!'' He grinned broadly at the thought. ''If the guests who are due to check out can't leave because of the fog, we've got over twenty-five rooms double booked. The phones are all tied up, the boiler isn't working right, and the staff hasn't been paid. Gramps is about to have a seizure, and Doris is threatening to quit.'' Clearly, Brian was enjoying every minute of the ongoing crisis. ''I just talked to a TV reporter dude. I should be on the news tonight. Fresh!''

Judith and Renie tried to share his enthusiasm, but had to make up for their lack of wholeheartedness with yet another generous tip. They had just settled in over scrambled eggs, Canadian bacon, hash browns, and toast when Evelyn arrived at the door, her eyes glistening with tears.

''All right, so *I'm* the fool!'' she declared angrily, brushing past Judith to throw herself on the sofa next to Renie. ''I suppose you're laughing your heads off at me!''

With a forkful of scrambled eggs poised at her mouth, Renie glared at Evelyn. ''I never laugh at anything before ten o'clock.''

Judith was more sympathetic than her cousin. ''What's wrong, Mrs. Frobisher?'' Not having an extra coffee cup, she offered Evelyn the rest of her tomato juice.

But Evelyn waved the glass away. ''You know every-

thing! Why didn't you tell me where Spud was last night?"
She drew her legs up under her body and hugged herself.
"Well?" Evelyn demanded, her skin as pale as the ivory
sweater she was wearing over matching slacks. "What
have you got to say for yourselves?"

"Evelyn," said Judith, putting the conversation on a
calmer and more personal note, "I have no idea what
you're talking about." She checked her statement. "Okay,
maybe I do. But I didn't know it when I was with you last
night."

Evelyn wiped at her eyes with shaking fingers. "Who
are you? Really?"

Judith gave a little strangled laugh and shook her head.
"Nobody. Ourselves. We're just a couple of cousins with
a knack for the unusual. Renie's dad always said we could
turn buying a quart of milk into a perilous adventure."

"It was a loaf of bread," Renie said with her mouth
full.

Evelyn regarded the cousins uneasily. "The point is,
you know about Spud and Desiree." Her hazel eyes were
accusatory, as if the alleged dalliance had been concocted
by Judith and Renie.

"All we know is that Alabama was looking for his wife
while you were worrying about Spud," said Judith pa-
tiently. "We also know—because Maria told us—that Desiree's rehearsal was over by five. The rest is pure
conjecture." She eyed the distraught Evelyn. "Perhaps you
know more."

Evelyn's taut, slim body unwound a bit. She dropped
her arms and allowed her feet to touch the floor. "Isn't it
obvious?" she replied, though there was doubt in her
voice.

"That depends," said Judith. "What does Spud say?"

Evelyn's mouth drew into a straight line and her eyes
flashed. "He denies it, of course."

Renie finished her second piece of toast. "Believe him.
The man's crazy about you."

Evelyn stared at Renie. "How would *you* know?"

Renie cut up her Canadian bacon and gave Evelyn a wry look. "We know everything. You said so yourself."

"You *are* laughing at me!" cried Evelyn. "You're Spud's friends!"

Judith's patience was wearing thin. "Renie hardly knew Spud, and I haven't seen him in thirty years. Give the guy a break. Desiree may have put a move on him. You're all under a lot of strain, trying to avoid getting implicated in Bob-o's murder. Even Desiree probably isn't herself."

Evelyn bridled. "She doesn't know who herself is! She's always playing a part, her favorite role being Desiree Sinclair, world-class tart! To make matters worse, we can't leave Port Royal because of this stupid fog! I can't let the au pair girl roast a turkey for the kids!" Evelyn started to cry again.

Judith and Renie traded looks of consternation. "The fog will lift," Judith said with more confidence than she felt. "It's Spud you're upset about. I gather he's been a faithful husband in general?"

Evelyn seemed taken aback by the blunt question. She stifled her sobs and sat up straight. "As far as I know. Oh, he's certainly had his opportunities. You can't work in the theater and not be faced with temptation every day. But except for—" She stopped, her expression suddenly faraway. "No, I'm being stupid. Years ago, when the children were small, and I was working so hard to get my agency going, I wondered if he was involved with someone else. It would have been my own fault," she added with a trace of bitterness. "Frankly, I was neglecting him."

Judith drank the rest of her juice and regarded Evelyn with compassion. "It happens. But as you said, you take very good care of each other. 'Protective,' wasn't that how you put it?" She took a deep breath. "Where did Spud go Monday night just before Bob-o was shot?"

Evelyn coiled like a snake, her small, perfect teeth bared. Judith and Renie both tensed, poised for a violent reaction. But the other woman relaxed almost at once, shaking her head in surrender. "I was afraid of this. Why haven't the police questioned him about it?"

"I'm not sure they know," replied Judith. "The person who saw him in the lobby may not have mentioned it." Judith was being deliberately cagey; she felt she might learn more by keeping Evelyn off-guard. "Well?" she pressed the point, like a boxer jabbing away at his opponent's open cut.

"I don't know," Evelyn said at last. She gazed at each cousin in turn. "I honestly don't know. Spud wouldn't tell me." In a sudden spasm of anxiety, she writhed about on the sofa. "Oh, God, I'm so scared!"

Rather diffidently, Renie put the hand that wasn't forking in food on Evelyn's arm. "Take it easy, kiddo. You don't really think Spud killed Bob-o, do you?"

Evelyn tried to regain control of herself. "No. Of course not. But what will the police think if they find out Spud was downstairs that night? And why won't he tell me what he was doing?" Her voice was filled with desperation.

Judith put her plate aside and stood up. "Let's ask. Where is he?"

A blank expression crossed Evelyn's face. "He stomped out. Maybe he's in the dining room. Or out walking. He does that sometimes when he's mad."

The vision of a clumsy Spud Frobisher, walking around in pea-soup fog, was more than Judith could handle. "Let's try the dining room." As both Evelyn and Renie started to rise, Judith put out a hand. "You stay here. Together. Don't worry, I'll be the soul of tact."

Renie rolled her eyes; Evelyn looked uncertain. But neither woman made an attempt to detain Judith. Three minutes later, after a frazzling ride in the elevator with an irate party from Nova Scotia who insisted the fog could last for three days, and thus ruin their entire lives, Judith entered the hotel dining room. To her relief, Spud was sitting at a corner table, smoking and drinking coffee.

"Hi," said Judith breezily, not waiting to be asked to sit. "I see you fled the war zone."

Spud's unhappy face flushed. "It sounds like Ev's been telling tales out of school."

Signaling for the waitress to bring her a cup, Judith noted that there was no evidence of food on the table. "Haven't you eaten?" she inquired.

Spud continued to sit with his chin on his fist, cigarette smoke swirling about him as if the fog had come inside. "I'm not hungry." He looked very much as Judith remembered him on an occasion thirty years earlier when Coach Humbert had benched him for fumbling three times in one game.

"Listen, Spud," said Judith as the cup and saucer arrived along with a fresh carafe of coffee, "Evelyn isn't mad so much as worried. She's afraid you're going to get arrested."

A startled look enveloped Spud's pink face. "For what? Telling Desiree to take a hike?"

"I thought so," murmured Judith, but continued before Spud could make a comment. "Wouldn't it be easier if you told her why you came down to the lobby Monday night?"

Judging from the misery in Spud's eyes, it wouldn't. "I can't," he said in a hopeless tone. "The fact is, if the police asked me, I could prove to them what I was doing. But I can't tell Ev." He stubbed out his cigarette and swigged down more coffee.

From where Judith was sitting, she could see the hallway that led from the Hepburn Street entrance. According to Sybil, Spud had come from that direction before he got into the elevator. The girl couldn't remember if he'd been wearing a coat, which, Judith figured, meant he probably wasn't. Therefore, in all likelihood, Spud had not gone outside. Judith stared at the trio of pay phones that flanked the wall opposite the dining room entrance, then looked squarely at Spud.

"Who did you call long distance?"

Caught in the act of pouring himself another cup of coffee, Spud sloshed the carafe's contents all over the tablecloth. "Who said I called anybody?" he asked belligerently.

Judith noticed that his hand was shaking. "Come on, Spud, it's not that hard to figure out. You used real money so the charge wouldn't appear on your hotel bill or your calling card. The only way you could prove that you'd made that call at a certain time was if it had been long distance. The phone company would have a record of it." She took a wild guess. "What time was it in Hong Kong?"

Spud looked as if he were about to cry. It crossed Judith's mind that before they got out of the Clovia, most of the Sacred Eight would wash away in a sea of tears. But Spud resisted the urge, instead making an awkward attempt to mop up the spilled coffee.

"I called Jonathan Castle," he answered on a defensive note. "We work together a lot, you know."

Judith fixed him with a shrewd, yet kindly stare. "I do know. It must give you great pleasure."

Spud's broad shoulders slumped. He crumpled up his soaked napkin and flung it on the floor. "Hell's bells! Who told you? Maria?"

"No. Not precisely." She gave Spud a little smile. "I gather that Jonathan knows about his real parents?"

To Judith's surprise, Spud shook his head. "Maria and I talked it over years ago, and decided against it. He was the kind of kid—well, young man, he was grown by then—who wasn't curious about that sort of thing. The couple who had adopted him were wonderful folks. There didn't seem to be any point stirring up trouble, especially since Maria didn't want Max to find out. And I wasn't crazy about Evelyn knowing I'd been an unwed father." The athlete's aging body sagged in the chair; the boyish face showed genuine remorse.

"Why did you call Jonathan?" Judith asked after an appropriate moment of silence. "At that particular time, I mean."

Having made his confession, Spud began to pull himself together. "I always call him once a month, on the third

Monday. It's a habit we got into early on in his career. He looked to me as sort of a . . . what do you call it, a sponsor? And I liked being able to help him out. It made up for . . . a lot of things.'' He turned away from Judith, wistful, yet proud. ''Jonny isn't just good-looking, he's got talent.''

''You and Maria made something wonderful together,'' Judith commented in a quiet voice. ''It's almost a pity that the world can't know.''

''Well, I'll be boiled in oil before I'll tell anybody,'' Spud asserted with fervor. ''I didn't know myself until Jonathan showed up in New York, and poor Maria went to pieces!''

''You mean she had a breakdown?''

Spud drew back in his chair, one elbow almost knocking over a plant stand. ''That's what ended her career. She hadn't seen Jonny since the day he was born. Oh, she knew where he was, and all that, even though she never told me he existed. Then along he comes, right off the bus from Oregon, and walks into the theater where I was auditioning actors for Alabama's new play. I didn't know Jonny from Adam, but Maria had stopped by on her way from rehearsal at the Met. She took one look at the names on the tryout sheet, found out which one was Jonny, and went into a regular tailspin! We had to call an ambulance.'' Spud shook his head at the unhappy memory. ''Maria never danced again.''

Judith emitted a low, faintly unladylike whistle. ''That seems like an awfully extreme reaction.''

Spud didn't agree. ''Not when you're the reigning prima ballerina of the dance world, and just married to the most respected theater impresario of our generation. Besides, she was always wound up pretty tight.'' Unexpectedly, Spud grinned. ''Remember the time Donnie Barksdale put the slug in her Pee-Chee folder and she freaked out so bad her folks had to come and take her home?''

Judith did, though the memory wasn't quite as vivid for her as it appeared to be for Spud. But slugs and Pee-Chees

were a far cry from illegitimate children and nervous
breakdowns. Or, Judith thought on reflection, maybe they
weren't . . .

The breakfast crowd was thinning out. Their waitress
reappeared to check the coffeepot, found it still half full,
commiserated over the wet tablecloth, and scurried off with
the promise of clean linen. Spud, however, was standing
up, jarring a passing busboy in the process.

"You really think Evelyn is more worried than mad?"
he inquired hopefully.

"Yes, I do." Judith had remained seated, craning her
neck to look up at Spud, who was holding the bill in one
hand and digging for coins with the other. "Spud—why
don't you tell her about Jonny? Your wife is basically a
very understanding woman."

Spud sighed. "You think so?" He seemed to be weigh-
ing Judith's suggestion. "No, I can't do it. It wouldn't be
fair to Maria."

There was some truth to his statement, Judith admitted
to herself. She was also impressed by Spud's old-fashioned
gallantry. Still, she believed—basically—that honesty was
always the best policy. But as much as she would like it,
she couldn't set all the affairs of the world in simple, logical order. "You'll have to do what you think best. But I'd
certainly put her mind at ease by reassuring her about
Desiree. And letting her know you made a phone call instead of plugging Bob-o"

"Ev doesn't think I did that," said Spud disparagingly.
He was moving through the dining room, leaving a trail
of jostled customers and rattling crockery in his wake.
Judith followed at a safe distance.

"Tell me something," Judith said, when they had
reached the privacy of the elevator. "Why did Birdwell
take Max to court?"

Spud let out a little rumbling chuckle. "You know about
old Dame Carmela?" He saw Judith nod. "She was
loaded. Her estate was divvied up between her daughter,
Sylvia, and her son—I forget his name, he's an ad exec or

something—but Dame Carmela couldn't stand Birdwell. When he married Sylvia, the old girl cut her daughter out of the will. Instead of leaving it all to the son, Carmela left Sylvia's share to Max. He'd always been her pet protégé.''

The elevator doors slid open, somehow without their usual jarring noises. "But what about Sylvia? She and Birdwell weren't married that long.''

Spud chuckled again, this time ruefully. "That was a tough break for Sylvia. Carmela died a month after the wedding. A year later, Sylvia and Birdie were separated.''

Judith stood at the door to Suite 804, fist poised to knock. "You mean she lost out on everything?''

Spud shrugged. "At least she got rid of Birdwell.''

"What happened to her?'' asked Judith, rapping on the door.

Spud shrugged again. "I don't know for sure. I think she remarried and moved to the States. Or Canada. I didn't ever meet her.''

"I don't suppose,'' said Judith as Renie opened the door, "you know why the marriage ended so fast.''

Spud burst out laughing, startling Renie. "Think about it,'' he said in a choked voice. "Besides,'' he added, as they entered the room and he inadvertently stepped on Renie's foot, "Sylvia smoked.''

FOURTEEN

JUDITH AND RENIE were never quite sure how the reconciliation between Spud and Evelyn Frobisher had taken place. All they knew was that Evelyn had greeted her husband with open arms, and after an exchange of whispered words, the couple had left, their faces wreathed in besotted smiles.

"What did you say to Evelyn while I was gone?" Judith inquired.

Renie looked blank. "Not much. We just talked a bit. I told her about you. And Dan."

Briefly, Judith shut her eyes. Her late husband had often been used by Renie as an example of what other wives should be thankful not to have to endure. "Thanks, coz."

"Sure," said Renie. "Want to go shopping?"

Judith's initial reaction was that she did not. Upon awakening, she had been convinced that the solution to the puzzle of Bob-o was at hand. She had all the pieces within her grasp, yet there was something missing. She hated to admit as much to Renie.

"Okay," she said. "Do we take a bus or cab it?"

Renie was at the window. The fog had thinned out just enough so that they could see halfway across Empress Drive. "Let's get a cab. It's only a four-dollar ride."

Five minutes later, they were in the lobby, avoiding the registration desk where an embattled Doris was fending off a TV news crew. "I wonder," said Judith, as Renie replaced the telephone that had a direct line to PAB Cabs, "when MacKenzie is coming by with those statements. Maybe we should hold off a bit."

A flicker of doubt passed over Renie's face. "He'll leave them with Doris. We can always come back here and have lunch somewhere in the neighborhood."

But Judith was uneasy. "I thought you were the one who was hell-bent for heading home."

Renie bridled. "I thought we both were. Or are you going to stand here and tell me whodunit?"

Judith sighed just as the PAB Cab pulled up outside, its red-and-white exterior looming up through the fog. "I wish I could. I almost can. But there's still something weird about this case."

"There's nothing weird about shopping," declared Renie, pushing the heavy hotel door open and marching down the stone stairs. "Come on, I feel like General Patton landing at Salerno. Let's hit those beaches! Let's wave those credit cards! Whoopee!"

But Judith didn't share Renie's enthusiasm. "You better not let Uncle Vince hear you talking like that," she said as she buckled her seat belt. "He was at Salerno, you know."

"Sure. Anzio, too. That's where he learned to drink Chianti out of a jug over his shoulder. Just think, tomorrow we'll all be together, eating that big fat fowl and stuffing ourselves until we puke."

The Iranian taxi driver's smoldering eyes seared the cousins with disapproval. "Where go?" he asked as if he didn't want to know.

"Royal Majesty Mall," replied Renie.

"Nowhere," said Judith, hastily unbuckling her seat belt. "I'm getting out."

"Wait a minute!" shrieked Renie. The cab, which had begun to pull away from the curb, screeched to a stop.

"Go or no?" asked the irritated driver.

"You go without me," Judith said, ducking out of the taxi. "I mean it, you planned on this, and in my present mood, I'd just be a drag. Meet me back here for lunch about one, okay?"

Renie started to protest, but Judith slammed the door shut, eliciting an angry look from the driver. It was all right, Judith told herself: Renie would overtip the poor man and make up for the inconvenience. Assuming, of course, that her cousin survived the journey. Judith noted with some alarm that the cab had shot off at a reckless speed, given the traffic and weather conditions of Prince Albert Bay on this foggy November morning.

Slowly, Judith mounted the short flight of stairs and reentered the hotel. The sudden brainstorm she'd had in the taxi now didn't seem quite so brilliant. The TV crew had departed, leaving Doris with a mere dozen or so frustrated guests who were trying to find out when the airport would be reopened. Birdwell was among them. He saw Judith, and detached himself from the herd.

"Really," he groused, "this is ridiculous! I'm not even flying! I hate airplanes! They aren't meant to stay up so high! Just look at the headlines, almost every day one of them falls down somewhere! But there's no connecting train going south between here and the States! Nobody told me that!"

Judith could have. Rail service between Port Royal and her hometown had been discontinued a decade ago, though the reason for it mystified potential passengers on both sides of the border. "You have to take a bus," she informed the agitated critic.

"That's absurd! I don't have a bus schedule! I have a train to catch for San Francisco at six o'clock tonight!" He was all but hopping up and down.

"I think," Judith said calmly, "there's a schedule posted over on that board." She pointed in the direction of the picture postcard display. "I noticed it yesterday."

"Where?" Birdwell peered in the direction of Judith's finger. "Oh! Excuse me, my eyes are really very poor. I can't seem to find an opthalmologist who can correct my vision. The medical profession is a disaster!"

With a small smile, Judith watched Birdwell bustle off to the hotel's bulletin board. He all but plastered his nose against the schedule, then headed for the elevator. Judith roamed about the lobby, trying to sort out her thoughts. At last, the desk area was cleared of traffic. Doris glanced about furtively, then sneaked a coffee mug out from under the counter and took a big sip.

"You're in the business," she said as Judith approached. "You'll understand."

"I do," agreed Judith, leaning on the desk. "Doris, what do you know about ducks and drakes?"

Doris choked on her coffee. "What?"

Judith made an apologetic gesture with her hands. "I know, it's a stupid question. I'm rambling this morning. Isn't there an old English rhyme, though?"

Doris had recovered herself. "Probably. It doesn't ring a bell." The phone jangled at Doris's elbow. "That does, though. Excuse me."

Judith resumed wandering the lobby. The Nubian lamp was turned on, to ward off the morning gloom. Two small children tumbled about on one of the cut-velvet sofas while their parents argued over the plan of attack on Port Royal's tourist attractions. The couple in matching tams and clashing tweeds came huffing and puffing through the main entrance. Their cheeks were rosy and their smiles friendly.

"Lovely, it is," the wife said to Judith. "Empress Park," she added by way of clarification. "You done it yet, luv?"

"No," responded Judith with an answering smile. "Isn't it a bit foggy for a walk?"

"That depends," said the husband, still panting from

his exertions. "Out past Smugglers' Point, the mist comes and goes. Then you get some smashing views. Peek-a-boos, as it were." His blue eyes twinkled at Judith.

At the desk, Doris slammed down the phone in a most uncharacteristic—and inhospitable—manner. "That does it! I quit!" She grabbed her forest-green cardigan and her brown leather shoulder bag from under the desk, and charged out through the little office.

"Well!" The wife put her hand through her husband's arm. "It's like I always tell Hubie here, things just aren't the same anywhere these days. Not even," she added mournfully, "at the Clovia." The couple nodded their tams in unison at Judith and walked toward the elevator.

Sybil bobbed up behind the counter, her pasty face quivering. "Blimey! What a place! I think I'll go back to the fish and chips shop on Piccadilly Island! If Mrs. Teel can't take it here, neither can I!"

Judith had strolled over to the desk. "What set Doris off?" she inquired.

"I really can't say," Sybil replied primly. "It was a guest, though." She lowered her head as well as her voice. "From the eighth floor." She gave Judith a knowing look, then shuddered as another elevator load of angry patrons stormed into the lobby.

Judith backpedaled away from the desk, making for the Hepburn Street exit. Fog or no fog, a walk in the park suddenly sounded like a terrific idea.

Crossing over to the Esplanade, Judith felt the damp against her cheeks, but her leather jacket kept her warm. She could see at least ten feet in front of her, though to her left, the bay was obscured, and on her right, the high rises were hidden from view. The paved walkway was strewn with crisp brown leaves and spiny horse chestnuts. Judith stopped to pick up a chestnut for luck. Carefully, she split the outer covering and extracted the smooth brown fruit. It was an old habit from the autumns of her childhood. Smiling, she tucked the talisman inside her pocket.

Empress Park began where the high rises left off, its

entrance heralded not by gates or signs, but a quaint old teahouse that had served four generations of Port Royal residents and visitors. Its French windows flirted with the fog as Judith passed by. She felt, rather than saw, other walkers. Port Royal was a city heavily influenced by the English, and its inhabitants preferred using their feet to driving their cars.

Beyond the teahouse and the tennis courts and the cricket pitch, the path divided into three separate trails. A wooden sign pointed to Smugglers' Point, the lighthouse, and Kitimat Cove on the left, to Princess Alexandria Yacht Club, Deadman's Cliff, and the zoo on the right, and in the middle, to the lawn bowling greens, the rose garden, and the Indian burial ground. Judith opted for the water view, hoping there would be one. If not, at least she would have avoided the stampede to welcome the new panda at the zoo. Deadman's Cliff and the burial grounds didn't suit her present mood.

Above her, in the virgin Douglas fir and western red cedar trees, she could hear the muffled cry of bluejays. Below, almost attacking her pant leg, were a pair of bold black squirrels. Unlike their gray counterparts across the border, they were not intimidated by Judith's efforts to shoo them away. For at least thirty yards, they scampered along beside Judith, then careened off into a clump of sword ferns.

The cool, wet greenery and the soft, gray mist soothed Judith's soul. She needed this peace, away from the hubbub of the hotel and constant flow of churning emotions among its guests. Her insights as to the identity of Bob-o's killer were falling into place. Judith was sure the solution was almost in her grasp. There were just one or two facts that didn't quite fit into logical order. That disturbed her, but Judith was convinced that if she used this quiet time to sort things through, everything would become clear.

Here, with the sound of the waves lapping at the shore, Judith no longer felt guilty about abandoning Renie. Her cousin would dash madly from boutique to salon to specialty shop, running up debts that would make what was left of Bill's hair stand on end. Judith smiled to herself again, and caught a glimpse of the lighthouse on the point. The foghorns sounded as if they were talking to each other.

She had gone about a mile when she realized her feet were getting damp. She really should have worn her boots, but she'd left them in the trunk of the car along with Renie's. Judith turned around, savoring the brief view of the water where a fishing trawler used radar to head for port. The fog now seemed to be dispersing on the bay, but settling in closer over the park. Judith felt the salt on her tongue and sniffed at the sharp, tangy air. She actually gasped when she heard the scream. A woman, she thought, pivoting around, and very nearby. Her heart began to thud as she tried to peer through the heavy curtain of gray. Another cry pierced the fog, then scuffling noises, and a sudden, ominous, silence.

Judith had frozen in place. Having turned about in every which way, she was unsure whether she was pointed toward the teahouse or headed deeper into the park. It dawned on her that for the past few minutes she hadn't been aware of anyone else on the path. Feeling an onset of panic, she started walking very fast. She knew there was a boathouse at Kitimat Cove. Surely she would meet someone soon.

Seconds later, a figure loomed up out of the fog, not six feet away. Startled, Judith let out a little cry of both fear and relief. She hesitated, blinking away the moisture on her lashes. Judith recognized the cashmere overcoat and the fedora. It was Max, and as he came closer, she could see that he had blood on his hands.

Judith turned, and ran for her life.

FIFTEEN

MAX ROTHSIDE CAUGHT up with Judith just before the path branched off to Smuggler's Point. He grabbed her around the waist with one hand, the other clamped over her mouth to stifle her screams. Judith struggled in his grasp, but Max was tall, strong, and very fit. She saw the smear of blood on the fingers at her waist, and felt her knees buckle.

"Please, Mrs. McMonigle!" His voice held an urgent, even pleading note. "Stop fighting me! I'm not going to hurt you!"

Judith didn't believe him for a minute. Although her body felt limp in his grasp, she desperately prayed for the strength to make one final, forceful effort to break free. Wriggling her head, she looked down: They were right at the edge of the trail that lead out to the point. As far as Judith could tell from her limited perspective and the drifting patches of fog, the dirt track took off along a cliff. She had no idea where—or how far—the drop-off went. The waves were very near; the cliff might plunge into the bay.

Summoning up all her energies, Judith bolted in Max's arms. The unexpectedness of her move loosened his grip, but he did not completely let go. They both toppled over, rolling together on the damp ground. Then, in one breath-catching instant, they were falling. Judith shrieked; Max cried out. The sounds still tore at their throats as they landed on soft, wet sand.

The distance between the upper ledge and the beach had been less than four feet. Max's fedora lay next to Judith's right foot. He was sprawled in an inelegant manner, his expensive overcoat a sodden mess. Judith felt bruised and dazed, but otherwise unhurt. She struggled to a sitting position, and looked around. The fog had lifted on the water to permit a narrow, horizontal view of the bay. A pair of ducks waddled across the sand, apparently intent on inspecting the latest pieces of flotsam and jetsam.

Judith contemplated flight. She had to get away while Max was still unconscious, yet all of her strength seemed to have been drained away in the tussle and subsequent fall. Feeling dull-witted and weighted down, Judith wondered if she were in shock. She blinked, and stared at the ducks. If memory served her from the bird book she had at home, they were blue-winged teals, whose plumage would not acquire its seasonal brilliance until after Christmas. Queer ducks, reflected Judith, verging on hysteria. She tried to check her rampaging emotions: Here she was, battered and filthy, sitting in the fog with a murderer, who, for all she really knew, was as dead as his victim. She had to act, to move, to think. Taking several deep breaths and gathering her strength, Judith watched the ducks watch her.

The fog hadn't lifted any further on the bay, but Judith felt as if the whole world was suddenly, miraculously, filled with light. She threw herself at Max, startling the ducks, who took flight across the beach.

"Max! Mr. Rothside! Are you okay? Please, wake up!"

Groggily, Max lifted his head. There was sand in his silver moustache; a matted piece of seaweed clung to his hair. He wiped at his face with his bloodied hands, and awkwardly raised himself on his elbows.

"Good Lord, what happened? Where are we?" His eyes were glazed.

"We took a little tumble," said Judith, now on her knees and helping pull Max up. "Can you walk?"

Max flexed his limbs. "Yes. It's my head that hurts." He tried to focus on Judith. "Are you all right? Poor thing, you're rather a wreck!"

"I'm okay. We were lucky." Clumsily, she patted the horse chestnut in her pocket.

Holding on to each other, Judith and Max stood up. His touch was firm, yet gentle. Judith understood why Maria was so anxious to keep his love, no matter what the cost. "Who hurt your hands?" she asked, but she already knew the answer.

Max, who now had his eyes in focus, read her thoughts. "You know, don't you?" he said solemnly.

Judith nodded dully. "Yes. Finally. I was so dense. I was looking at everything the wrong way."

In silence, they tramped along the beach for a few yards until they found a set of wooden steps sunk into the earth. "Watch your footing," Max cautioned. "It'll be slippery."

It was. Judith slipped twice going up, but Max was there to steady her. In the distance, a siren mingled with the foghorns. Judith allowed Max to take her arm as they walked toward the teahouse.

"Where is she now?" Judith inquired as another black squirrel darted across their path.

"I don't know," Max replied, his rich voice heavy. He paused, listening. The sirens sounded closer. "I tried to go after her, but I lost her in the fog. She ran off through the woods. Deadman's Cliff, I'd guess. It's a very steep drop."

Judith shivered. They resumed walking, but now at a brisker pace. To the lone jogger who huffed and puffed as he passed by, they should have looked like a strange pair, bloodstained, mud-stained, and filthy. But the sinewy young man was plugged into his Walkman, totally self-absorbed.

"When did you know for sure?" Judith inquired of Max.

He was brushing sand from his fedora. "Not until just now. I went to Robin's bank. She'd changed her name, of course. But there it was, listed as a joint account. Strange as it may seem, I had never met her. She had some phobia about visiting her mother in New York. Still, I wonder why Sylvia chose such a plain sort of name for herself." He gave Judith a rueful little smile. "I've always found 'Doris' quite dull, don't you?"

"Listen, Birdbath," bellowed Desiree in a voice made even huskier by three gimlets, "the bitch was your wife. She set me up! Why shouldn't I want to take you apart and put all the pieces back in the wrong places?"

Birdwell de Smoot stood so close to Desiree that his glasses almost touched her green crepe de chine blouse. "She set all of us up! Anyway, I haven't seen the wretched woman in almost thirty years! She left me, and ran off and married somebody else! Then she married that idiot, Robin! His imitation of a downy woodpecker was a disgrace!"

"How could you know, Birdwell?" chimed in Alabama, fiddling with his pipe while trying to juggle a glass of bourbon. The entire Rothside party, including the cousins, had gathered for farewell cocktails in Suite 800. The fog had all but lifted, with word coming down that the airport would reopen by three p.m. Angus MacKenzie was supposed to be there, but the press of business had detained him. "Let's face it, Birdie," Alabama went on, "you can't see your hand in front of your face. Why don't you get some decent glasses?"

"Stop that!" raged Birdwell. "You're spitting on my head! And don't you dare light that horrible pipe! Where's my atomizer?" He wiped at his bald pate, then allowed

Mildred to feed him a piece of pickled herring. Her ministrations seemed to have a calming effect. "All right," muttered Birdwell, "I'll admit I didn't recognize Sylvia. But my poor eyesight doesn't prevent me from being one of the world's most perceptive critics! Your new *glasnost* thoroughbred racing play, *Boris's Horse Is Behind* is . . ." For once Birdwell seemed at a loss for words. ". . . *poopy!*" he declared. "So there!"

"You just don't understand the social and political nuances," retaliated Alabama, finally giving up on his pipe and giving in to his bourbon. "Wait until you see a full production."

"I couldn't stand it," remarked Birdwell, as Mildred tugged timidly at his arm. "The script was enough to make world peace seem like a bad idea." But his words were less heated, and he brightened at Mildred's offer to fix him a nice cheese plate.

Judith watched him strut off in the direction of the buffet, Mildred close to his side. Maria, clinging to a rejuvenated Max, smiled tremulously at both cousins. "I can't believe how clever you were, Judith! and how brave Max was! However did you figure it all out?"

Spud, with his arm around Evelyn, had moved into the circle. "You ought to tell all of us how you did it. I got to admit, I'm still pretty confused."

Judith, who was feeling the effects of her terrifying morning in the park, began to demur. Renie, however, waved a strip of lox at her cousin. "Go ahead, this will be your only chance to take center stage with a crew like this. Besides," she mouthed in Judith's ear, "you took so long in the bathtub that I still haven't heard all of it."

Judith looked around the suite with its art deco furnishings and sea of curious faces. She owed it to them, she supposed. Or perhaps she owed it to herself. As if on cue, the others had seated themselves, and grown remarkably quiet. Judith allowed Max to pull out the white piano bench so she could sit in the middle. Alabama handed her a fresh scotch.

"I made a terrible mistake," she confessed. "I got it in my head right from the start that one of you had to be the killer. It was those photographs, I suppose, and the fact that Bob-o was probably shot on the seventh or eighth floor. The evidence could have pointed to all of you, though it began to narrow down to Desiree."

"No sweat," said Desiree, hoisting her glass. "I might have enjoyed playing the unjustly accused murderess."

But Judith smiled wryly and shook her head. "No, you wouldn't. None of you wanted to be involved. That was perfectly understandable, *given the fact that you were all innocent.* I should have seen that. You knew each other so well, and for such a long time. You're close enough that you can even fight with one another, just like a family. Surely if one of you had killed Bob-o, the others would have been suspicious. But you weren't."

"They're not *that* clever," put in Birdwell. Desiree thumped him on the head. But softly.

"Doris—or should I call her Sylvia?—was *very* clever," Judith went on. "From what Lui told my cousin a little while ago, she's worked here for several years. Her second husband died of cancer in 1979. That was Mr. Teel. She married him after she left England, I think. I don't know why she changed her first name, unless it was to disassociate herself completely from her Finch-Pitkins family ties after Dame Carmela disinherited her. Maybe, like a bird, she wanted a change of plumage. I'm guessing that her hair was dyed." Judith glanced at Birdwell for confirmation.

"What? Oh, yes," agreed Birdwell. "She was a mousy blond. Like Mildred here." Mildred giggled.

Judith took a sip of scotch and continued: "Over the years, she must have talked to, or been talked at, by Bob-o. She learned that he had a lot of money. It was, she discovered, money that should have been hers." Judith turned to Max. "It was, Max, *your* money."

For once, Max was faintly disconcerted, even embarrassed. "Well, yes. I'd never felt right about inheriting that obscene sum from Dame Carmela. I was doing very well on my own. When Helen died, and Robin became unstable, it occurred to me that I could use that windfall to help feather Robin's nest. So to speak," he added with a self-deprecating smile. "After all, Robin was my brother-in-law through his marriage to my half-sister, Estelle. My other sister, Suzanne, had married well, and didn't need any extra income. But I worried about how Robin would get along in his new life. I set up a trust fund for him at a New York bank, and checks were sent every month." His face was touched with irony. "Maybe I shouldn't have done it. Robin didn't seem to want the money."

Evelyn broke in, turning to Maria. "Did you know about this?"

Maria's long lashes fluttered. "My, no! Max never troubles me with that sort of thing! I might worry."

There was a pause. The Sacred Eight turned its collective attention back to Judith. "Somewhere along the way, Doris—I really can't stop calling her that—figured out the connection with all of you. Maybe it was last year," Judith said to Max and Maria, "when you visited and helped Bob-o sort out his invoices. It was shortly afterward, at any rate, that she and Bob-o were secretly married."

Alabama had resumed fussing with his pipe. "How did Robin ever keep a secret?"

"Maybe he didn't," answered Judith. "But he jabbered so much, who would listen to him? And if he told five hundred tourists he had a wife name Doris, who would have cared?"

"What about Mrs. Wittelstein?" asked Evelyn, holding Spud's hand.

Judith shrugged. "I suspect she probably turned a deaf ear, too. And I'll bet Doris rarely went near the Tudor Arms."

Desiree was looking skeptical. "Sure, Robin was an old geezer, but how could Doris keep him from moving in with her? Or asking her to live with him in his ghastly little hovel?''

"She stalled him," replied Judith. "She would have been good at it. Anybody who's coped with all kinds of irate guests over the years wouldn't have any trouble talking around a poor old addled popcorn vendor." Judith shifted her weight on the piano bench. She was growing stiffer by the minute. "No doubt she hoped he'd keel over of natural causes. But he didn't, and then she saw a golden opportunity. All of you, people he'd known in London, including his ex-son-in-law and his brother-in-law, were coming to the Clovia. You'd make prime suspects. All it took was setting the scene. She began by sending strange notes to Maria, knowing her . . . ah . . . artistic temperament would be unsettled. Birdwell might resent Bob-o because he'd gotten the money that should have come to him and Sylvia in the first place."

Quibbling, Birdwell pointed a finger at Judith. "I would have killed Max, not Robin!"

Max's gaze was humorous. "But you didn't. You only tried to sue me."

Behind his glasses, Birdwell lowered his eyes. "And lost. But you must admit, I was a good sport about it, Max."

"So was I," said Max, his expansive nature never more in evidence.

"Then," Judith went on, "there were Desiree and Alabama. If Helen's death hadn't been an accident, they were the logical suspects. Bob-o might have known that one— or both—had killed Helen. If so, they would want to silence him."

"That's about the only way anybody could shut him up," remarked Desiree, turning to Alabama. "How come nobody did it sooner?"

Judith continued in a matter-of-fact tone while avoiding Evelyn's gaze. "Spud might have been involved with Helen. At least a case could have been made for that as a motive for getting rid of her. That same motive would apply to Evelyn as well. Again, Bob-o's silence could be bought with a bullet.''

Spud made a disparaging noise. "Helen was pretty as a picture, but she drank. Lips that touch liquor will never touch mine." He jostled Evelyn's arm, spilling her diet soda on the rug. "Right, sweetie?"

"You better be," murmured Evelyn, with a sidelong glance at Desiree's gimlet glass.

"As for Max," Judith resumed, feeling very tired, "he might have wanted to stop making those payments to Bob-o. Or Maria, if she'd known, might have wanted him to quit throwing money down a rat hole. But in this instance, there was also the matter of the threatening letters which had been sent to Maria.''

Maria went pale and groped at her pearl and ruby choker. "Oh! But I thought you promised . . .''

Judith interrupted smoothly. "You thought I didn't realize that Doris wrote those notes? I didn't, at first. But it was the easiest thing in the world for her to say they'd suddenly appeared at the hotel desk or under the door. It was also a cinch for her to use the Clovia's master key to get into everybody's rooms. Even if she'd been caught, she could have come up with a plausible excuse. Of course, Doris had nothing incriminating to hold over you, Maria. But human nature being what it is, she calculated that the notes would upset you.''

Maria's white face flooded with relief. "They certainly did," she acknowledged ruefully.

Judith's gaze flickered over Mildred, who was squirming next to Birdwell. "Somehow," said Judith, "Doris got a gun. She arranged for Bob-o to meet her on the seventh floor at a specified time. She told Sybil she was going to the rest room, but of course she wasn't. She took the freight elevator, which is in that little alcove, and can't be seen from the desk, then she got out and waited for Bob-o. The passenger elevator door opened, and she shot him.'' She paused, pressing her palms together, as if offering a prayer for the late popcorn vendor's soul. She could only surmise that Mildred's anxious query about the hotel safe had been posed to Doris, who might have guessed there was something more sinister than Krugerrands in Suite 805. "Then," Judith went on, "she used her master key to get into Birdwell's room and hide the gun outside the window in the ivy."

"What?" Birdwell all but flew off the black divan. "*My* room? *My* window? *My* ivy?"

Judith noticed that Mildred was growing more distressed. "Doris had made sure the window would open easily beforehand. I assume she chose your window, Mr. de Smoot, just to throw suspicion around and confuse the issue. Then she probably took the freight elevator back down, maybe to the second floor, where she could walk the rest of the way and not be seen as easily coming from the guest rooms."

Spud was scratching his head. "Where'd she get the gun in the first place? You can't buy one up here."

It seemed to Judith that Mildred was about to faint. "Where and how she got it doesn't matter," Judith said blithely. "If she intended to break the law by committing murder, then procuring an illegal handgun wouldn't bother her a bit. That," said Judith pointedly, "was her downfall. People who thumb their noses at morality should learn to stop before it's too late."

Judith couldn't be sure if her message had sunk in on Mildred, but the other woman's shrinking attitude indicated that perhaps it had at least made a dent. "Anyway," Judith continued, "Renie and I found the gun." This time she ignored Birdwell's expression of outrage. "Then it disappeared again. The leaves were blowing off the ivy during the storm. At this point, Doris might have wanted to plant the gun on Desiree. Or maybe she wanted it to defend herself. She realized the gun would be exposed by morning, took advantage of Birdwell's absence, and found it was already gone. She must have panicked a bit, not knowing if the police had found it. She started checking the vacant rooms, maybe all of them, or perhaps she got lucky and went to ours first. But she made a special trip to do it. She was off duty that night, and claimed she came back to straighten out the payroll. But Brian said this morning that the staff hadn't been paid.''

Desiree motioned for Alabama to refill her glass, but he shook his head and handed her a smoked oyster instead. "Why did she pick on me?" Desiree demanded. "I hardly even spoke to the blasted woman.''

"She tried to spread the blame, but in your case, it was your hair," said Judith. "Bob-o had taught Tootle those little rhymes. 'Wearin' o' the green' indicated a redhead. You wear a lot of green, Desiree." Judith saw Desiree look down at her blouse. "So, of course, did Doris. To add fuel to the fire, she swiped some of the decorations off your stage costumes and laid a false trail of glitter. But she couldn't be sure that Tootle wouldn't recite verses that might be more incriminating. So she strangled the parakeet, using another trip to the ladies' room as an alibi, or else slipping out in all the confusion after the police were called in. She'd probably finagled a key out of Bob-o which wouldn't have been too hard, given the fact that she was his wife. She also put your picture in the dumpster, to make it look as if you wanted to avoid any connection with Bob-o. And if anyone, such as Mrs. Wittelstein, had seen a tall redhead going into Bob-o's place, you would have fit the description perfectly, Desiree.''

"Aaaaargh!" moaned Desiree, clutching Alabama's arm for support. "Doris looked about as much like me as I look like a lamp-post! Hey, Birdbread, when you get your eyes examined, take Mrs. Wittelstein with you!''

Alabama, lost in thought, idly stroked his wife's hand. "What an irony, that except for Birdwell, none of us had ever met Doris—ah, Sylvia.'' He looked at Max. ''Why didn't you meet her in court?''

Max glanced at Birdwell. ''We only got to the deposition stage. Birdie handled all that.''

Alabama wasn't quite finished with his ruminations. ''I have to admit, I never suspected her. She must have had a split personality.''

''What she had,'' put in Max, ''was professional training. She'd studied to be an actress. Isn't that true, Birdie?''

The little critic nodded unhappily. ''She did indeed. But she was terrible. I wrote her up in a scathing review.''

''Is that how you met?'' asked Renie, smearing caviar on a toast point.

Birdwell scowled. ''No, no. That was on our honeymoon.''

Judith couldn't prop herself up any longer. She rose, gingerly stretching herself. ''That's it. This morning, Max went to the bank and discovered that Robin and Doris O'Rourke had a joint account worth over a million dollars. Any withdrawal required both signatures. Bob-o, being a miser, wouldn't touch it. Doris had to get rid of him to get at the money. Because of the strike, the police had only been able to make a phone call so they hadn't actually seen the bank records. When Max made his discovery, he called the hotel to ask Maria to meet him downtown after he'd gone to police headquarters.''

''But I was out on the Esplanade, sitting on a bench, brooding,'' Maria admitted with a little laugh.

Max, seeing how weary Judith had become, took up the tale: ''I rang the desk, and told Doris I was at the Bank of Newfoundland, headed for the police station, and not to tell Maria if she saw her before I could call back. I didn't want to worry Maria, of course.'' He gave his wife a tender look. ''Doris's reaction was unexpected, to say the least. She must have thought I was threatening her. It dawned on me that the Clovia's Doris and Doris O'Rourke were one and the same. I didn't want to confront her at the hotel, so I told her to meet me at the teahouse in Empress Park.''

"My reckless husband," sighed Maria, glowing all over.

Max tipped his head to one side. "Just because she was married to Robin didn't mean she'd killed him. But Doris lost her head. She believed I knew everything. She told me right off she was Sylvia Finch-Pitkins. Then she drew her gun.'' He bit his lips. "I'm sure she intended to use it.''

Maria gripped Max's arm tight. "Oh, my darling, how did you stop her? I still can't take it all in!''

Max caressed her long fingers. "We were standing by the wishing well behind the teahouse. I jumped her—it was risky, but I had to do it. We struggled; I scraped my hands on the rough stones. The gun fell down the well. Someday, maybe, if the police ever settle this strike, they'll find it. Then again, maybe they won't bother.''

This time, Judith definitely noticed relief flood Mildred's face. But it was Evelyn who spoke:

"Somebody said she'd quit her job. That was a ruse, I take it. Was she going to run away?''

Judith was walking up and down in the open space between the baby grand piano and the semicircle of chairs and sofas. "Yes. I'm sure she thought I was on to her when I asked a dumb question about ducks and drakes. She choked on her coffee. I just thought she was reacting to my inanity. Then the call came through from Max. She must have been convinced the net was closing over her from all directions. I suppose she figured she could get at the money later.''

"But," said Evelyn with a shudder, "she killed herself instead.''

A silence followed, broken only by a rap on the door.

"Oh!" exclaimed Maria, "it must be that poor old man to get our luggage. Or that nice young one."

It was neither. There were indeed two men framed in the doorway. One of them was Angus MacKenzie. The other was Joe Flynn.

SIXTEEN

JUDITH HAD NO trouble closing her suitcase for the return journey. Not only was there no wayward cat to contend with, but it seemed that half her wardrobe was in the laundry bag. So was much of Renie's, though for a vastly different reason. Bringing her luggage out into the sitting room, she took one last look around their quarters at the Clovia.

"Except for a corpse in the elevator and a homicidal desk clerk, I really like this place," said Judith. "Someday, I want to come back."

Angus MacKenzie was fingering his battered hat and looking pensive. "You're more than welcome. In fact, I'm thinking of offering you a job." He glanced at Joe, who was standing by the window, admiring the view of the now fogless bay. "Unless, of course, you Yanks have already signed her up."

Joe's expression was ambiguous. "It's on my agenda." He was looking much the same as when Judith had seen him in August, except perhaps a little trimmer around the middle and more rested. His red hair had a few strands of gray, especially at the temples, and his green eyes, with those dancing gold flecks, were as mesmerizing as ever. "Magic eyes," Judith had always called them. The spell they'd cast over her twenty-five years ago had never been lifted.

MacKenzie looked faintly bemused, as if he didn't know quite what to make of Joe's reply. Judith thought she did, and suddenly felt giddy. Renie didn't hear the remark, being preoccupied with her concealment of Bill's Cuban cigars in the Royal Doulton teapot she'd bought for her mother as a Christmas gift.

"You gave Mrs. McMonigle quite a lot of help with your information out of London," MacKenzie was saying. "I take it you've known each other a long time, eh?"

Joe's round face was wearing its most ingenuous expression. "We go way back. I coached her field hockey team. She played under me for a couple of years."

Judith tried to suppress the choking fit that overcame her. The provocative remark had caught Renie's attention, spinning her around to give Judith a stupefied look. But Angus MacKenzie seemed to take Joe's words at face value.

"Mrs. McMonigle isn't the only one who appreciates your help," he said. "We're so shorthanded that it would have taken us several days to get around to making those overseas contacts. I hope your department paid for the calls."

"They're covered," Joe replied casually. "Frankly," he went on, now sounding more like a policeman and less like a rogue, "I couldn't see how all that old background would be much use."

Judith had more or less recovered. At least she'd fought back the urge to choke, though she was still tempted to strangle Joe. "It was the part about Helen's accident that gave me a lot of ideas. I must write to Paul and thank him especially for taking the trouble to contact Scotland Yard."

Joe looked blank, hands shoved in the pockets of his carefully tailored gray slacks. "Scotland Yard? What are you talking about? Paul didn't contact anybody at the Yard.''

Puzzled, Judith stared at Joe. "I'm referring to your off-the-record remarks about Bob-o suspecting that . . . Wait a minute, where's that fax?" She dug into her purse and produced the now-wrinkled document. "Here, see for yourself, the part that begins, 'Judith: Here's a bit of information that might be of help.' ''

Joe, with MacKenzie leaning over his shoulder, read through the message. "Hell, I didn't give you this stuff! All I sent was this first part, the data on Robin O'Rourke and a couple of sentences about his daughter, Helen.''

The cousins and the policemen all looked at each other with curious expressions. It was Joe who spoke up: "Who actually received the fax at the hotel?"

Judith let out a little groan. "Doris. She must have added all that stuff about Helen's death just to make us think there was something fishy. And," she noted with irritation, "it worked." She tapped the fax with her finger. "I should have known better. You wouldn't have called me 'Judith'. You'd have said—ugh—'Jude-girl.' ''

"Of course I would," Joe replied easily. "Since when did I do otherwise?" He caught her aggravated glance, and held it with those magic eyes.

"Rats!" Judith turned away, crumpling up the fax. She started to pitch it at the fireplace, then changed her mind. "Here," she said to MacKenzie, "keep this, if for no other reason than it lifts any cloud hovering over Helen's demise. No wonder everybody I talked to insisted it was an accident! It was. I'm surprised the Sacred Eight didn't jump me for assigning them motives which never existed.''

"By then," said Renie, "they were too relieved to have everything over and done with. For all you know, Bob-o might have suspected foul play. Didn't Mrs. Wittelstein say he yapped a lot about ghosts and cowards and all sorts of things in connection with Helen's death?"

Judith grimaced. "That's right. She did. That's odd.''

Her face worked in cogitation, then she broke into a grin. "No, it's not odd! It's just show biz! Spud was directing Desiree in *Blithe Spirit,* remember? Noel Coward, right?" Judith struck a triumphant pose.

Joe gave Judith a nod of approval. "Clever girl. I still like the part about the ducks."

Judith was gathering up her shopping bags, allowing Joe and MacKenzie to carry their suitcases. "It came to me in a flash. Of course I didn't know Doris's last name was Teel until this morning when Sybil mentioned it. But that was just after Doris had blown a gasket when I asked her about 'ducks and drakes.' Earlier, Renie had said something in the cab about 'fowl.' Finally, along came that pair of teals, waddling out of the fog, just like a dream. It's a good thing they weren't mallards."

"They usually are," said MacKenzie as they approached the elevator. Birdwell and Mildred were already there, waiting for the car to come up from the lobby.

"I'm going to write a book." Birdwell declared, as if the others had come out into the hall for the sole purpose of hearing his announcement. *"I Married a Murderess.* No, no, that's too sensational. *Who Is Sylvia?* No, that's been done." He turned to MacKenzie. "It's too bad you didn't get to arrest her. If she'd gone to the electric chair, I could call it *Roast Duck."*

"We don't have capital punishment," MacKenzie said, more gloomy than usual.

The elevator arrived. Joe scanned it with a professional eye. "It was a cunning plan. She didn't even have to get in, so she could avoid leaving any trace of personal evidence." He turned to MacKenzie as they all crowded inside. "Do you have any idea where she got the gun?"

MacKenzie looked straight ahead as the doors rattled shut. Judith felt Mildred tense at her side. "Not a clue," said MacKenzie solemnly.

"I'm going to economize," Mildred suddenly said, seemingly apropos of nothing. "This trip has made me realize I'm not living strictly within my income."

"Good for you, Mildred," said Judith, making an attempt to pat the other woman's arm. "Where will you start? I wouldn't advise investing in Krugerrands. Their sale in the United States was outlawed in 1988."

Mildred blushed and giggled. "It's a good thing I don't have any," she replied, ignoring Birdwell's puzzled glance. "I'm starting to conserve right away, by driving Birdwell to meet his train. As a thank-you, he's very generously offered to take me to San Francisco with him for a few days. Mr. Rothside said I could use a little time off after all this stress." She craned her neck to look at Birdwell, who was humming to himself. "We could save even more money by driving all the way down the coast. Then we could stop off in Sweet Home, and you could meet Mother, Birdie."

Birdwell did not appear to be wildly enthused about being introduced to Mildred's mother. On the other hand, he didn't take off on one of his customary tirades. Judith found his attitude promising. The elevator jolted to a stop. Sybil was at the desk, looking healthier and heartier than usual.

"I've been given Doris's job!" Sybil exclaimed under her breath to Judith and Renie. "Isn't it lucky she turned out to be a killer?"

"It's . . . wonderful," Judith replied, groping for the proper adjective.

Maria was crossing the lobby, swathed once again in her sable. Max stood by the main entrance, apparently waiting for their cab. "You're not paying for your room," Maria asserted, taking Judith's hands. "Not after all you've done. Max and I—and the others—will never forget it!" She enfolded Judith in her arms, then whispered rapid-fire words: "I'm going to tell Max the truth. I think. Bless you."

Maria stepped back, smiling with a bit more confidence than usual. At the main door, Max was doffing his fedora and signaling that their taxi had pulled up. Lui scurried across the lobby to help them with their luggage.

"Where's your car?" Judith asked Joe as they headed for the parking garage.

"Downtown at headquarters," Joe replied, avoiding her gaze.

Judith gave him an inquiring look. "When are you heading back? We're going to stop in Three Rivers for dinner at Pie-Oh-My!. You could meet us there."

"I can't." Joe plucked a piece of lint from his navy blazer. He glanced at MacKenzie, then turned to Judith as they reached her car. "I've had some experience with labor negotiations over the years. Since I've got the week off with nothing else to do, I decided to offer my services to MacKenzie as a gesture of international cooperation. I'm staying over for a few days. I'll meet with one of the guild representatives tomorrow. It isn't a holiday here."

Judith's black eyes narrowed in anger. She had assumed that Joe had traveled the one hundred twenty miles for the sole purpose of lending her moral support. Or something. She could hardly believe that he'd use his hard-earned—and rare—time off to volunteer his expertise in a labor dispute on the other side of the border. Then she saw the hint of the little lost boy that still resided somewhere deep inside Joe Flynn, even at the half-century mark.

"You can eat Thanksgiving dinner with us," she blurted.

But Joe gave her his half smile, and shook his head. "No, I can't. Gertrude would see to it that the turkey wasn't the only thing getting stuffed."

Judith considered, while Renie twitched anxiously, waiting for the trunk to be opened so that she could safely stash her illegal loot. "The keys, coz," murmured Renie.

Judith handed them over to Renie, but kept her eyes on Joe. "It's holiday time. Mother will be ticked off, but she won't physically harm you. I promise."

Joe was dubious. "My job's dangerous enough, but it's never prepared me for coping with Gertrude," he said with a grimace. "Give me a good old serial killer every time. I'll bet she even threw the hibiscus I sent her into the garbage.''

"You sent that plant?'' Judith laughed. "Oh, dear! That's funny!'' Suddenly she sobered. "Oh! I don't want to leave those flowers you had delivered to the hotel. Maybe I can get Brian to bring them down.''

But MacKenzie was dolefully shaking his head. "Sorry, fruit and flowers and such can't be transported across the border. Apple maggot quarantine and all that.''

Judith looked momentarily crestfallen, even as MacKenzie lifted Renie's suitcase into the trunk. "Well, have them sent down to Sybil as a present on her promotion,'' said Judith.

"A nice idea,'' agreed MacKenzie, then peered more closely into the trunk. "What's this?'' he inquired, holding up a clump of sod.

Renie jumped. "Nothing! I'm under my legal limit of purchases! We were here three days! I only bought cheap stuff! I never buy Cuban cigars!''

But MacKenzie was lifting the lid of the shoe box. "Dahlias? Peonies? Begonias?'' He poked about among the tubers. "Oh, my, you shouldn't be carting this sort of thing across the border.'' He cocked his head at Judith. "Why *are* you hauling them about in your car, eh?''

Judith leaned on the roof of her blue compact. "It's a long story.'' She shot a look at Joe. "It all began when I was playing field hockey under Lieutenant Flynn. I got ejected from the game.'' She saw Joe actually blush, and turned her gaze back to MacKenzie. "Let's just say that you ought to post a travel advisory that reads as follows: 'Do not attempt to bring live plants or dead husbands into Canada.' ''

Begonia tubers, Cuban cigars and all, the cousins were back in the States an hour later. Traffic had been heavy at the border, due to the American holiday coming up. Harried U.S. Customs and Immigration officers waved on all but the most suspicious-looking types, mainly from

Southern California. Thanks to Angus MacKenzie's decision to overlook Judith and Renie's peccadilloes, they were home free. Or at least headed in that direction.

"Do you think he'll come?" Renie asked Judith from out of nowhere.

Judith knew what her cousin meant. "No." She kept her eyes on the crowded freeway, the waning sun striking the left-hand side of the windshield. "I'm still not sure why he came up to Port Royal in the first place."

"Maybe he thought you were in danger," Renie suggested. When Judith didn't reply, she changed the subject. "Tell me," she inquired as they wound through the dense forests that formed the foothills of the great mountain range to the east, "how did you really figure out it was Doris? Was it her unprofessional manner in hanging up on a guest, or getting our reservation screwed up in the first place?"

Judith gave Renie a sly, sidelong glance as she clicked on the turn signal for their exit to Three Rivers. "Alabama asked me the same thing, being deep into character analysis," said Judith. "I told him what I intended to tell CLIP-TV, had they asked me. Which," she added, slowing the car down to forty miles per hour on the off ramp, "they thankfully did not."

"Well? What was it?" Renie had one eye on Judith, the other on the sign of a giant steaming crust which denoted the location of Pie-Oh-My!.

"Simple," replied Judith, pulling into the restaurant parking lot. She gave Renie a puckish grin. "A little bird told me."

Auntie Vance was swearing like a sailor as she stirred the gravy, Uncle Al was expounding on his latest scheme to get rich at the dog track, Uncle Vince was dozing off by the fire, and Bill was smoking a Cuban cigar while he tried to watch the traditional Thanksgiving football game on TV. Mike and Kristin had dashed up to the top of Heraldsgate Hill to a convenience store to get the whipping cream which Uncle Al's girlfriend, known to the family as Tess of the Timber Mills, had forgotten to bring. Aunt Deb was being waited on by all three of her grown grandchildren while Gertrude plotted a new way to booby-trap her sister-in-law's wheelchair.

"If I greased the wheels with turkey fat, I could send her right into the aspidistra," Gertrude chortled as Judith elbowed her way in besides Auntie Vance to check the green beans.

"Knock it off, Mother," reproached Judith. "You know darned well you're more fond of Aunt Deb than you'll ever admit."

Gertrude leaned on her walker and gave Judith a sly look. "I could start a fire under that contraption and see if she's as crippled as she pretends."

"Shut up, knotheads!" shouted Auntie Vance, wielding a long wooden spoon. "Do you want to eat this gravy or wear it?"

Accustomed to Auntie Vance's little ways, Judith smiled and moved to the cupboard to get down the serving bowls. "That turkey should be done. I'm going to take it out and let it rest for half an hour."

"*I* should be able to rest that long," grumbled Auntie Vance, the only living human being who had been known to get the better of her sister-in-law, Gertrude, and live to talk about it. She was also the only one in the entire clan who could feed up to forty without flinching, take care of tiny tots and teenagers alike without turning a hair, and make people laugh when they should have cried. "Move it, goatbreath," Auntie Vance said to Judith, "I need to get more flour. Your kitchen's so disorganized, I don't see how you could run a third-rate cathouse, let alone a classy bed-and-breakfast joint. Sheeesh!"

Judith smiled some more. Gertrude leaned on her walker as Sweetums wandered by, sniffing at her bedroom slippers. "Judith does just fine, all things considered. Stop picking on my girl." She gave Sweetums a clumsy kick and her daughter a flinty look. "But you *were* an hour late getting home last night. You said *eight* o'clock, not nine. And you come up with the lamest excuses! Customs agents and begonia tubers! You think I'm an idiot?''

Judith kept her expression bland. She and Renie had not wanted to worry their mothers about their involvement in the Clovia murder. ''It couldn't be helped,'' Judith said noncommittally as the front doorbell rang. ''Drat, that's probably Mike and Kristin. He must have forgotten his key again.''

By the time Judith reached the entry hall, Renie was already there. So was Joe Flynn, standing in the doorway with a shopping bag in his hand. Judith stopped short, her mouth agape.

''Joe! I thought you were staying in Port Royal!''

It wasn't Joe's style to look sheepish, but he came close. ''They're getting things under control up there. I thought if I stayed on, my presence might be construed as interference.'' He moved aside as Renie closed the door behind him. It was almost dark, with the autumn air clear and crisp, and a golden moon on the rise. ''Where,'' asked Joe, ''is your mother?''

Around the corner in the living room, Uncle Al, Tess, and Aunt Deb craned their necks to get a glimpse of the new arrival. Bill snarled at the Detroit Lions' defensive secondary. Uncle Vince snored peacefully, his mouth open, his head to one side.

Judith was trying to steer Joe out of her family's line of vision. Renie cooperated by twirling into the living room, a cow-shaped oven mitt on her head. ''Twenty minutes to turkey time, folks! Come on, kids, help get Nana ready to roll!''

''I'm glad you came,'' Judith breathed, getting Joe as far as the dining room.

His green eyes twinkled. ''So am I. So far. But listen, Jude-girl, I don't think we'd better make a habit of this. Yet. It may be two, three, even four months before I hear from the chancery.''

Judith's face hardened. "What's taking them so long? Now I know why the archbishop wears that tall, peaked hat—it's to cover up the point on his head!" She fumed briefly, then calmed down, and turned a penitent face to Joe. "I'm sorry, I'm just not sure I understand why we aren't supposed to see each other. What's the problem?"

Joe regarded Judith with a wry expression. "Remember what my enclosure card said? The one I sent with your flowers?"

"Sure," replied Judith. "It was cryptic. 'Mum's the word.' "

"There's nothing cryptic about *your* mum," said Joe. "She makes her feelings pretty plain."

As if to prove his point, the swinging door to the kitchen was flung open by Gertrude, clumping her way across the threshold. She saw Joe, banged the walker down, and let the door fly back, hitting Sweetums smack in the whiskers. The cat howled, but Gertrude was unmoved. Her beady eyes narrowed and her chin quivered. She didn't speak for what seemed like an eternity. When she did, the words were low and raw:

"Joe Flynn, you son of a bitch. Get out of *my* house!"

Joe had been known to charm the warts off toads, or at least a reasonable facsimile of such an unlikely achievement. He started to smile, to speak, to bow, even to demur. Instead, the hand that held the shopping bag shot out at Gertrude. "Here," he said. "Truce."

Gertrude eyed the shopping bag as if it contained a live grenade. "I told you to take a hike," she said in her rasping voice. "What do you mean, prowling around my girl when you're a married man? Haven't you got any *morals?*"

Joe looked around as if he might actually have misplaced his morals somewhere in the dining room. "To be honest with you, Mrs. Grover, I was just about to say the same thing to Jude—to Judith." He gave both women a tight smile. "You're absolutely right, I wouldn't be here at all if I had anywhere else to go."

Only the faintest dimming of Gertrude's bright little eyes revealed that she was the least bit touched by Joe's plight. "What about one of those do-good shelters or mission places downtown? Don't they pass out free meals on Thanksgiving?"

Her retort annoyed Judith. "Mother, don't be so mean! I asked Joe to come!" She grabbed Gertrude by the sleeve of her baggy chartreuse cardigan. "May I remind you, it's *my* house, too?"

"Faugh!" Gertrude growled at Judith, yanking her arm free. "The last time I talked to this shanty Irishman, I told him to go to the devil. I haven't changed my mind in over twenty years!"

Puzzled, Judith looked from her mother to Joe. "When was that?" During Judith's four-year romance with Joe, Gertrude hadn't deigned to speak to him more than five or six times. And while always sharp-tongued, Judith didn't recall her mother ever being so specific in telling Joe off.

Gertrude avoided her daughter's probing gaze. "It was a long time ago," she mumbled.

The kitchen door had opened a crack, no doubt Auntie Vance, satisfying her curiosity, thought Judith. The living room had grown very quiet, except for the squeaking of Aunt Deb's wheelchair as she edged ever closer to the scene of conflict. Even Bill had stopped cursing the Lions and was half turned toward the dining room.

Joe spoke up in a matter-of-fact tone. "It was when I called from Vegas, the morning after Herself and I got dead drunk and eloped." He paused, pointing an accusing finger at Gertrude. "You wouldn't let me talk to your daughter. You hung up on me and took the phone off the hook."

Gertrude thrust her chin up at Joe. "So what? It served you right for running out on my girl."

Judith felt her legs go weak, and had to brace herself on the marble-topped Victorian washstand that she used for an impromptu bar. *"You* called *me?"* Her voice was very faint.

"Of course I did." Joe looked angry now, his round face dark, the gold flecks turned to amber in his eyes. "I knew I'd made a terrible mistake."

Judith wanted to cry. Or murder her mother. Or beat Joe into the floor. Or shoot herself. It was all too bizarre, too ironic, to discover that perhaps she had misjudged Joe Flynn for more than twenty years. At the very least, she had not been quite fair to him.

Gertrude was looking a bit chagrined, if still pugnacious. Joe continued to proffer the shopping bag. Auntie Vance opened the kitchen door a good six inches and poked her bleached blond head into the dining room. "Come on, half-wits, we've got a dinner to serve. Get the lead out before I cut up that ugly cat and put him in with the giblets."

Slowly, Gertrude took the shopping bag by its handles. She eyed Joe suspiciously before she looked inside. "Chocolates!" she exclaimed. "Hey, five pounds of Granny Goodness Dark Creams and Chewy Centers!" She was weakening now, digging into the bag for the second gift, a slim package wrapped in gold foil with a russet bow. "What's this? Don't just stand there, you dumbbell," she said to Judith, "give me a hand."

Judith complied, unwrapping the foil and handing the bow to Auntie Vance, who made as if to plaster it on Gertrude's rump. Judith showed the wooden box to her mother, and then clicked open the little brass latch.

"A cribbage board!" cried Gertrude. "Now there's a really useful present!" She started to grin at Joe, caught herself, and pursed her lips. "You can't buy your way into this old heart, kiddo." Her glance strayed to the crib board with its finely polished wood grain. "You can give it a try, though. At least this once.'' Briefly, her wrinkled face softened. She watched the others file into the room, led by Aunt Deb in her wheelchair. ''Maybe,'' muttered Gertrude, ''there are still some things to be thankful for.'' With a hitch of her hips, she clumped to her place at the far end of the table, just as Mike and Kristin came through the front door. ''Okay,'' called Gertrude, ''let's say grace. This old pilgrim could eat Plymouth Rock!''

Bill intoned the prayer in his best lecture-lector style. Judith surveyed the long oval table, now augmented by two extra slats in the middle to accommodate the large gathering. The entire crew was happily immersed in passing around turkey and dressing, cranberry sauce, creamed onions, green beans, giblet gravy, mashed potatoes, sweet potatoes, and Renie's not-so-famous rolls, which, for once, had turned out to be edible. In the kitchen on the counter, the pecan, mince, and pumpkin pies awaited their dollops of whipping cream.

Judith let out a little sigh of pleasure at the sight of her loved ones piling their plates, talking and laughing, teasing and taunting. Some of the places were empty, chairs from the past that had been pulled away for good. But the faces remained, familiar, locked in memory, easily recalled by a word, a thought, a gesture. Grandpa and Grandma Grover. Her father. Uncle Cliff. Dan.

Judith glanced at Joe, who was squeezed in between Tess and Aunt Deb. He leaned forward, handing Judith the butter plate before he took the beans from Tess.

''I'm putting together a new field hockey team come spring,'' he said in a low voice, his ingenuous expression in place. ''Interested?''

Judith tipped her head to one side as she placed a pat of butter on her plate. ''Maybe.'' She gave Joe a sweet little smile. ''It all depends on whether or not you can give me a real good puck.''

Joe spilled the beans.

CHECK INTO THE WORLD OF MARY DAHEIM

WHAT COULD BE more relaxing than a well-deserved respite at Hillside Manor, the charming bed-and-breakfast inn set atop Heraldsgate Hill? Well, for Judith McMonigle Flynn, the ever courteous proprietress, hand-to-tentacle combat with an irritated octopus might, on occasion, seem like a quieter pastime than running her beloved inn.

Daily worries for Judith include whether she'll be able to pay the utilities bill, whether she'll be able to keep the inn at full capacity during the busy season, whether her supply of hors d'oeuvres will satisfy her guests, whether her crotchety mother will keep out of the way, but most importantly, Judith always worries where that next body will turn up . . .

It's not that she goes out in search of murders to solve—after all, she doesn't deliberately try to compete with her husband, Homicide Detective Joe Flynn, on his own turf—it's just that murder and mayhem seem to find her. And what's a gal supposed to do?

Grab her ravenous and reliable cousin Renie and hit the trail after the latest killer, before this energetic and entertaining hostess is put permanently out of business.

JUST DESSERTS

A WIDOW OF three years, Judith McMonigle decided to convert her family home into the charming—and therefore destined to be successful—Hillside Manor bed-and-breakfast, which will provide her with a steady income (she hopes) and a place to live for herself and her not-so-gracefully aging mother, Gertrude. In business for just over seven months, Judith suddenly wishes she hadn't gone out of her way to accommodate the Brodie clan . . . except for the fact that the corpse in her dining room, which may put her out of business, also brings the local police onto the scene. . . .

"She's pretty good at what she does," remarked Judith in an undertone. "I wonder if Oriana thinks she's getting her two grand worth?"

Over the flutter of unsettled noises, Madame Gushenka was speaking again: "Far off, bleak, isolated. A handsome bird in a concrete cage." Her voice rumbled into the very depths of her chest, then suddenly brightened. "There is music, too. Such pretty notes! Or are they? Greed, deception creep onto the stage." The tone had changed again, now overtly sinister. "Wrongs not righted, the past swept under cover, while over the ocean, a crowd roars, then goes silent. Disaster strikes! The night goes black, the sky is empty, hush . . . hush . . . ssssh. . . .''

The last utterances had slowed, then begun to fade away. Judith and Renie almost banged heads trying to press closer against the door. They were steadying themselves when they heard the crash, the screams, and the sounds of chairs being overturned, crystal shattering and china breaking. Even as Judith fumbled for the kitchen light switch, the dining room sounded as if it had erupted into a stampede. Renie threw open the door.

The illumination from the kitchen showed a scene of utter confusion, with everyone clustered around the head of the table. Lance was struggling with something or someone, Ellie was whimpering and clutching at Harvey, Gwen was verging on hysterics, Oriana was deathly pale despite her makeup, Otto was swearing like a sailor, Dash was trying either to help or to hinder Lance, and Mavis was shrieking for order.

''The lights!'' called Judith, and was amazed when Oriana immediately obeyed, bringing the chandelier up to full beam. Gwen stared at the blaze of shimmering crystal as if hypnotized and Lance stepped back, revealing Madame Gushenka, sprawled face down on the table, one hand on the cards, the other clawing at the azalea's vivid blooms. Her black hair spilled onto the Irish linen, and the brilliant veils seemed to have wilted like weary petals.

''She's out like a . . . light,'' said Lance, peering up at the chandelier.

''It must be a trance,'' Oriana said, but her usually confident voice was uncertain.

''Get back,'' Harvey ordered, assuming his best operating-theater style. ''Give the poor woman room to breathe.'' As the others, including the distraught Ellie, moved away, Harvey felt for a pulse, first at the wrist, then at the neck. His sallow face sagged as his search for a vital sign grew more frantic. ''My God,'' he exclaimed. ''She's dead!''

FOWL PREY

*JUDITH AND HER cousin Renie are heading north to Brit-
ish Columbia and the Hotel Clovia for a pre-
Thanksgiving getaway. But when an addled and
impoverished popcorn vendor is murdered along with
his foul-mouthed parakeet, a local policeman's suspicions land on the visiting Americans, Judith and Renie.
Meanwhile, the cousins suspect one of the "Sacred
Eight"—a strange collection of showbiz glitterati gathered at the historic hotel. And unless Judith and Renie
can find the murderer among the glitzy group, their
goose will be cooked!*

Renie was about to respond when the cousins both
heard another noise, this time very faint—and very near.
Their eyes darted to the bathtub where the shower curtain was pulled shut. With the poker again held aloft,
Judith stood at one end of the tub while Renie guarded
the other. Renie yanked at the curtain, revealing a cowering Mildred Grimm.

"Well, Mildred, first you show up half-naked in the
middle of the night, then you come to take a shower
with your clothes on. What gives?" asked Judith, putting
the poker down.

"You'd never understand," whined Mildred, gingerly climbing over the mahogany surround.

"Could we try?" asked Judith, keeping her exasperation at bay.

Mildred stepped out of her low-heeled pumps, which apparently had gotten wet in the tub. "You wouldn't believe me," she said, not looking at either cousin.

"You'd be surprised what we'd believe about now," remarked Judith, as the trio emerged from the bathroom, went out through Renie's bedroom, and into the sitting room. "We presume this handiwork is yours, not the police's?" Judith made a sweeping gesture with one hand while replacing the poker with the other.

"Yes." Mildred drooped, a pitiful thing in her baggy blue sweater and pleated skirt. "I'm sorry, I would have put everything back if I'd had time."

Renie was already straightening the sofa cushions. "Sit down, we'll have a drink, we'll talk. What were you looking for, Mildred? More library cards?"

Whatever color Mildred possessed drained away. She collapsed onto the sofa like a rag doll. "How did you know?" she gasped.

"We were there," said Judith, closing the drawers on the end tables.

"Yes." Mildred sighed. "I saw you. But I didn't think you saw me."

Renie was at the phone. "What will you have, Mildred?"

Mildred opened her mouth, started to shake her head, then reconsidered. "A martini. Very dry. With a twist."

"Drat." Renie replaced the receiver. "No dial tone. I'll run downstairs and give the bar our order." She was gone before Judith could say "scotch."

With only one cousin confronting her, Mildred seemed to revive a bit. "I tell you, it's not believable."

"Let me decide," said Judith, sitting in the armchair opposite Mildred. "You owe us an explanation. You broke into our room, you ransacked our belongings. We could have you arrested.''

''I know.'' Mildred's face crumpled again. ''But that will probably happen anyway. Only on a more awful charge.''

''Of what?'' asked Judith, but the catch in her voice told Mildred she already knew.

The close-set blue eyes welled up with tears. ''Murder. Bob-o was killed with my gun.''

HOLY TERRORS

*CATERING THE ANNUAL brunch and Easter egg hunt is
enough of a hassle for bed-and-breakfast hostess Judith
McMonigle. Add to that, murder by a scissors-happy
fiend in a bunny suit and the return of her ex-beau, Lieutenant Joe Flynn, and Judith is up to her elbows in some
serious unsolicited snooping . . .*

Joe's casual air masked his tenacious professionalism,
just as the well-cut tweed sports coat camouflaged the
spreading midriff Dooley had mentioned. His receding
red hair was flecked with gray, yet his round face retained its freshness, despite over two decades observing
the seamiest slices of life. At his side stood Woodrow
Price, a uniformed officer on the verge of thirty and his
next promotion. A stolid black man with a walrus moustache, Woody Price had displayed a hidden reservoir of
talents during his previous adventure at Hillside Manor.

But it wasn't Woody Price's serious dark gaze which
held Judith mesmerized at the back door. Rather, Joe
Flynn's green eyes, with those magnetic flecks of gold,
turned her faintly incoherent.

"You're early," she blurted. "It's still two weeks to
go. But who's counting?" Judith giggled and mentally

cursed herself for sounding like a half-baked teenager instead of a poised middle-aged widow.

Joe's mouth twitched slightly, showing the merest hint of his roguish smile. "This is business, not pleasure. I've yet to bring Woody along on a date." He put a highly buffed loafer over the threshold. "May we?"

Judith actually jumped. "Oh! I didn't mean . . . Sure, come in, I just heard about what happened up at church . . ."

Gertrude's rasping voice crackled from the kitchen: "Is that Joe Flynn?" She didn't wait for confirmation. "Where's he been for six months? One lousy cribbage board and a box of chocolates won't buy this old girl! There was a caramel in with the creams, and it wrecked my partial plate! Get that bastard out of my house!"

As always, it was useless for Judith to argue over the legal rights of ownership to Hillside Manor. "Mother," she pleaded over her shoulder, "you know why Joe hasn't called on us since Thanksgiving. That was the bargain. Now he's here about Sandy Frizzell's murder."

"Baloney!" snarled Gertrude, wrestling with her walker as she tried to get up from the dinette table. "Joe's here because you got your hair dyed like a two-bit hussy! Out!" Her thin arm flailed under cover of a baggy blue cardigan. "Beat it, and take your chauffeur with you!"

"Mother!" Judith was aghast. "Don't be so ornery!" Agitated, she rushed to Gertrude's side. "Settle down. Do you want to be arrested for impeding justice, you crazy old coot?"

While she was still seething, Gertrude's voiced dropped a notch. "Justice, my foot! If there were such a thing, Joe Flynn would have spent the last twenty-odd years in prison for breach of promise! But you, you gutless wonder," she raged on, wagging a bony finger in her daughter's face, "you just rolled over and married Dan McMonigle! Is that justice, I ask you?"

DUNE TO DEATH

HAVING FINALLY MADE it to the altar, bed-and-breakfast hostess Judith McMonigle and Detective Joe Flynn head out for their overdue honeymoon. Settling into a cozy, costly cottage on Buccaneer Beach it seems like a dream come true. However, their newly wedded bliss is shattered when a dune buggy accident puts Joe in the hospital in traction and Cousin Renie shows up to keep Judith company. And to make a bad situation worse, the landlady shows up garroted to death in their living room . . . and Judith is on the case!

A soft mist had settled in on the MG's windshield when Judith and Renie reached the parking lot. The air was cool and damp, but the wind had died down. It was almost ten by the time they returned to Pirate's Lair. To Judith's relief, the house was dark, but she had remembered to leave a light on in the garage. The faint sound of music could be heard drifting from the We See Sea Resort next door. Judith decided they should build a fire in the cottage's stone fireplace. The cousins gathered wood and kindling to bring inside. Judith noticed that more boxes seemed to be missing from the garage. She gave a mental shrug—if Mrs. Hoke were moving her belongings, that was fine—as long as she didn't keep popping into the house itself. Maybe, Judith thought with a wry smile, she'd taken home a crate of dulcimers.

Renie was already in the kitchen, flipping on the lights. "Have you opened the damper yet?" she asked, heading for the living room.

"No," replied Judith as Renie switched on a table lamp by the beige sofa that sat across from the fireplace. "Let's make sure we do it right. I wouldn't want to set off the smoke alarm."

The words were hardly out of her mouth when Renie set off her own alarm. A piercing scream brought Judith vaulting around the sofa and across the floor. Renie stood frozen, the kindling clutched in her arms like a newborn baby. At her feet was Mrs. Hoke, long arms and legs at awkward angles. At her side was the bright pink kite the cousins had tried to fly in vain that afternoon.

And around her neck was the long, strong string. Her face was a ghastly shade of purple and the gray eyes bulged up at the cousins.

Judith and Renie knew she was dead.

BANTAM OF THE OPERA

AS TIME GOES on, the bed-and-breakfast continues to do well, gaining a reputation that keeps Judith hopping for most of the year. In fact, Hillside Manor has begun to draw some high caliber celebrities, including obnoxious opera star Mario Pacetti, who threatens to eat Judith out of house and home. Judith's attempts to satiate the significantly statured songster seem of minor significance once the threats on his life draw his attention away from his next meal—which could possibly be his last. . . .

"Hey, Jude-girl," Joe called after his wife. "Where's my gun?"

Judith gnashed her teeth. During her four years of widowhood she had forgotten how men, even sharp-eyed homicide detectives such as Joe Flynn, couldn't find a bowling ball in the bathroom sink. Suppressing the urge to tell her husband to look in the vicinity of his backside, Judith opened her mouth to reply. But Joe had spotted the holster and was grinning with the pleasure of discovery.

"Hey, how'd it get there?" he asked in surprise.

"Gee, I don't know, Joe. I suppose it grew little

leather feet and walked, meanwhile tossing socks and shirts every which way. Are you taking that with you?'' It was Judith's turn to evince surprise.

But Joe shook his head. ''No need. I'll ditch it in the closet. Or what about that little safe you've got?''

Judith rarely used the safe, but considered it an excellent repository for Joe's .38 special. ''It's in the basement, behind the hot water tank. I think.''

''Right.'' Joe was filling his shaving kit; Judith headed out into the little foyer which served as a family sitting room. On her left, the door to Mike's room was closed. On her right, the door to Gertrude's former room stood ajar. As if, Judith thought with a pang, it was expecting Gertrude Grover to return at any moment. Judith consoled herself that by Monday she might have some good news for her mother. If the Swedish carpenter's estimates were relatively reasonable and his schedule wasn't too busy, Gertrude might be home for Christmas. Of course Judith must discuss it more fully with Joe, but not now, with his departure at hand.

She had just descended the short flight from the third floor when she heard a tremendous crash and a piercing scream. The sounds emanated from the front bedroom. Judith raced down the hallway and pounded on the door.

''Mr. Pacetti! What is it? What's wrong? Mr. Pacetti?'' Judith's heart thumped along with her fists. Fleetingly, she wondered if her insurance agent had already increased her coverage as she'd requested the previous day. It was a callous thought, she realized, since Mario Pacetti might be in a lot more trouble than she was.

A FIT OF TEMPERA

JUDITH AND RENIE are headed for their family's back-woods vacation cottage for some much needed R&R. But shortly after they've unpacked their bags they find out that someone has painted their world-renowned neighbor, artist Riley Tobias, permanently out of the picture—and has artfully managed to frame Judith for the crime!

"Let me make some coffee," Judith suggested, then remembered that the fire had gone out. "Or some pop? A drink? Ice water?" She grimaced slightly at the thought of chipping chunks off the ice block.

But both Kimballs declined the offer of beverages. Indeed, Ward was on his feet, fingering his beard and gazing out the window. Mount Woodchuck stood watch over the forest, the clouds dispersed along the river valley.

"I think I'll head over to see Iris," Ward said, touching Lark's shoulder. "The law should be gone by now, and if not, I'd like to hear what they've found out. If anything. Lark?"

His daughter shook her head. "I told you, I'd rather not play out a farce with Iris. She doesn't like me any more than I like her."

Ward Kimball sighed with resignation. "As you will, dear heart. I'll amble over there. I shouldn't be long." He sketched a courtly little bow and was gone.

"Come on, Lark," Renie urged, "have a beer. A sandwich? A couple of hot dogs?"

Judith heard the hunger pangs and made a face at Renie. "Don't force food and drink on people, coz. Not everyone is a Big Pig."

But Lark said she would like a glass of wine after all, if the cousins had any. They didn't. She settled for a beer. Judith and Renie joined her, trying to be companionable.

"I suppose," Judith mused as she sat down next to Lark on the sofa, "that Riley never married Iris because his first bout with matrimony was so unhappy."

To the cousins' surprise, Lark laughed. "No, it wasn't. Riley just didn't like the idea of the institution. Not when he was young, anyway. It wasn't part of his philosophy then. He was into Kerouac, and all those British Angry Young Men. But he changed. Riley matured late, but fully." She held her bottle of beer as if it were a case of jewels.

Renie cut to the heart of the matter. "Then why didn't he marry Iris?"

Lark's laughter took on a jagged edge. "He didn't love her." The beautiful, unworldly face turned from cousin to cousin. For one brief moment, Judith could have sworn that Lark Kimball was not only seeing but studying her hostesses.

"Did he tell you that?" Renie, as usual, had sacrificed tact.

"Of course he did. Why should he love her?" Lark sounded defensive. "She's well connected in the art community; she's supposedly glib, handsome, and articulate. Useful, in other words. But she's also a rapacious conniver. It didn't take him twenty years to figure that out."

"Yes, it did," retorted Renie. "They were still together when he died."

"That's only because he couldn't figure out how to get

rid of her.'' Lark's voice had risen and her face no longer looked so unwordly. Indeed, she was blushing, and her jaw was set in a hard line. ''Riley needed some time to tell her how he felt. How *we* felt.'' She flounced a bit on the sofa. ''He wasn't merely my teacher, he was my lover. And we intended to be married. As soon as he told Iris to go to hell.'' Lark Kimball sat back on the sofa, now smiling serenely.

MAJOR VICES

JUDITH AND RENIE would rather be boiled in oil than cater the seventy-fifth birthday party for their batty Uncle Boo Major, the billionaire breakfast mush magnate. But fortunately, their duties keep them in the kitchen and away from most of their contemptible kin—that is until the birthday boy is found blown away behind the locked den door. And now a plethora of wills are popping up all over the place making everyone suspect, Judith and Renie included.

Pandemonium broke out in the den. Aunt Toadie whirled on Jill, trying to tear the will out of her hands. Derek embraced his daughter, which wasn't easy, since he had to fend off his aunt's clawing fingers. Holly fanned herself with her hand and leaned against one of the radiators. Aunt Vivvie beamed—and fainted again. Judith called for Mrs. Wakefield and the smelling salts.

It was Renie, however, who showed up. "What the hell . . . ?" she muttered, encountering the chaotic scene.

"Derek won," Judith said in her cousin's ear. "Jill found the will."

"Well." Renie stared at Aunt Vivvie, who was lying on the parquet floor and making little mewing noises.

"Did you say smelling salts? I think she's coming around."

Renie was right. Vivvie was not only conscious, but also smiling, if in a trembling, anxious manner. "Oh, my!" she gasped out, allowing Judith to prop her into a sitting position. "Oh, my, my! Bless Boo! My son is so deserving!"

"Bunk!" shouted Toadie. "Let me see that will! It must be a phony!"

With an air of victory, Derek waved a hand at his daughter. "Let her read it, Jill. Let everybody read it. I always knew Uncle Boo loved me best." His off-center smile revealed his gold molar, making him look vaguely like a pirate.

Toadie snatched the document from Jill's grasp. She read hurriedly, then sneered. "This thing is three years old! He wrote this just after Rosie died. Do you really think he didn't make another will?" Toadie crumpled the legal-sized paper and hurled it at Derek. "I should make you eat that, you swine!"

Trixie's blond head bobbed up and down like a puppet's. "That's right, Mummy! Uncle Boo promised *us* his money! And the house! And . . ." Trixie took a deep breath, her cleavage straining at the deep ruffled neckline.

". . . *everything!* Let's go through those other books!"

Chaos reigned in front of the open bookcase. Shoving, pushing, and otherwise stampeding one another, the four Rushes, including a rejuvenated Aunt Vivvie, vied with the two Grover-Bellews. Books began to fly from the top shelf. Her librarian's sensibilities enflamed, Judith called a halt.

"Wait!" she cried, practically vaulting over the desk. "Stop!" To her amazement, the combatants did, staring at her with varying degrees of curiosity and hostility. Swallowing hard, she made a calming gesture with her hands. "I have an idea. There's a better way to find that will than to tear this place apart. Would all of you agree to a truce and to appointing Renie and me as neutral searchers?"

Aunt Toadie's face turned mulish. "We would *not*. Why should we trust you two?"

MURDER, MY SUITE

EVER SINCE JOE Flynn walked back into Judith's life and finally married her, Judith has begun to breathe a little easier. Life is good for Judith, who loves being surrounded by her devoted husband, her delightful son, her bosom buddy of a cousin, Renie, and even, in a rare tender moment, her mother. That is, until life takes a devilish turn when gossip columnist Dagmar Delacroix Chatsworth descends on Hillside Manor with a flurry of lackies and her yappy lapdog Rover, who seems to think he owns the joint. But Judith is ever the professional, gritting her teeth and bearing the barrage, even when things become fatally frenetic. . . .

Judith was at a loss. She abandoned guessing at Dagmar's veiled intentions. "You certainly cover everybody's peccadilloes. Do you ever get threatened with lawsuits?"

For a brief moment Dagmar's high forehead clouded over under the turban. "Threatened?" Her crimson lips clamped shut; then she gave Judith an ironic smile. "My publishers have superb lawyers, my dear. Libel is surprisingly hard to prove with public figures."

The phone rang, and Judith chose to pick it up in the

living room. She was only mildly surprised when the caller asked for Dagmar Chatsworth. The columnist already had received a half-dozen messages since arriving at Hillside Manor the previous day.

While Dagmar took the call, Judith busied herself setting up the gateleg table she used for hors d'oeuvres and beverages. At first, Dagmar sounded brisk, holding a ballpoint pen poised over the notepad Judith kept by the living room extension. Then her voice tensed; so did her pudgy body.

"How dare you!" Dagmar breathed into the receiver. "Swine!" She banged the phone down and spun around to confront Judith. "Were you eavesdropping?"

"In my own house?" Judith tried to appear reasonable. "If you wanted privacy, you should have gone upstairs to the hallway phone by the guest rooms."

Lowering her gaze, Dagmar fingered the swatch of fabric at her throat. "I didn't realize who was calling. I thought it was one of my sources."

"It wasn't?" Judith was casual.

"No." Dagmar again turned her back, now gazing through the bay window that looked out over downtown and the harbor. Judith sensed the other woman was gathering her composure, so she quietly started for the kitchen.

She had got as far as the dining room when the other two members of Dagmar's party entered the house. Agnes Shay carried a large shopping bag bearing the logo of a nationally known book chain; Freddy Whobrey hoisted a brown paper bag which Judith suspected contained a bottle of liquor. Another rule was about to be broken, Judith realized: She discouraged guests from bringing alcoholic beverages to their rooms, but a complete ban was difficult to enforce.

The bark of Dagmar's dog sent the entire group into a frenzy. Clutching the shopping bag to her flat breast, Agnes started up the main staircase. Freddy waved his paper sack and shook his head. Dagmar put a hand to her turban and let out a small cry.

"Rover! Poor baby! He's been neglected!" She moved

to the bottom of the stairs, shouting at Agnes. The telephone call appeared to be forgotten. "Give him his Woofy Treats. Extra, for now. They're in that ugly blue dish on the dresser."

Judith blanched. She knew precisely where the treats reposed, since she had discovered them earlier in the day, sitting in her mother's favorite Wedgwood bowl. Anxiously, Judith watched the obedient Agnes disappear from the second landing of the stairs. Rover continued barking.

"I thought the dog was a female," Judith said lamely.

Dagmar beamed. "That's because he's so beautiful. Pomeranians are such adorable dogs. Rover is five, and still acts like the most precious of puppies. Would you mind if he came down for punch and hors d'oeuvres?"

Judith did mind, quite a bit.

AUNTIE MAYHEM

JUDITH AND RENIE are taking in the London countryside for an unharried weekend at a real English manor. However they find the weekend anything but relaxing with Aunt Petulia, Ravenscroft House's aged mistress, holding court to her many relations. Then a box of sweets poisons Aunt Pet. Now Judith and Renie are up to their American necks in a murder most British.

Judith and Renie both recognized the neighborhood; some of the Grover ancestors had lived there in the late nineteenth century. "But you spend weekends at Ravenscroft House," Judith noted.

"Oh, yes," Claire replied with a tremulous smile. "At least some. London makes me nervy." To prove the point, Claire looked as if she were on the verge of an anxiety attack.

Renie was nodding. "We've got a cabin in the woods, about an hour outside of town." She referred to the ramshackle structure that had been built a half-century earlier by their fathers and Grandpa Grover. "Of course it's sort of falling down. We don't go there very often."

Claire put a hand to her flat breast and leaned back in the chair. "Oh! I know! These old houses are so stress-inducing! The heating, the electrical, the plumbing!''

''Actually,'' Renie murmured, ''we don't exactly have plumbing. Or electricity or heating. The outhouse is collapsing, too.''

Claire sympathized. ''Outhouses! My! We call them outbuildings. But I know what you mean about repairs. Such a challenge! Judith—may I call you that, I hope? Thank you so. Margaret said you renovated your family home. The one in the city. Into a bed-and-breakfast. I shall hang on every word. I swear.''

Judith assumed a modest air. ''I'll do my best. Hillside Manor had some serious problems, too.'' Fondly, she pictured the Edwardian house on the hill, with its fresh green paint and white trim, the bay windows, the five guest bedrooms on the second floor, the family quarters in the expanded attic, and the enclosed backyard with the last few fruit trees from the original orchard. There was a double garage, too. And the remodeled toolshed where her mother lived. Gertrude Grover had refused to share a roof with her son-in-law. She didn't like Judith's second husband much better than her first one.

''It *was* a challenge,'' Judith finally said, thinking more of coping with Gertrude than of the renovations. ''It's expensive. I had to take out a loan.''

Claire's high forehead creased. ''My word! A loan! Charles should hate that!''

Trying to be tactful, Judith made an effort to put Claire's mind at rest. ''I'm sure my situation was different. I'd been recently widowed and had no savings.'' Dan McMonigle had blown every dime on the horse races or the state lottery. ''My husband wasn't insurable.'' Dan had weighed over four hundred pounds when he'd died at the age of forty-nine. ''We had no equity in our home.'' After defaulting on the only house they'd ever owned, the McMonigles had lived in a series of seedy rentals, and had been about to be evicted when Dan had, as Judith put it, conveniently blown up. ''In fact,'' she went on, feigning serenity, ''I had no choice but to move in with my mother. That's when it occurred to me that it didn't make sense for the two of us to rattle around in a big old house. My son was almost ready for college.''

''How true!'' Claire positively beamed, revealing small, perfect white teeth. ''That's precisely what I've told Charles. Why maintain a second home with so many expenditures and taxation? Why not turn it into something that will produce income?''

''Exactly,'' Judith agreed. ''The main thing is to figure out if you're going to run it or let someone do it for you.''

Claire's smile evaporated. ''Oh, no. The main thing is Aunt Pet,'' she insisted, her rather wispy voice now firm. ''First of all, she has to die.''

NUTTY AS A FRUITCAKE

WITH ALL THE comings and goings around the bed-and-breakfast, Judith finds it comforting to know that, should her aging mother require her assistance—beyond the meals she serves her every day and the errands she runs—Gertrude is right on the property, living in the converted toolshed. Although Judith and Gertrude have their moments, this mother-daughter relationship is an affectionate one, depending on how you look at it. . . .

"They're questioning the neighbors," Naomi said in a breathless voice. "First, Mrs. Swanson, then the Rankerses, and finally, me. Nobody else is home—except your mother."

"*My mother?*" Judith gaped at Naomi, then jumped out of the car to look down the driveway. She saw nothing unusual, except Sweetums, who was stalking an unseen prey in the shrubbery.

"They're questioning her now," Naomi added, backpedaling to her own property. "Don't worry, Judith. I'm sure she'll be treated with respect."

That wasn't what concerned Judith. With a half-hearted wave for Naomi, she all but ran to the toolshed. There wasn't time to think about the awful things Gertrude could say to the police, especially about Joe Flynn. Judith yanked the door open.

Patches Morgan was standing by the tiny window that looked out onto the backyard and the Dooleys' house. With arms folded, Sancha Rael leaned against a side chair that had originally belonged to Judith and Dan. Gertrude was sitting on her sofa, smoking fiercely, and wearing a tiger-print housecoat under a lime-and-black cardigan. She glared as her daughter came into the small sitting room.

"Well! Just in time, you stool pigeon! What are you trying to do, get me sent up the river?"

Judith's mouth dropped open. "What? Of course not! What's happening?"

With his good left eye, Morgan winked at Judith. "Now, now, me hearties, this is just routine. But," he continued, growing serious, "it seems that certain threats against Mrs. Goodrich were made by Mrs. Grover. You don't deny that, do you, ma'am?" His expression was deceptively benign as he turned back to Gertrude.

Gertrude hid behind a haze of blue smoke. "I make a lot of threats," she mumbled. "It's my way. I can't remember them all."

Judith stepped between Gertrude and Morgan. "Excuse me—who told you that my mother threatened Enid?"

Morgan's good eye avoided Judith. "Now, I can't be revealing my sources, eh? You know that anything we might regard as a threat has to be investigated when there's a homicide involved."

"It was years ago," Judith said, then bit her tongue. "I mean, it must have been—*I* don't remember it. Either," she added lamely, with a commiserating glance for Gertrude.

Sancha Rael stepped forward, a smirk on her beautiful face. "This threat involved a family pet. It had something to do with"—she grimaced slightly—"sauerkraut."

Gertrude stubbed her cigarette out. She shot Morgan and Rael a defiant look.

Judith didn't know whether to grin or groan. She did

neither. "Look," she said to Morgan, "this is silly. I can't believe you're wasting the city's time interrogating my mother. Does she look like the sort of person who'd take a hatchet to somebody?"

Morgan eyed Gertrude closely. "In truth, she does," he said. "Where were you Wednesday morning, December first, between seven and eight-thirty A.M.?"

SEPTEMBER MOURN

JUDITH HAS AGREED to run a high school chum's bed-and-breakfast for a few days. So off she goes with cousin Renie for B&B sitting in the rustic splendor of Chavez Island. But when one odious blowhard tries to horn in on their dinner one night, Renie beans him with a china dish and moments later he takes a deadly tumble down a flight of stairs. Now Judith must find the real killer and prove coz Renie innocent.

Hodge bristled. "Lips that touch liquor will never touch mine."

Defiantly, Renie took a big swig of bourbon. "You can count on it, Burrell. I wouldn't touch you with a ten-foot pole."

"Let's all calm down," Judith urged, as she counted the simmering prawns. There were an even dozen. Divided by three, that made four apiece. Renie wouldn't be happy to share.

"We're having dinner for two," Renie asserted. "Beat it."

Though appalled by her cousin's attitude, Judith knew she had to side with Renie. "It's a rule," she insisted. "Mrs. Barber doesn't do dinner."

"Mrs. Barber isn't here," Hodge countered. "H. Burrell Hodge is." He wedged himself between the table and the matching bench. "Ah! Do I smell garlic? H. Burrell Hodge is fond of garlic!"

"Guess what?" Renie said, placing a knee on the bench next to Hodge. "I'm not fond of rude people who try to steal my dinner. You're not eating our pasta, but you might end up wearing it. Am I being clear?"

Hodge glared at Renie. "You're very maddening," he averred, picking up the silverware that had been intended for Renie. "H. Burrell Hodge doesn't give in to silly threats from mouthy women who drink too much. Where are my prawns?"

"That does it!" Renie was enraged. She snatched up the heavy blue-and-pink plate and cracked it over Hodge's head. The plate broke. Hodge let out a howl of pain. Clutching his head with one hand, he made a fist with the other.

"Damn your hide! I'm reporting this to the authorities! You assaulted me! I'll sue!"

Judith was staring at Hodge in horror, but the unrepentant Renie had gone to the cupboard to get another plate. "I'll use a skillet next time," she snapped. "Did you think I was kidding about the prawns? R. Grover Jones doesn't kid about *food*!"

WED AND BURIED

JUDITH McMONIGLE FLYNN'S son Mike is getting married and the Hillside Manor B&B is packed to the rafters with relatives. However, the joyous occasion is dampened for Judith when she spies a tuxedo-clad gent tossing a bridal-gowned beauty off the roof of a nearby hotel. Judith's determination to find the killer could put some stress on her own marital bliss with policeman husband Joe, but she's not about to take a honeymoon from amateur sleuthing until she's gotten to the bottom of the homicidal hanky-panky.

"I feel awful," Judith declared after they had driven around the block four times to find a parking place and waited ten minutes for a table. "I think it's the heat."

Joe was scanning the long list of microbrews that were written in various shades of colored chalk above the bar. The Heraldsgate Pub was crowded as usual, but Judith and Joe had been lucky—their table was at the far end of the long, narrow establishment, and, thus, not quite in the center of noise and bombast.

"The heat?" Joe replied rather absently. "Maybe." The green eyes finally made contact with Judith. "How about the corpse? You pegged the wrong one, Jude-girl.'' A faint smile touched Joe's mouth as he started to reach for her hands.

Abruptly, Judith pulled back. ''Hey! I pegged *somebody*! You're ticked off because I knew there was a dead person at that hotel. You thought I was hallucinating.''

Joe's grin was off-center. ''You're having one of your fantasies. Nobody was pushed off a roof. The dead man didn't die from a fall. He was stabbed.''

Judith gaped. ''Stabbed? With a knife?''

Joe was noncommittal. '' 'With a sharp instrument' is the way we put it. No weapon was found. Dr. Chinn says he'd been dead about forty-eight hours. He'll know more after the formal autopsy.''

''Stabbed,'' Judith echoed. Then the rest of what Joe had said sank in. ''What do you mean? 'Whoever he is'?''

Joe shrugged. ''Just that. The guy had no ID. He looked to be about thirty, just under six feet, a hundred and forty pounds, not in the best of health, signs of poor nutrition. But you're right about one thing—he was wearing a tuxedo.''

Judith's eyes sparkled. ''So he was the man I saw on the roof.''

SNOW PLACE TO DIE

JUDITH MCMONIGLE FLYNN is more than ready to hang up her oven mitts, but her effervescent Cousin Renie needs help catering the telephone company's annual winter retreat. Judith gives in because the pay is good, never thinking that there would be a killer cooking up mischief on the premises. But when Judith and Renie discover the frozen garroted remains of the previous company caterer, they know that they are on the trail of a killer who would like nothing better than to put the two cousins in the Deep Freeze.

"When do you make your presentation?" Judith asked, forcing herself out of her reverie.

"Friday," Renie answered, no longer placid. "I told you, it's just for a day. Can't Arlene Rankers help you throw some crap together for these bozos? Bring her along. You'll be up at the lodge for about six hours, and they'll pay you three grand."

"Arlene's getting ready for her annual jaunt to Palm Desert with Carl, and . . . *three grand*?" Judith's jaw dropped.

"Right." The smirk in Renie's voice was audible. "OTIOSE pays well. Why do you think I'm so anxious to peddle my pretty little proposals? I could make a bundle off these phone company phonies.''

"Wow." Judith leaned against the kitchen counter. "That would pay off our Christmas bills and then some. Six hours, right?"

"Right. We can come and go together, because my presentation should take about two hours, plus Q&A, plus the usual yakkity-yak and glad-handing. You'll get to see me work the room. It'll be a whole new experience. I actually stay nice for several minutes at a time."

Judith couldn't help but smile. Her cousin wasn't famous for her even temper. "How many?" she asked, getting down to business.

"Ten—six men, four women," Renie answered, also sounding equally professional. "All their officers, plus the administrative assistant. I'll make a list, just so you know the names. Executives are very touchy about being recognized correctly."

Judith nodded to herself. "Okay. You mentioned a lodge. Which one?"

"Mountain Goat," Renie replied. "It's only an hour or so from town, so we should leave Friday morning around nine."

Judith knew the lodge, which was located on one of the state's major mountain passes. "I can't wait to tell Joe. He'll be thrilled about the money. By the way, why did the other caterers back out?"

There was a long pause. "Uh . . . I guess they're sort of superstitious."

"What do you mean?" Judith's voice had turned wary.

"Oh, it's nothing, really," Renie said, sounding unnaturally jaunty. "Last year they had a staff assistant handle the catering at Mountain Goat Lodge. Barry Something-Or-Other, who was starting up his own business on the side. He . . . ah . . . disappeared."

"He *disappeared*?" Judith gasped into the receiver.

"Yeah, well, he went out for cigarettes or something and never came back. Got to run, coz. See you later."

Renie hung up.